CATCH ME WHEN I FALL

Bridget—
Sweet dreams,

Vicki Leigh

CURIOSITY
QUILLS PRESS

A Division of **Whampa, LLC**
P.O. Box 2160
Reston, VA 20195
Tel/Fax: 800-998-2509
http://curiosityquills.com

© 2014 **Vicki Leigh**
http://www.vleighwrites.com

ISBN 978-1-62007-486-2 (ebook)
ISBN 978-1-62007-487-9 (paperback)
ISBN 978-1-62007-488-6 (hardcover)

For Grandma,
who first showed me what it meant to love a good book,
and who, even when the world told her she was blind, found a way to read.

TABLE OF CONTENTS

CHAPTER ONE

I nvisible, I leaned against the wall at the back of Eva's bedroom, waiting for her to fall asleep and for the Nightmares to arrive. The crows' feet around Eva's eyes crinkled as she smiled and shut the book she'd been reading before smoothing her blankets out around her and flicking off the light.

"Do you always have to be so brooding? While most people die, you get to continue to live. You should be more grateful," my partner, Marlene, said.

Ignoring her, I closed my eyes. As Protectors of the Night—me a Dreamcatcher and she a Dreamweaver—we were both sworn to guard humans for the rest of eternity. Marlene created dreams; I fought off Nightmares. Which meant I was spending nearly every day in battle, and I would never get to see the Heavens. When I died—for good this time; I *was* already dead—I would just cease to exist. Lost in a black void. Not much of an eternity, if you ask me.

Marlene gave an exasperated sigh and stepped away to do her job. "Just be on alert, okay?"

When wasn't I? Not like I hadn't been doing this for two-hundred years or anything.

I'd been just seventeen, sent from England to fight in what was now called the War of 1812. Why I'd wanted to be a soldier, I no longer knew. I could've stayed in my family's home, the son of an Earl, and have married and fathered children. But instead, I'd gone overseas to the Americas and died. Not my cleverest move.

Now, I was still that young soldier, just in a different kind of war. Good versus evil. The cliché kind. I'd agreed to this afterlife because I couldn't bear to be away from the family I'd left behind. But when the last of my kin were finally gone… I never should've tried to cheat death.

The smell of sulfur hit me and my hair stood on end. I uncrossed my arms, opened my eyes, and grabbed the daggers from my weapon belt.

Marlene was still straddled over Eva, her hands hovering above the woman's head. The dream she created shone above Eva's bed, like a movie projector played video on the wall. Standing on the balls of my feet, I waited for the attack.

The first Nightmare entered the room through the wall by the door, its scaly, humanoid body twisting like a character from an exorcism movie. Stepping toward it, I gripped my daggers tighter and raised a blade like an American football quarterback prepping to lob a pass. The beast's red eyes glowed as it slithered toward the bed. I wasted no time throwing my dagger. The blade stuck in the creature's skull right between the eyes. The glow in the monster's beady eyes faded as it crumbled to the floor without a sound.

Grimacing, I tore the blade out of the Nightmare's head and wiped the black blood from my knife before pulling out a lighter and setting the beast on fire. The twisted body burned as fast as the oil in a Kerosene lamp, then turned to ash. Remembering how difficult it'd been to get rid of Nightmares' corpses before someone invented the lighter, the corner of my mouth twitched. I could build a house with all the wasted matches.

"Something's wrong," Marlene said, panic coating her voice. "Her mind... it's like I can't pull the memories anymore."

The dream above the bed flickered like a television before the power went out. I'd protected enough people to know what was happening.

"Just do your best. Give her something to hold onto as she passes."

Marlene looked at me, her lips in a frown. This had been her first real case, taking over when my former partner transferred to a more difficult assignment. "You mean..."

I nodded, and Marlene turned away with tears in her eyes.

Maybe I should've been sad, but I'd watched over cancer patients, kidnapped girls, and soldiers. I'd even protected a little six-year-old boy who died in a coma after a drunk driver killed him. Eva was my first charge who had lived a full life and died in her sleep at a normal age. She deserved to go peacefully like this. And if I were being honest, as someone who had died young—and would remain so forever—I was jealous.

Turning away when the scent of sulfur hit my nose again, my eyes searched the room for the second Nightmare's point of entry. The monster crept through the far corner near the window with a snakelike hiss, claws extended from its hands. I waited until the creature was a little closer to us before stepping forward to throw my blade.

Its claws contracted and the Nightmare's hiss died, but I threw my blade anyway, ridding the world of one more evil. Still, I knew what had happened, why the monster was no longer interested in feeding.

Eva was dead.

With my arms crossed over my chest, I stood at the back of the funeral home, invisible to human eyes. Exhaustion filled every muscle and joint in my body, but I needed to pay my respects. Eva might not have known I was there, but after spending every night with her for eighty years, I felt like I at least owed her a goodbye.

A hand touched my shoulder.

Jumping, I dropped my arms from my chest. "Bloody hell!" I hated when she did that.

"Always so stoic, Daniel. You make it easy." Samantha smiled from ear to ear. Since she'd become a Dreamcatcher almost one hundred years ago, she'd been what they called my "understudy."

Every Protector of the Night spent about one hundred years as an understudy before taking their trials and becoming a lead. If anything were to happen to me on a mission, Samantha would take over in my place. Our charge always held priority in our eternal lives and should never be left alone during the night for more than a minute—that's all a Nightmare needed to attack a person's mind. And the more a Nightmare invaded someone's head, the more that human suffered from insanity—insanity that often led to violence or suicide.

But the likelihood of Samantha having to step in for me was slim-to-none, and we both knew it. Besides, until she took her trials, I wasn't going to let her fight on her own. Call it a dated notion, but I was responsible for her. Our souls were dead, but our bodies still worked like the living. We could still bleed—and die. The last thing I wanted was for her to get hurt. So, Samantha had resorted to playing pranks on me in her everlasting downtime.

"Doesn't that get old?" I crossed my arms again and stared straight ahead. Standing like this had become my usual pose when I was either bored or didn't want to be bothered. Right now, it was the latter.

"Nope." She mimicked my stance and watched one of Eva's granddaughters bend over the casket to touch Eva's hand. The granddaughter burst into tears and fell into her husband's arms.

"Why do you watch this?" Samantha asked.

"What do you want, Sam?"

"Giovanni's asking for you."

I sighed. Giovanni was our Leader and the second oldest in the entire company. He had mastered the arts of both Catching and Weaving, a prerequisite for leading the Protectors of the Night. He was a royal pain in the ass, but no one avoided him. They'd be benched for a century. And as I'd yet to take more than a few months off, I didn't want Giovanni to break my streak.

"All right. Let's go." Uncrossing my arms, I closed my eyes to evaporate to Rome. When I reopened them, I stood in the grand foyer of Il Palazzo di Santo Stefano, our twelve-story mansion where Catchers and Weavers trained and lived when we weren't on assignment. The building sat right in the middle of the city, but when living humans walked past our front door, they thought they were passing a laundromat that reeked of dead cat and horse shit. It's how we kept them out. If any of them could look through the veil, though, they would see a brick fortress that rivaled the most beautiful castles in Europe.

I stomped my black boots on the cream-colored marble floor as I crossed the room, wondering what Giovanni could want with me right now. We usually got at least a week of down time after our charge passed on. The Tuscan-gold walls blurred as I took two stairs at a time up to the twelfth floor, just wanting to get this over with. The staircase split each floor in half, and I turned right toward Giovanni's study.

Samantha stayed on my heels and paused next to me as I knocked on large, double doors of finished, cherry wood. From inside, Giovanni's burly guards opened them. Immediately, I was hit with the smell of Giovanni's cigar and coughed. I had never enjoyed the smell of cigar when I was alive. It was no different now that I was dead.

I passed Seth, Giovanni's understudy and my best friend, and nodded a "hey" in his direction. My feet trudged across the white carpet to the ornate, cherry desk in the middle of the office. A laptop sat open on it, a sign of Giovanni's recent technological undertaking, and files were tossed about. I rolled my eyes at his inability to keep anything organized.

"You called for me, sir?"

Behind the desk was a wall-sized window Giovanni continued to stare through, watching the city as if he hadn't heard me. But I knew he had.

"Shall I come at a later time?" I asked.

At this, Giovanni turned around, staring at me with eyes so black I could see my reflection in them. His dark brown hair had been slicked back today into a small ponytail. I wondered if he knew how much he resembled Dracula with his hair like that. Still, he would've blended in with any Italian on the street, so I supposed that's what he was going for.

"No, *per favore*. Sit." He motioned to the dark brown, leather loveseat opposite his desk. I took my seat, moving a gold pillow from underneath me as he continued. "I heard Eva passed earlier this week. How did it happen?"

"In her sleep, sir. She was comfortable."

"That's good to hear. It'd be a shame if she died in fear after all these years. Now tell me, how many times did you have to fight off the Nightmares for her?"

"Twenty-five thousand and twenty four, sir."

"*Mamma mia*," he said, his eyes wide. But then he leaned back in his seat, and his face drew back into apathy. "Is that all?"

My jaw clenched. *Nobody* had gone as long as I had without a break. Any human who died at an old age usually had two Catchers protecting them over their years. Even a week of relaxation kept us from getting overworked and burnt out.

I balled my hands before speaking. "Yes, sir."

At this, Giovanni stood up. "Well, then I think we must do something about that. You're my star player. I can't have you getting rusty."

I hated when he used sports references like I wasn't risking my eternity every night.

"How would you feel about taking on a tough case?" His eyes filled with wonder. If I wasn't so exhausted, I might have been more excited to know what had made our serious boss so intrigued.

"Forgive me, sir, but I did just finish a very long assignment. Might I have at least a year to refresh?"

Giovanni stared at me then shrugged. The reaction was so out of character it unnerved me. He turned to Samantha and pointed. "You. How would you like to take on a very dangerous case? It could be the highlight of your career."

A wave of heat ran through my body as I snapped my head to stare at her. The last thing I wanted was for Samantha's first charge as a lead to be a difficult one. She could be killed. Giovanni needed to give her a young child with a short lifespan. There'd be fewer chances to fight Nightmares that way.

Samantha perked up. "I'm ready, sir. Absolutely."

I jumped up. "No way. She is *not* ready, Giovanni."

A flash of anger sparked in his eye at the use of his first name. "And who else should I go to, Daniel? If not you, then I want the Catcher you trained. One of you two will do it, whether you like it or not."

My jaw twitched. He was using my understudy as a way to get to me. I wanted to push him and his cavalier attitude out the window he stared through so often. "Fine. I'll do it."

Samantha's face reddened. I'd pulled the rug out from underneath her. But she was immature, impatient and had yet to Catch on her own. If she hated me, so be it. At least she'd still exist.

Giovanni smiled in victory. "Glad to hear you're on board. I'll send Seth to your room later with the file. For tonight, enjoy your dinner and get some rest. You will need it."

I turned and stormed out the door, past Seth's apologetic eyes and Samantha's hateful stare. What I wouldn't give to trade places with Eva right now. At least then I'd be on my way to the Heavens instead of putting my eternity on the line for another stupid assignment.

CHAPTER TWO

S itting at the dark oak desk in the far corner of my bedroom, I shoveled food into my mouth while reading through my original copy of *A Tale of Two Cities*, one of my favorite novels. After two hundred years of Dreamcatching, I'd had plenty of time to collect books. I'd probably read this one fifty times.

"Come in," I said when someone knocked on my door. I marked my page with a leather bookmark and turned in my chair to see who'd come to visit. Seth. Standing, I greeted my friend with our "secret handshake." We'd seen people do one of those fancy handshakes once, and it just kind of stuck. I smiled a little as our hands moved back and forth like floppy fish.

"You not goin' to your party?" Seth asked, his Alabama drawl still strong fifty years after his death.

"I never have." Although it was a nightly event—Protectors celebrating the peaceful passing of their charges—I had yet to attend one of my own congratulation parties. Something about celebrating death bothered me.

"Come on, man. You could at least enjoy a few beers, find some pretty lady to follow you upstairs." He wiggled his eyebrows.

I shook my head and smirked. His thoughts were always in the gutter. "Why don't you give me the file, and then you can go downstairs and party for the both of us?"

Seth smiled and held out the file. I took the manila folder and sat back in my chair. The corner of the desk bumped one of my bookshelves and nearly sent books falling to the floor. Seth plopped down on my bed and hung his legs over the edge, his dark skin in extreme contrast to my off-white comforter. People often said my room looked like a hospital with white walls and white bed sheets. But I preferred life simple.

"So where you goin' next?" Seth asked.

When I opened the file, the first things I noticed were her eyes. They were hazel, and the gold in them framed her pupil like the sun on a bright, summer day. She had soft, feminine features, lightly tanned skin, and long, brown hair the color of a dark chocolate Hershey bar. The strands looked like they would be soft to touch. She was pretty. I glanced at the name. Kayla Bartlett. How could she be a tough case?

"Well?" Seth probed.

"Ohio. There's a girl there who lives…" I'd been so immobilized by her face, I hadn't yet checked where she lived. "In a mental ward." And there was the catch. Great. Giovanni was sending me to a loony.

"Is she hot?" Seth jumped off the bed to peek over my shoulder. "Damn, she's fine."

"And insane." Snapping the folder closed, I made a mental note to check the rest of the details when Seth was gone.

"So? When she gets naked, it won't matter if she's all there or not." He bounced from side to side and pretended to smack an imaginary girl's behind while he bit his lip in a display of ecstasy.

I shook my head and used a phrase I had heard in passing by one of the newest Catchers. "You, my friend, need to remember to think with your upstairs brain."

Seth burst out laughing. "Man, did you really just say that?"

I couldn't help but smile. I wasn't always without a sense of humor. "Tell you what. I don't want to go to my 'party,' but I could use a good beer. Want to go to *Bellandi's*?" I hadn't seen my best friend in months, and if I was going to be in the United States for god-knows-how-long, I didn't really want to sit in my room all night by myself. There'd be plenty of alone time when I was holed up in a flat in Columbus. As long as we didn't reveal ourselves to our charges, there was no rule that said we couldn't exist amongst the living.

"Yeah, man. I'll change and meet you there." Seth held his hand out to me for a fist-bump.

When he evaporated from the room, I returned to my desk and opened the file.

Replacement position for Jessica Atwol who was mortally wounded in combat, along with her understudy.

Kayla Bartlett, 16, was referred to St. Mark's Home for the Mentally Challenged by her mother, Meredith, a neurosurgeon at St. Andrews Medical Center. Her father died in a drunk-driving accident when she was ten-years-old. She claims that on her sixteenth birthday she burned a man alive with her own hands. Her psychiatrist has diagnosed her with post-traumatic stress disorder, clinical depression, and possible schizophrenia.

Great. There wasn't going to be a single night when the Nightmares didn't try to invade. The beasts loved to pick on those with a tortured past, especially those that would be easy to break—like the insane.

Following Giovanni's rules, I lit the file on fire and tossed the papers in my metal rubbish bin. But those eyes—her eyes—never left my mind.

After twenty minutes of waiting outside of *Bellandi's*, Seth finally appeared. "You are the slowest Catcher I know," I said.

"Sorry, man. Giovanni caught me before I left and had me shred some papers. Took me five minutes to get the damn thing to work."

I opened the door to the bar. "Yeah, right. I know you were performing your beauty routine."

With a playful glare, Seth shoved me inside and then followed.

Bellandi's was our usual place when we were both in Rome. The bar was the only one I knew that served my favorite British ale, *Worthington White Shield*, and Seth enjoyed the half-naked women parading around the room, serving the customers. It felt like ages since I'd been in here, and I relished in the familiarity of the place—the hardwood floors and paneling of the brightly-lit room; the drinks cabinet that covered the entire wall behind the black, marble-top bar; the lingering smell of cigarettes and whisky; and the heavy beats of music screaming out of the stereo in the far corner.

Corporeal—if we touched anything while invisible, we'd go right through—we grabbed stools at the bar and watched the current *calcio* game.

"Samantha's been waitin' for you to get back," Seth said.

I sipped my beer. "Has she?" I'd made the mistake of sleeping with her about twenty years ago after my mentor's funeral. Even after being a lead for about sixty years by that point, I'd still been extraordinarily close to him, and his death had wrecked me. She'd handled the rejection surprisingly well when I told her the sex had been a mistake—hell, she had to considering I was *her* mentor—but our relationship was never quite the same after that.

"You should give the girl a chance, Daniel. She's a great Catcher, your understudy, not to mention beautiful—"

"The fact that she's my understudy is precisely why I shouldn't. And I don't feel for her that way. I'm enough of a gentleman to know she deserves more than that."

"Whatever, man. You've just been different. I don't like seein' you all, I don't know, depressed."

The bartender replaced my empty beer with another, and I swallowed deep. It was true I'd been different lately, distant. But I wouldn't say I was depressed. Tired of this afterlife, yes. Did I care if a Nightmare killed me? No. But I wasn't suicidal.

"Don't worry about me," I said.

Seth shook his head and called for a second drink. As the bartender filled the glass, another group of Catchers walked through the door. Ivan, their leader, spotted me and smirked.

In my training, Ivan and I had been at the top of our class. I'd grown up in one of England's noble families, trained from birth how to fight, and Ivan had been raised in a Russian war family. We were perfectly matched, and at the end of our training period, we'd been the last two standing in the Catchers' Competition. For hours we'd fought, neither one of us yielding to the other, until finally he'd tired. My stronger stamina had been my saving grace, and I landed the finishing blow after two hours and five minutes. Since then, he and his posse had been relentless in their hatred of me.

"So, I see they're letting the swine in, too?" Ivan led his group to where Seth and me sat at the bar.

I ignored him and stared straight ahead at the TV. Seth, on the other hand, loved confrontation. He turned around in his stool to face Ivan. "Why don't you mind your own business?"

"This is my business," Ivan replied in his thick, Russian accent. "You two are in my bar."

"Last I checked, this bar belonged to Nico Bellandi."

I closed my eyes. *Seth, shut up.*

Ivan grabbed Seth's shirt collar and tugged him off his stool. "If you don't get out of my bar, negro, the counter is going to belong to your face."

Standing up, I smacked his hand off Seth's collar. "Shove off, Ivan."

"Don't touch me, Tinker."

Ignoring the insult, I dropped cash on the bar and shifted Seth toward the door. "Come on. There's no point in fighting with him."

"Yeah," Seth said, "I guess he can't help being a prick."

We hadn't gone five feet when Ivan spoke. "Ouch, I'm hurt. Did you kiss your mother's *pizda* with that mouth?"

Seth stopped in his tracks and turned to face him, his hands balled into fists. "What did you say?"

15

I jumped in front of him and placed a hand on his chest. "Seth, don't."

But he knew as well as I did how to translate Russian. If I didn't get Seth out of here now, he was going to beat the living shit out of Ivan.

Ivan crossed his arms over his chest and raised his eyebrows, taunting Seth. "You heard me. Tell me—did she beg for it after a while?"

Seth clocked him in the jaw. *Damn.* Ivan flew backward into his friends, knocking one of them to the ground. They jumped into action. While one went after Seth, another swung at me. Dodging the punch, I grabbed his arm. With one hand on each side of his elbow, I tugged down while bringing my knee up to strike. I heard the snap of his elbow when the joint hit my knee. His arm bent in half and with a cry of pain, he fell away.

Ivan's elbow caught my nose as I spun around. Swearing, I stumbled into the bar stool behind me, my nose gushing blood. Ivan's fist came for my face again. I spun out of the way and heard the crack of knuckles when he punched the countertop. Grabbing the back of his head, I smacked his skull into the hard marble.

By now the bartender was yelling at us to cease fighting or get out, but Ivan wasn't letting up. Our fight escalated into a boxing match. Again he swung at me, but I blocked his fist and backhanded him into a table. The people sitting there had been smart enough to move when the brawl broke out, but their drinks hadn't. The glasses shattered.

I took a second to glance at Seth who had taken down one of the other Catchers and was now in his own boxing match with the last of Ivan's posse. His bottom lip was swollen and bloody, but other than that, he didn't look too bad.

Ivan caught me off guard and picked up the table, throwing it at my head. I ducked just in time and swore when the table soared over the bar into the drinks cabinet, breaking almost every bottle in it. Glass flew everywhere, and I covered my head.

Before I could drop my arms, Ivan body slammed me. Glass cut through the back of my shirt into my skin as we skidded across the floor. I ignored the sharp pain and brought my arms up to block more punches. When I saw my opening, I flipped Ivan off me, and he sailed over my head into the bar.

I jumped up and spun around, ready to block another attack, but Ivan lay limp on the ground. My chest rose and fell as I tried to catch my breath, and my hands shook at my side. Adrenaline coursed through my body. I pressed my fingers to Ivan's neck. His heartbeat pounded against my fingers.

Thank god. Leaving Seth to fight for himself would've been a shitty thing to do, but I still didn't want to kill the guy.

"*Fuori, ora! Chiamo la polizia!*" the bartender yelled, threatening to call the police if we didn't leave now.

"*Mi dispiace per il disordine.*" I apologized for the mess, throwing a wad of cash at the owner, then grabbed Seth's arm. We needed to get out of here before the police arrived and accused the man of insanity for talking about people who fought then disappeared. We walked down the road until we were sure no one saw us then evaporated back to the mansion.

CHAPTER THREE

After sleeping for exactly seven hours—as I always did—I showered and dressed in my usual outfit: dark wash jeans, black T-shirt and black boots. Running a comb through my dark blond hair, I winced when the teeth raked tender spots on my skull. Seth and I had gone to the medical wing upon our return to the mansion for a healing serum, but the effects hadn't quite kicked in yet. I still looked like a raccoon with dark purple bruises surrounding my blue eyes.

Samantha caught me on my trek to the dining hall, her curly, blonde hair bouncing in a ponytail as she jogged to catch up with me. "Hey!"

I pinched the bridge of my nose and turned to greet her. "Hey, Sam."

She crossed her arms over her chest. "Seth tells me your new charge is some psycho. Maybe I should be thanking you for stealing her from me." Except I could tell she wasn't thanking me. Her eyes burned with rage.

"Back off. I had a rough night."

"Yeah, I can see that."

My jaw twitched. "And you *should* be thanking me because you're not ready yet to take something on like this."

"Oh yeah? How would you know? You look like you ran face-first into a moving train."

I walked away, unwilling to deal with her shit today, and about flipped when she followed me.

"You're never here anymore. You have no idea what I'm capable of. You go to funerals and movies and concerts like you're still some freaking human while I stay here and train with Seth. You have no right telling me what I can and can't do."

I stopped and stared at her. Did she not realize I was trying to protect her? "Actually, I do."

Her hard, chocolate brown eyes stared into mine as she unfolded her arms. "Fine. Have fun with your psycho." She spun around and stormed away before I had a chance to respond.

Shaking my head, I jogged down the stairs to the first floor and passed beneath the oversized, crystal chandelier in the grand foyer. The morning sun from the mansion's gigantic front windows bounced off the crystal, casting little rainbows to dance on the gold wallpaper. I entered the carpeted hall on my right and headed for the double-doors at the end. As I reached for the handle, they opened and a blur of waist-high, red hair flew at me.

"Daniel!" Tabitha yelled as she clutched her tiny arms around me.

Tabitha had been recruited the same day as me, and she was one of the only individuals anymore who could put a smile on my face. She had become like my little sister. Her energy, her enthusiasm, and her unyielding compassion warmed my soul every time I saw her. Those traits were what also made her a Dreamweaver.

"Tabbi, what are you doing here? I thought you were training in Canada." I hugged the forever-twelve-year-old girl gently to my forever-seventeen body, afraid that if I squeezed too tight, her tiny frame would break. She had died of starvation on the streets of Northern Ireland in 1814 after giving her last piece of bread to a little boy who was shivering under blankets. Or at least that's how she explained it to me.

She stepped back, looked up at me with her gray-blue eyes and replied with a thick, Irish accent. "I'm your Weaver."

My heart stopped. A loon would be receiving regular visits from the Nightmares. If I didn't want Sam to be a part of this assignment, I definitely didn't want Tabbi to be involved. Samantha could at least take care of herself.

I placed my hands on her shoulders and spoke quietly. "I will talk to Giovanni. You shouldn't be taking on something like this when you haven't been a lead yet." Weavers usually trained twice as long as Catchers—forming dreams to fit individual personalities was a hell of a lot harder than fighting creatures that simply acted on instinct. Last I knew, Tabbi hadn't even taken her trials.

Her eyes glassed over. "But I have. Please don't talk to Giovanni."

"You've been a lead?"

Tabbi rolled her eyes. "Don't you read your emails? They gave me this old guy with dementia and made me pull memories from his head. There were, like, none left, but I still managed to find one from his childhood when his dad took him to this bike shop. And then he showed him how to ride the bike, and he was so happy. And when he was dreaming, he had this big smile on his face. Giovanni said I was the best he'd ever seen, that I was the fastest, and I really made the dream come alive with all the colors and everything."

She was rambling, trying to convince me that she could handle Weaving for Kayla. Although I didn't like it, if what she was telling me was true, she was wicked good. Dementia was a nasty disease and most Weavers struggled to navigate inside the mind of someone suffering from the illness. Even the ones who'd been leads for a long time.

I sighed and dropped my hands from her shoulders. "All right. Well then, if you're sure you're up to this, I would be happy to have you as my partner."

Tabbi grinned from ear to ear and slipped her hand into mine like a little sister would, and we crossed the dining hall to eat breakfast and go over the details with Seth. We sat at a round, white table covered with silver plates of Italian sausage, scrambled eggs and buttered toast. Around us, a few of the other tables were occupied, and the "hired help"—as Giovanni liked to call them—wandered the room, cleaning up after the Catchers and Weavers. They were the only humans allowed inside our hidden mansion, and they were sworn to secrecy of our existence.

Seth handed us disposable mobile phones and yellow, rubber bracelets. On them was the name of our charge. Giovanni liked to color-code the humans based on how difficult and dangerous they were deemed to be. Most humans fell into the green category, like Eva had been, and about twenty percent were yellow. Red was uncommon, but I'd seen Catchers and Weavers wearing the bracelets several times over the years. The color was usually designated for people like Adolf Hitler or H.H. Holmes. Most of the Protectors on red-level humans didn't last long, and Catchers always caught in pairs.

Tabbi and I slipped the yellow bracelets round our wrists, marking each other as partners.

"You both read through the file?" Seth asked as he scooped scrambled eggs into his mouth.

Tabbi and I nodded.

"Cool. Well, you guys know what to do. Take the day to get oriented with her, and make sure you perform the ritual so you know when she's fallin' asleep. Giovanni's rented out adjacent apartments at a complex in Columbus. They sound pretty sweet."

Giovanni liked for us to live in the same city as our charge so our bodies adjusted to the time zone change. It was our souls that were dead and held the powers the Angels gave us. Though we couldn't age—and we could choose to be invisible—we still needed to eat and sleep like the rest of the living. We could choose to remain in Rome since evaporating was easy, but going that distance often took a toll on a Protector's body. And the last thing we needed was to protect our charge while exhausted.

Seth handed us a slip of paper with the apartment building's address and our keys. "If anything weird happens, report to Giovanni immediately, but otherwise, he has you on a weekly report schedule. Mondays, I think. Oh, and because I have to say this or he'll kill me, remember the oath you swore to serve and protect. And remember our first Law: On penalty of 'termination,' under no circumstances will you reveal yourself to your charge."

One of the nice things about being a Dreamcatcher was that you were a close relative of the spirit world. You could not be seen unless you chose to be. All you had to do was close your eyes and picture where you wanted to go, and when you opened them, you would be there. And anything or anyone you touched, while corporeal, could go invisible or travel with you. So when moving across the world, you were done in about five minutes.

The flats Giovanni had chosen for Tabbi and me were much nicer than I anticipated. The one I had spent eighty years in when I watched over Eva had been a studio piece of shit with beer-stained carpet and a sliding door that didn't open. My new apartment overlooked McFerson Commons, a beautiful park in central Columbus whose focal point was an ornate, stone arch that reminded me of Rome. The place was a one bed, one bath apartment with a separate living room, dining area and kitchen. Everything was clean and well maintained. The walls were painted a light gray color, and the carpet was spotless and white.

Tabbi decided to "fix" my apartment, so I leaned against a wall and watched as she disappeared and reappeared with rugs, lamps, and other pieces of furniture. By the time she was done re-arranging everything, my flat looked like it could have belonged in a magazine.

"That's better." Tabbi plopped down on my sofa with a smile on her face.

"Yes, and now all those stores are without their merchandise. You better hope no one needed that navy blue rug or… what the heck is that?" Tabbi had hung a picture on the wall above the sofa of what looked like a black and white candy cane—if they had painted on an acid trip.

"It's a *zebra*." She gave me a look that suggested I was an idiot for not being able to understand abstract artwork. Or, at least, that's how I interpreted her.

"Ah, I see. I can't imagine anyone wanting that, so you should be safe." I smiled at her.

"Ha, ha. Very funny." She stood up. "So, are we going to go visit Kayla?"

Uncrossing my arms, I straightened up. "If you're done making my place hideous, then sure."

Tabbi stuck her tongue out at me then made sure the front door was locked. Although the humans couldn't see us or hear us unless we wanted them to, our furniture was definitely real. We didn't need anyone breaking in and stealing anything—one reason Giovanni had us burn our charges' files. Nixon's Dreamcatcher had left a piece of information out once about that Watergate scandal. It was supposed to be part of the weekly report he sent to Giovanni, but the file had been intercepted. Didn't play out well for Nixon—or his Catcher.

Tabbi took my hand. Together, we closed our eyes and brought up the image of Kayla in our minds. When we opened them, we stood in her room.

Kayla sat in a rocking chair, staring out her window at the courtyard below, dressed in the white outfit that identified her as a patient. Her dark brown hair fell in waves over her left shoulder, and her full lips were tight in concentration. With pastels, she sketched the profile of one of the patients sitting in the courtyard.

Kayla's large, hazel eyes flickered over the features of the old man below. She was more attractive than I could've imagined, so much more stunning than in the picture Giovanni gave me. I couldn't take my eyes off her.

A knock at the door made her jump. She turned her head as a nurse wearing SpongeBob SquarePants scrubs waltzed in with a glass of water in one hand. The other carried a small paper cup.

"How are you feeling today, Kayla?" the nurse asked.

"I'm all right." Even her voice was beautiful. The way she said the words were as if she was singing, her tone a melodic alto sound.

"Glad to hear it, sweetie. I brought your medicine. You should take it before you come down for lunch. You had a rough night."

Kayla pouted as she took the small, paper cup and swallowed the pills with the glass of water.

"What's she thinking?" I asked Tabbi. As a Dreamweaver, she could read humans' minds. Weavers were limited in the fact that they couldn't read other Protectors, but if a human was within a certain radius of Tabbi, she could focus on the person's thought pattern and hear what they were thinking.

Tabbi shook her head. "It's all a jumbled mess. She's trying *not* to think. And the nurse thinks she's crazy. They gave her a shot two nights ago. The nurse hopes they won't need to use it again tonight."

They used a tranquilizer on Kayla? She couldn't weigh much. How could she possibly be a danger?

The nurse took the glass back from Kayla and told her they'd be back for her in thirty minutes for lunch. Kayla returned to her chair and continued working on her portrait.

"Why did they give her the shot?" I asked.

"She was screaming, and when the nurses tried to calm her down, she fought them. She scratched one and wouldn't wake up. She kept screaming, 'He's going to hurt me! Don't let him hurt me!'" Tabbi shuddered, and I frowned.

"Are you sure you're going to be able to handle this?" I'd seen some pretty freaky stuff before. But from what I'd read in the emails she sent, Tabbi had only helped Weave for old people who lived happy, quiet lives in nursing homes. She'd yet to see anything like this.

Tabbi's green eyes bore into mine. "Stop babying me, Daniel."

I raised my hands in defeat. There was no point in arguing that she was still, technically, a child. "All right, sorry." I returned my attention to the beautiful girl in the chair. Who would want to hurt her?

CHAPTER FOUR

W
e followed Kayla to her dining hall for lunch. The room was large with white walls and a white, tiled floor. Steel tables and chairs were bolted to the ground. Kayla sat near a window in the far corner of the room with one other boy, a red-haired, freckle-faced kid with glasses that covered the top half of his face. He spoke with a bit of a lisp, and he rocked back and forth as he conversed with Kayla. Still, he appeared to be quite intelligent.

"Did you ever read Charles Darwin's theory on evolution? Maybe we're not crazy at all, but instead, we're fundamentally different from the rest of the universe because we can see things and hear things. Maybe we're supposed to be part of this super army that protects other people like us when the zombie apocalypse takes over the world and destroys all the people who haven't mutated like us."

Okay, maybe he was crazy.

Kayla smiled. "So, we're going to be like X-Men during a zombie apocalypse?" She listened with intensity, as if she was truly interested in hearing what he had to say, and although his idea was absolutely idiotic, she had replied with a level of kindness I never would have managed. Impressive.

"Exactly! Ooh, I know. You could be Rogue, and I'll be Cyclops."

Kayla's head tipped backward as she exploded with genuine laughter. "Why Rogue? I mean, maybe I want to be Storm. She's badass, you know."

"Yeah, but you're pretty, like Rogue."

Kayla blushed as if she hadn't gotten those kinds of comments a million times. "Well, thank you." She patted his hand.

He smiled and looked down at where her fingertips touched the back of his hand. Then he looked over his shoulder and glared. Kayla's instant frown made me spring up on the balls of my feet.

"No, you're wrong!" He yelled at an empty spot in the room.

Kayla grabbed his wrist. "Marcus, calm down."

He snatched his wrist out of her grasp and turned in his chair toward whatever invisible person he screamed at. "No! I don't have to listen to you! She's my friend." He stood up and marched over to the empty space, swinging like he was backhanding someone.

Kayla jumped from her seat and stood in front of him. She placed her hands on his upper arms. "Marcus, they aren't going to hurt you."

"Get off me!" He shoved her away from him, hard. Not weighing much, Kayla flew into the chair behind her. Bolted to the floor, the chair didn't budge. She yelped in pain and crashed to the ground.

I took a step toward her, every fiber in me wanting to make sure she was okay. But then I remembered what I was and ground my teeth.

Seeing the violence, the nurses rushed in. Two of the bigger men grabbed Marcus as he fought them, eventually having to resort to a tranquilizer to calm him down. Two others jogged to Kayla where she sat on the ground, her eyes wet with tears. She clutched her side where her ribs had hit the metal chair. I balled my hands into fists, angry that I could do nothing but watch as the nurses helped her to her feet and led her out of the cafeteria.

After Marcus' outburst, Kayla had been taken to the first floor where the medical part of the asylum was located. They'd run x-rays and eventually treated her for a bruised rib. But she still winced every time she breathed.

With my arms crossed over my chest, I watched Kayla converse with her psychiatrist.

"How many times have we told you not to intercede when Marcus is having an episode?" the psychiatrist asked. The name on her coat read Dr. Malcolm.

"I know." Kayla's eyes dropped to the floor.

"Then why did you confront him?"

"I just wanted to help."

Dr. Malcolm's stare was intense. She folded her hands in her lap and sighed. "Kayla, it's not up to you to fix Marcus. You know that."

Kayla nodded but didn't look up at her doctor.

"You have a good heart. But sometimes you need to take a step back and let the people who can help intercede. Do you need a sedative tonight?"

Kayla raised her head and shook it *no*.

"Okay. Well, push the call button if you change your mind." She patted Kayla's knee and stood.

Kayla nodded and, with a soft smile, Dr. Malcolm left the room. Kayla whimpered as she rose from her chair and lay on the bed. She took a well-loved teddy bear out from under her blankets and gripped the stuffed animal tight, her dark hair falling into her face as tears overflowed.

I turned to Tabbi. "Let's do the spell now and go relax before nightfall."

Tabbi nodded. She placed her small hand in mine, and together we crossed the room. In our invisible state, anything we touched—though we could feel the objects—would be undisturbed on the other side of the veil. It was the only way a Dreamweaver could touch a human without the human knowing they were there. Tabbi placed her hand over Kayla's heart and waited for me start speaking.

"*Cum vota nostra, nobis iurare ad protegendum. Angeli ligare nose simus unum.*"

Tabbi spoke the words alongside me: "With our vows, we do swear to protect. Angels, bind us so we may become one." When Kayla's skin under Tabbi's hand flashed blue, we knew the spell worked. Now, if Tabbi focused hard enough, she would be able to get inside Kayla's head and see what Kayla saw, feel what Kayla was feeling, even if they weren't in the same room. The spell helped us stay connected to our charge. Then whenever Kayla needed us outside of her normal sleeping pattern, like a nap, Tabbi would alert me, and I'd evaporate to wherever Kayla was.

"Whew. Humans are complicated," Tabbi said, removing her hand from Kayla's chest.

"If you could read Protectors' minds, I think you'd find we're complicated, too."

Tabbi shrugged. "Probably. Hey, you want to get food?"

I chuckled at her sudden change in thought. "Sure."

We evaporated.

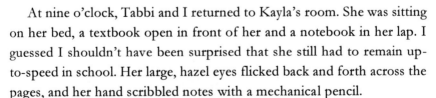

At nine o'clock, Tabbi and I returned to Kayla's room. She was sitting on her bed, a textbook open in front of her and a notebook in her lap. I guessed I shouldn't have been surprised that she still had to remain up-to-speed in school. Her large, hazel eyes flicked back and forth across the pages, and her hand scribbled notes with a mechanical pencil.

Following a knock at her door, Kayla slid her notebook into the pages of her textbook, marking where she'd left off, and set her book on the floor. She stood with a wince as a nurse entered with more medicine.

"How are you feeling?" the nurse asked.

"I'm still in a lot of pain. Was there nothing else Dr. Malcolm could give me?"

"The doctor prescribed you more Vicodin, but if you still can't sleep, let us know." She handed Kayla the small, paper cup. Kayla took the pills and downed them in one big gulp of water.

The nurse turned off the light and left the room, then Kayla crawled into bed. Within minutes her soft snores filled the room.

"Okay, kiddo. You're up," I said to Tabbi.

Tabbi's eyes tightened in concentration as she climbed onto the bed, positioning one leg on either side of Kayla's body. She leaned forward, tucking her red hair behind her ears, held her hands close to Kayla's face and closed her eyes. The dream Tabbi created for Kayla shone on the wall above her bed.

At the beach, a young Kayla was carried on the back of a man I guessed was her father. He had the same dark hair and the same hazel eyes, and their smiles were identical. Kayla's arms linked around his neck, and her legs wrapped around his waist. Laughing, they barreled into the ocean until the water got deep enough for her father to fall backward. With a squeal, Kayla and her dad disappeared under the waves. When their heads popped back up, they were both still laughing.

What had happened to force this happy child into the one locked away in the asylum?

I continued to watch Kayla's day at the beach until the sun peeked over the horizon here in Ohio. The clock on the other side of the room read seven in the morning. How had we not received a visit from any Nightmares?

Frowning in confusion, I tapped Tabbi's shoulder. "Come on. Nightmares only come out when it's dark. Let's get some rest."

Tabbi's eyes opened, and she moved her hands away from Kayla's head. The dream playing above the bed flickered into nothingness.

I knocked on Tabbi's door around one o'clock. Lunch would soon be over at the asylum, and Kayla would return to her room. Giovanni demanded we watch our charge for two days to really get to know them. Sometimes I felt like I was going to the zoo.

Tabbi cracked open the door and glared at me through the gap. "Ten more minutes?"

I shook my head with a smile. "I know the first few days are rough, but you know how Giovanni gets when we don't follow directions."

She rolled her eyes and closed the door. Ten minutes later, she emerged in sweat pants and a too-big T-shirt. "Okay, let's go. But for the record, I sleep until four." She stuck her hand in mine, and together we evaporated.

An older woman sat on the bed across from Kayla. She had auburn hair that twisted into a bun on the back of her head. She was dressed in very expensive business clothes, and the white coat of a doctor draped over the same rocking chair where Kayla painted. It didn't take me long to figure out this was her mother. Their facial features were too similar. I listened to their conversation.

"How are you feeling?" Kayla's mother asked. She placed her hand on Kayla's knee.

"Fine." Kayla fidgeted with her fingernails.

Kayla's mother removed her hand. "The doctor tells me you had a good night last night. She said she put you on new medication. Do you think it's working?"

"I don't know."

"Well, what about your group therapy? Is that helping?"

Kayla shrugged and stood from the bed to stare out the window at the garden below.

"Have you been playing your violin lately?"

"No."

"Are they not letting you? I thought I made it very clear that music helps you."

"I don't want to play."

A look of horror split her mother's face. "You don't want to play?" She spoke every word as if it was its own sentence.

Kayla's body snapped around so fast I would've had whiplash had I been in her shoes. "No, *Mom*. I don't want to play. In fact, you can take it with you." She stomped across the room, pulled out a case from under her bed and threw the violin in her mother's lap.

Kayla's mother's eyes reddened. "But you love your violin."

"No, I *loved* my violin. Past tense. As in I don't want anything to do with the life I had before you and your boyfriend ruined it."

Pain and anger radiated off Kayla like heat from a furnace on a cold day. And I wasn't the only one who felt her fury. Tabbi shot me a sidelong glance, and Kayla's mother stood up from the bed, her cheeks flushed. She left the violin where she once sat, patting the box.

"Its home is here with you." She crossed the room to where her doctor's coat laid and threw it on. Then she grabbed her purse and walked to the door. With her hand on the door's handle, she turned back around to her daughter. "I love you, Kayla-Bear. When you're ready to come home, just let me know." She left the room without waiting for a word from her daughter.

Ten seconds later, Kayla collapsed to the floor in heaving sobs. My heart lurched in my chest. I took a step forward, my body aching to hold her in my arms. Then, realizing what I was again about to do, I snatched my hand away.

What the hell was that? I had never felt like this before, not even when I was still human myself. Tabbi stared at me with a raised eyebrow, and I fought the urge to clear my throat. "You know, I think we've seen enough. What do you say to getting in a nap before nightfall?"

"Yes, please!"

When she slipped her hand into mine, I evaporated us back to the apartment building.

CHAPTER FIVE

After Kayla's emotional breakdown—and my near slip-up—I'd tried to force myself to sit down in front of the television and pay attention to *Sportscenter*. But my attention had only stayed on the show for about twenty minutes before returning to her. Annoyed, I'd found a late afternoon course on OSU's campus and hid, invisible, at the back of the room, listening to the professor lecture about imagery in eighteenth century literature.

Now, I stood next to Tabbi in Kayla's room, watching as she put finishing touches on the portrait she'd drawn of the old man sitting in the courtyard. The in-progress version had already impressed me, but her finished product was incredible. She used only pastels, yet the picture looked life-like and had captured so much beauty of the garden below.

The door to Kayla's room opened. A heavy-set nurse walked in with Kayla's usual nighttime cocktail. "Lights out, Kayla."

Kayla closed her crayon box before taking the cup of water and swallowing her medicine.

"Push the button if you need us," the nurse said, leaving the room.

Kayla climbed into bed when the nurse flicked off her light. Her soft snores were our cue. I pulled two daggers out of my belt while Tabbi went to work.

Above the bed, the dream Tabbi weaved came to life. This time, Kayla stood on a stage in a long, black gown. She brought her violin up to her left shoulder and placed her chin in its rest. In her right hand was the bow, and after taking a deep breath, Kayla moved the bow across the violin's strings.

Music filled the room, each note on perfect pitch. It was a beautiful, melancholy tune that she played with so much emotion the song took on a life of its own. The melody sped up and slowed down in just the right places, grew louder and fell softer in a way that told a story. Goose pimples rose on my arms.

I closed my eyes and listened to the music, letting the notes transport me to a place of serenity. Only when the last note played and her dream filled with an eruption of claps and cheering did I open my eyes. The Kayla in the dream wore a smile that made me smile in return. She was so beautiful, so happy. And she looked so confident, like she knew where she belonged.

Then the scent of sulfur filled the air.

Bugger. The Nightmares were coming.

Moving closer to the bed, I gripped my daggers tight in my hands. Tabbi sensed my movement and glanced in my direction. I knew she felt them too.

"Just keep working. I'll keep you safe."

Tabbi nodded and weaved another dream.

The first Nightmare came through the wall at the far side of the room. The creature slithered through the white stone until its whole scaly body was in view. Breathing through my mouth—the sulfur smell was intense—I threw my dagger. My blade, spelled to kill what was already dead, entered its skull right between the eyes. The beast hissed as it fell to the floor. I quickly disposed of the monster, lighting its body on fire, then waited for the second.

From behind the first came the other, the Nightmare's glowing, red eyes staring holes into me. *Got you, bitch,* I thought, bringing my hand back to throw my dagger. But through the window came a third, through the door a fourth, and near the rocking chair came a fifth.

What the hell? Nightmares never came out in fives. I might have gotten five in one night before, but never at the same time.

Yanking my mobile of my back pocket, I sent a "1-1-2" text—standard emergency number in Italy—to Giovanni. He would document the message and send Samantha to help me. Before I could stuff the phone back into my pocket, the Nightmare from the door rushed me, the nails in its claw-like hands extended like a cat's. I blocked the beast's first slash and kicked it in the stomach, sending the creature flying into the wall. It hit with a thud and fell to the ground.

A Nightmare neared the bed from the window. Sprinting, I leapt over Kayla's body, slicing off the hand of the Nightmare before it could touch her. The monster screamed, its voice earsplitting, like a baby's cry through a megaphone. I groaned at the sound, knowing if I covered my ears, I would lose my defense. The Nightmare sliced at me with its other hand, but I chopped that one off, too. Again the beast shrieked, and I kicked it into the window while fighting the urge to cover my ears.

Ready to throw my dagger into the Nightmare's head, a blow to my side sent me flying into the wall next to Kayla's bed. My shoulder hit the wall with a crunch, and the knife fell out of my hand. I swore and, with my good arm, back-handed the Nightmare that was still on top of me. My fist hit cheekbone. The creature's face snapped sideways, and its moment of stunned silence was all I needed. With the dagger still in my hand, I sliced through the Nightmare's neck. Black blood spattered onto my clothes, and I pushed the creature off my body.

Before I had a chance to get up, Tabbi's scream filled the room. I snapped my head in her direction to see a dagger in her back—my dagger. The Nightmare on the far side of the room must've taken the blade from the one I had killed earlier and thrown it—something I'd never seen before.

"No!" With a grunt, I jumped from the ground. My left shoulder was dislocated, but I wasn't going to let Tabbi die. I ran to her and threw my arms around her, evaporating to Giovanni's room.

Our sudden appearance startled him. "What the—"

"I called for backup. Why didn't you send Sam?"

Seth and one of Giovanni's guards, Rosado, sprinted to where I knelt on the ground with Tabbi. Her face was wet with tears, and she squirmed in pain. Rosado picked her up and carried her out of the room. Seth stared at me with fear in his eyes.

"Seth, go with Daniel now. I will send Samantha immediately," Giovanni said.

Grabbing Seth's arm, I evaporated us to Kayla's room. She writhed on the bed, screaming in terror. A Nightmare had taken Tabbi's place as soon as we left.

On the wall above Kayla's head, the nightmare played. A man twice her age—and twice her size—crushed her against a desk and stuck a dagger in her side. I rushed the beast and tackled it off the bed onto the floor.

Wincing at the pain shooting down my left arm, I balled my hands into fists and beat the Nightmare mercilessly. The monster rolled on the floor underneath me, its cries making my eardrums ache. But I didn't stop. The creature's shrieks only made me want to end its existence more.

I hit the beast again and again, its bones crushing beneath my fists. Black blood coated my knuckles, and all I could smell was sulfur. But I hit the hairy creature again, determined to make the bastard pay for hurting Tabbi. It wasn't until Samantha's hands rested on my arms that I stopped.

"Daniel, it's gone. The fight's over." Samantha's eyes peered into mine. I knew her well enough to see the fear in them. Jumping up, I took a step toward Kayla's bed. But before I could reach her, the door to the room burst open and three nurses ran to her bedside, speaking to her and trying to wake her. When Kayla finally did, she shook like she'd been outside in negative degree weather too long.

"Call for Dr. Malcolm," one of the nurses said as she sat next to Kayla on her bed, rubbing her back.

I stood there, watching, my chest tightening. With a growl, I evaporated to Rome and landed in Giovanni's office. When he wasn't there, I ran down the steps to the hospital wing on the fifth floor. Samantha, knowing me as well as she knew herself, chased after me.

"Daniel, slow down. You don't want to do this."

"Back off, Sam."

She grabbed my arm. I smacked her hand away and barreled through the doors into the medical ward. As expected, Giovanni was there, checking in on Tabbi who was still crying.

I rammed Giovanni up against the wall. "This is *your* fault! I called for backup. I followed protocol. And now Tabbi's wounded and my charge was attacked. What the *hell* happened?"

Giovanni's face glowed red. He pushed me off. Samantha placed a hand on my chest before I could retaliate.

"Your frustration is understandable, Daniel, but if you take one more step out of line, I will bench you."

I stood there, my heart pounding and my hands clenched at my sides. Giovanni adjusted his shirt and stormed out of the wing without a second glance in my direction. Watching him go, I pictured running after him and slamming his arrogant head into the wall, but I forced myself to stay put until I'd had a moment to calm down.

Tabbi's cries stopped. Turning away from Samantha, I entered Tabbi's room. She was asleep, her bright red hair like fire around her head. An Indian woman stood next to the bed, taking her pulse. The stone she'd used to intensify her healing abilities still glowed in her hand. I recognized her from when she healed one of my previous, almost fatal injuries. Trishna, a witch and the leader of our allied coven.

Not entirely human, witches and warlocks—or the Magus, as they were collectively called—were the only beings in the supernatural realm we actually had relations with. Not surprising Trishna'd been called in to assist with healing Tabbi.

I stepped back into the hall knowing Tabbi was in safe hands then jumped when a short, thin man appeared out of nowhere, his black hair falling into his face.

Bartholomew spoke with a thick, Middle-Eastern accent, "Daniel, are you injured?"

Bartholomew was our Keeper and the oldest Protector in existence. Rumor said he was picked by the Angels themselves to watch over humans in B.C. times, and he was the one who decided who was chosen as a Protector of the Night. Bartholomew knew everything about everything, including medicine—though some injuries were beyond his abilities. Like Tabbi's.

Almost as if on cue, the pain in my shoulder throbbed. I was coming down from my adrenaline high. "My shoulder. I think it's dislocated."

He nodded and led Samantha and I to a different room. "Sit." He pointed to the table in the middle of the room. I followed his instructions and avoided Samantha's gaze. Did she really have to be here for this?

"I need to reset it." He rested his left hand on the top of my shoulder and placed my arm between his side and right arm. "Three, two, one—"

I managed to spout off every swear word known to man in thirty seconds and swore again when he stuck a long needle in my shoulder, pumping my joint full of the same healing serum I'd received the night before. Bartholomew handed me a sling and a bottle of painkillers.

"That should heal in a day or so. Take the medicine as needed, but remember the pills will make you drowsy."

Nodding, I slipped my arm into the sling with a grimace. "May I ask you a question?"

Bartholomew stared at me, his eyes wide. He wasn't used to people of my level coming to him for advice. Usually it was just Giovanni. "Well of course, my boy. What do you need to know?"

"How often do Nightmares show up in groups of five?"

"Five?" Bartholomew's eyebrows rose. "I suppose... Well, I haven't heard of it happening since the fourteen hundreds. Why?"

"The girl I'm protecting had five Nightmares come after her tonight, all at the same time. I didn't know if that was common."

Bartholomew stroked his goatee. "No, not really. I don't know what to tell you. I can look into it for you, see if there are any others receiving multiple Nightmares."

I got off the table. "Brilliant. Thank you."

He waved his hand and wandered toward the door, still lost in thought. "I'm here to serve." He disappeared into the hall.

Following him out the door, a knot formed in my stomach. What was it about Kayla that drew so many Nightmares to her—and what would I do if it happened again?

CHAPTER SIX

I popped the pain pills as soon as I got to my flat and plopped on the sofa. Covering my eyes with my good arm, I couldn't help but wonder if Bartholomew would alert Giovanni to something that shouldn't have been mentioned. If there *was* something about Kayla that attracted the Nightmares, Giovanni would pull her protection, just like he had with Hitler. I couldn't let that happen.

The drugs hit me, and my eyes drooped like they were attached to hand weights. If I didn't get to my bed soon, I'd pass out right here. Forcing myself up from the sofa, I stumbled through the apartment until someone knocked on my door. With a groan, I wobbled to the door. Samantha and Seth stood on the other side.

"What are you two doing here?" I asked.

"Giovanni sent us," Seth replied. "After I told him how many Nightmares there were, he made Kayla a level red." He handed me a red, rubber bracelet. "He sent Samantha to help you, and me to 'formulate a report on the frequency of your visits from the Nightmares.'" He mimicked Giovanni's Italian accent.

"Brilliant." I grabbed the bracelet and stepped back, leaving the door open and bracing the wall as I made my way toward my bedroom. Samantha said something, but I was almost asleep, which meant she sounded like the teacher from *Charlie Brown*. Before I could ask her to repeat herself, I fell face first on the bed.

Sunlight woke me, and I sat up, groaning at the pain in my shoulder. Bartholomew's shot had definitely worn off. I let my arm out of the sling and stretched it out, swinging it in a circle. At least the pain was less than when the injury took place—and I still had good mobility.

Glancing at the clock, I jumped out of bed. Just after nine o'clock. Why had no one awakened me while Kayla slept? Still wearing the same, bloodstained clothes as yesterday, I stormed into the living room. Seth was passed out on the sofa. I smacked his feet, and he jumped.

"Jesus, Daniel. What the hell?"

"Why didn't you wake me up?" I asked.

"Because we thought you could use the sleep."

"Damn it, Seth, you guys could've gotten hurt."

He rolled over and waved his hand at me like I was a pesky fly. "Relax. Tabbi's temporary replacement showed up, so I helped Sam catch. There were only two Nightmares anyway."

I still couldn't believe they would leave me. "I'm coming with you tonight."

"Fine, fine. But please shower first. You smell worse than Giovanni's cigars."

Rolling my eyes, I left him to shower and change. Giovanni better give Seth and Samantha their own places soon. If Seth had to crash on my sofa, Samantha was probably on Tabbi's. After a while, they were going to want a bed. And if Samantha was as messy as I knew Seth was, Tabbi would kill her the minute she tripped over a dirty shirt on the floor.

I tried making myself lunch, but now that I wasn't bogged down by anger or pain—or drugs—my thoughts returned to Kayla. What had happened after we left? Had Dr. Malcolm been able to calm her down? The memory of her writhing on the bed filled my mind, and food no longer sounded appealing. Shutting off the stove, I ran my hand down my face and glanced over at Seth who was out cold. He probably would be for hours.

Damn it, Daniel. I tried to remind myself I couldn't get attached to my charge, but I knew nothing would stop me from checking in on her. Resolved, I closed my eyes and evaporated to Kayla's room.

Kayla sat in her chair, her feet propped on the seat and her knees under her chin. She wrapped her arms around her legs as she stared at the garden below. Her eyes were swollen and red, as if she'd cried so hard there were no more tears left to fall.

She'd tied back her dark brown hair at the nape, and her ponytail ran halfway down her spine like a thick, dark brown stripe in her white uniform. She turned when a nurse knocked on her door.

"Time to go to therapy," the nurse said as she stepped into the room.

Kayla frowned but rose from her chair and followed the nurse out the door. I stayed close behind, not wanting to miss a moment. My boots stomped on the floor, echoing down the corridor.

36

Wait, why are my boots making noise?

I caught my reflection in the glass of one of the doors—something that only happened if I were corporeal. *Shit!* After glancing down the hall to make sure no one was looking, I stopped walking and focused on making myself invisible again. In a flash, my reflection disappeared from the window. I ran my hands through my blond hair and let out a sigh of irritation. *Snap out of it, Daniel.* If I was still acting like a fool tomorrow, I'd ask to be reassigned. Or benched. I was tired, anyway. Maybe it was time I took a long break.

Kayla was in a large room on the floor below. It was about the size of my living room and covered in brown shag carpet. White folding chairs were arranged in a circle in front of a large whiteboard, but the rest of the room was bare. Kayla took a seat as the others filed into the room. I stood near the whiteboard and watched the others join her.

Kayla's friend from the lunch room, Marcus, grabbed a chair next to her, and across from Kayla sat a girl with pink hair and braces. Two others sat in the empty chairs—one a very heavy-set man who kind of reminded me of a young Santa Claus, and the other a boy, maybe in his mid-twenties, who had burn marks down the left side of his body.

Dr. Malcolm was the last person to enter. She closed the door behind her and took the chair opposite Santa Claus. She pulled out a notebook and pen and jotted a few notes.

"Glad to see you all came today. Unlike last time, let's make this meeting one where we all support each other, okay? Now, how is everyone doing?" she asked.

Santa Claus answered first. "There was a rat in my room today. Same one as last time. You promised they'd take care of the rat."

Dr. Malcolm scribbled a note while answering. "One of the nurses checked, Hunter. They couldn't find a rat."

"Well, he was in there."

"I had a rat in my room once. It was before the fire that tried to *kill me*!" the burn victim yelled.

I raised an eyebrow.

"Donald, if you continue with the outbursts, I will have you returned to your room."

He sat back in his chair and fidgeted with a loose string on the bottom of his shirt.

"Kayla, you had a bad night last night. How are you feeling today?"

"Fine." Her voice was strong, but her body gave her away. Her eyes fell to the floor, and she clasped her shaking hands in her lap. I frowned. Her bad night was my fault.

Dr. Malcolm stared at Kayla, her lips also in a frown. She saw right through Kayla, too. She tapped her pen on her notepad. "Would you like to share more about how you're feeling?"

Kayla shook her head.

"This therapy isn't going to work if you aren't willing to talk about how you're feeling."

When Kayla shrugged, Dr. Malcolm sighed. She continued with the other patients, but my gaze remained on Kayla. Hers never left the floor, and she quickly wiped a falling tear from her cheek. She tried to remain strong, but I could tell she was breaking on the inside.

For the rest of the hour, Dr. Malcolm asked questions of her patients and jotted notes. When the session was over, she returned her attention to Kayla.

"Kayla, I'd like for you to stay a minute." When the others had filed out of the room, Dr. Malcolm closed the door and sat across from Kayla. "You were pretty shaken up last night, so I didn't have a chance to get much information from you. I'd like you to tell me what happened."

"It was another dream."

"The same as last time?"

Kayla nodded. "I grabbed the gun and tried to shoot him, but I kept missing. Then he burst into flames, just how I... wanted him to."

Dr. Malcolm paused, calculating her response. "You mean, just how you remember?"

Kayla's eyes fell to the floor.

Dr. Malcom sighed. "Kayla, we've talked about this. You need to start believing that what you thought you saw was your brain's way of protecting you during the attack —"

"I know what I saw!" Kayla yelled. She gripped the seat of her chair and fought the tears that pooled in the bottom of her eyes.

Dr. Malcolm spoke calmly. "This is why you're here, Kayla. What you saw was your mind's reaction to what that man did to you. As soon as you come to terms with this, the dreams will stop feeling so real and you can move past the pain."

The word "attack" brought up memories from my past I'd tried to forget. I'd died saving two women from the brutality of savage men. By the way Kayla's face looked right now, I was positive I knew where this was going, what happened to her. Having heard enough, I balled my hands into fists, closed my eyes and evaporated to Rome.

Tabbi was awake when I arrived, though my sudden appearance startled her. "Jeez, Daniel. You could've at least knocked."

"Sorry." I sat in the chair next to her bed and tried to appear unfazed. "How are you feeling?"

"Better. Trishna did a good job healing me, but Bartholomew wants to keep me one more night until he's certain I can return to work." She squinted at me. "What's wrong?"

Damn. Can't hide anything from her. "When you read Kayla's mind, did you read all of it?"

Tabbi scrunched her small nose. "Well, yeah. It is my job to know my charge." She spoke like I was stupid to forget. I would've smiled if my heart wasn't already consumed with anger.

"Then you saw what happened to her the night she was attacked."

Tabbi frowned. "Yeah."

"Was she raped?"

Tabbi shook her head. "Here. Let me show you what happened." She held her hand out to me.

Since I was Tabbi's partner in protecting Kayla, I could see what she saw in Kayla's mind once I linked hands with her. The connection was part of the supernatural bond we'd created with Kayla when we performed our ritual the first day we were assigned to her. I grabbed Tabbi's hand and closed my eyes. Within seconds, I was in Kayla's head, seeing through her eyes and feeling her emotions. I had *become* Kayla.

Kayla hummed as she chopped vegetables for her salad on the island in her kitchen. Someone knocked on the front door, and she glanced at the clock on her microwave. *I thought I told Renee not to come until seven.* Kayla set the knife down and walked through the immense house to the foyer then opened the door. Matt, her mother's boyfriend, stood on the other side with a bouquet of flowers in his hands.

"Hi, Kayla. Is your mom home?"

Aww, Mom's going to love this. Kayla shook her head with a soft smile. "She's at work until four, but I'll let her know you stopped by. Want me to put the flowers in a vase?"

"Okay. Well, can I at least come in and leave a note to go with it?"

Kayla nodded. "Sure."

Matt smiled and stepped inside the door. Kayla led him through the house to the kitchen and took a vase out of a cupboard. "So, what's up with the flowers?"

"Oh, you know. Just thought your mom would like them."

Kayla giggled. "You know her well." She turned around to hand the vase to him and stopped. The flowers were on the counter, and Matt stood just inches from her. A slow smile rose on his face. Kayla's heart raced. "Um, if you'll just let me get to the flowers, I can, you know."

Matt grabbed her wrist as she tried to push past him. "The flowers can wait. They're not the real reason I'm here. You are."

"Let me go." Kayla stared right into his eyes though the hairs on her arms rose and her palms sweated.

But he didn't. Instead, he slammed her against the kitchen counter and tried to plant his lips on hers. The vase fell to the floor and shattered.

"No!" she shouted and turned her face. Kayla shoved Matt's face away from hers.

He growled in annoyance. "Don't fight me, Kayla. I don't want to hurt you."

Matt leaned in to kiss her again, but Kayla slapped him.

"Behave!" He hit her back, punching her in the eye.

Kayla squealed and tried to struggle out of Matt's hold, but he pushed her harder until the edge of the counter dug into her back to the point of pain.

"Let me go! Help!" she screamed.

"Shut up!" He hit her again.

She didn't quiet. Instead her screams turned into cries. She squirmed, slapped him and kicked his shins, but all she seemed to do was fuel his desire. His lips found her neck as he held her wrists against the cold marble of the countertops, and he kissed up her chin to her lips.

Then he slid his tongue into her mouth. Kayla bit down, and Matt jumped back with a curse. "You little bitch!" He took one hand off of her to slap her.

She reacted quickly and brought her knee up, hitting him between the legs as hard as she could. His moment of shock was all she needed. Kayla squirmed out of his grasp and ran through her house and up the stairs, knowing her mother's gun was in the desk drawer in her room. After being home alone all the time, she'd stolen it from her mom's safe and tucked it away in her bedroom as a safety precaution.

Her paranoia was about to pay off.

With shaky hands, Kayla grabbed the revolver out of her desk. She turned around, her finger on the trigger. Matt entered the room, his face red and his teeth bared. The knife Kayla had been using to cut her vegetables was in his right hand.

Kayla pulled the trigger, her heart racing in her chest. Matt jumped as the bullet flew past his head. Kayla whimpered and pulled the trigger again. The bullet missed.

Four more times she shot at him, and Matt shrunk away each time. But Kayla's hands were too shaky. The gun had a wicked kick, and she never once hit her target. Her chin trembled as Matt stalked toward her, a fiendish smirk on his face. She grabbed a metal trophy off her desk and held the award like a baseball player at the plate, ready to strike when he neared her. Her palms were clammy and her legs weak. When he was close enough, she swung.

And missed.

Matt's dagger entered her left side. Kayla dropped the trophy with a scream as blood poured from her body. He grabbed her arms and flung her onto the floor. Kayla sobbed, both at the burning pain in her stomach and the fear coursing through her veins. She held her hands out in front of her, praying she would die before her mother's boyfriend raped her.

Warm, awkward tingles ran from the tips of her toes into her palms, like her body had been asleep but was now waking up. Matt stood near her feet, unbuckling his belt. Kayla sobbed, begging God for help. Then, without warning, Matt went up in flames.

I ripped my hand out of Tabbi's and jumped from my chair like I'd sat on something sharp. My shaking hands raked through my hair, and I paced around the room, my heart pounding in my ears. The room blurred. I wanted to drag Matt out of Hell and kill him again. At least he'd gotten what he deserved.

"Daniel?" Tabbi asked.

"Give me a moment." I took a deep breath and tried to slow my pulse.

"She really did produce those flames, didn't she? I hadn't felt it before, but this time, it was like it came from inside her," Tabbi said.

I nodded. Kayla *had* set fire to her attacker. She was telling Dr. Malcolm the truth.

Something lurched in my chest. Kayla needed to know she wasn't crazy. Staying away from her now was going to be even more impossible than before.

I never should've taken Tabbi's hand.

CHAPTER SEVEN

S amantha was waiting for me when I returned to my flat. She sat on the sofa and, as usual, watched *Judge Judy*. She idolized that woman a little too much sometimes.

"Make yourself at home," I said.

Her head whipped around at the sound of my voice. "Where have you been?"

I grabbed a Coke out of the fridge before responding. "Visiting Kayla."

Samantha turned off the TV. "You need to be careful, Daniel. If anyone were to find out you were there alone and outside of her sleeping pattern, they might—"

"No one's going to find out, Sam. And besides, Kayla doesn't know I'm there."

"Fine. I was only trying to help. Giovanni has spies everywhere. Why *are* you so interested in her, anyway?"

I glared at her, already angry with myself for developing unwanted feelings. She didn't need to judge me, too.

Samantha held her hands up in defeat. "Whatever. Tabbi's replacement is Hendrik, by the way. Thought I'd warn you."

I groaned on the inside. Hendrik was a wanker, and he was one of Giovanni's favorites. The two of them *had* to have been lovers. Giovanni's preference for men was no secret.

"Thanks for the heads up," I said.

"Yeah." Samantha walked to the door to leave. "Oh, it's your turn to report in to Giovanni. Tomorrow morning, he'll expect to see you in Rome."

I let her leave without saying another word.

At exactly nine o'clock, I showed up in Kayla's room to do my job. Samantha, Seth and Hendrik were already there. Kayla twisted her hair into a ponytail and flipped off the light. I must've missed the nurse coming in to give her medicine. She crawled under her bed sheets, lay on her back and closed her eyes.

"I hope you protect me better than you protected your last Weaver," Hendrik said to me.

I gripped one of the daggers on my belt. "Keep talking and see what happens when my blade misses."

Samantha glared at me. Seth coughed to hide his chuckle. I fought the smirk that wanted to show, especially when Hendrik's face turned red.

Before Hendrik could reply, Kayla's breathing slowed. "Better get to work, mate," I said, waving Hendrik away.

Hendrik's face turned a brighter shade of red, then he positioned himself over Kayla's body.

Above the bed, Hendrik's dream played. In it, Kayla wore a soft yellow, strapless gown. Her hair was curled over one shoulder, and her smile lit up the room.

Kayla walked down the stairs of her house to a large foyer where a boy in a tuxedo waited for her. He eyed Kayla like she was just another girl he expected to bed before the night was over. An eagerness to smack that arrogant grin off his face jolted through my body, especially when he placed a hand between Kayla's shoulder blades and led her out the door.

Stop it, Daniel! She should've been able to dream about her junior prom, or wherever the hell she was going. I shouldn't have cared that she was being led out her front door looking like that with a boy who wasn't me.

The first Nightmare dropped into Kayla's room from the ceiling like Tom Cruise in *Mission Impossible*. Its surprise attack caught me off guard for a moment, but I jumped into action and grabbed its foot, pulling the monster as far from the bed as possible. The Nightmare flipped around to attack me, and I dug my blade under its jaw. The beast screeched in pain before collapsing to the floor, its hands grasped around its neck as black blood sprayed from the creature's throat. I wiped my hand and my blade on my handkerchief and kicked the bastard to the corner of the room for later disposal.

Samantha watched my every move. I was about to tell her to mind her own business when a Nightmare crawled through the wall behind Seth.

"Seth, drop!" I yelled.

He fell to the ground without hesitation, and I threw my dagger between the Nightmare's eyes.

"Everybody move closer to the bed and face out. They're getting wiser."

Samantha and Seth obeyed my instructions. I stood at the foot of the bed with Samantha on my left and Seth on my right. Hendrik was already facing the headboard, so he'd shout if any tried to get in that way.

Two more Nightmares came in a similar fashion as the first, then three more entered through the walls. I grabbed one from the ceiling and threw it into the Nightmare on the far side of the room. Then I grabbed the other beast and threw it into the one directly across from Samantha. They crashed into each other like a bowling ball into a pin.

Knowing Samantha could handle those two and Seth would quickly dispose of his Nightmare, I ran at the two on the far side of the room. I threw my remaining dagger into the back of one of the Nightmare's heads as it stood. The beast flopped to the ground, and the other—who was missing an ear—hissed a warning at me. But I didn't back down.

I ducked when the Nightmare swiped at my face with clawed hands, and I jabbed the monster in the stomach. The butt of my hand punched the creature in the nose when it bent over with a groan. The Nightmare's head tipped backward, and I used that moment to kick its legs out from under it. The beast fell to the floor with a yelp of surprise.

I tore my dagger out of the dead Nightmare's head while the one-eared guy scrambled to its feet. Black blood oozed from the creature's nose. It screeched at me like an angry hawk that couldn't catch its prey, and I waited for the Nightmare to strike.

"Come on, bitch. Hit me."

Instead of swiping at me again like I expected, the monster tried to tackle me. But I recovered quickly, using the Nightmare's momentum to toss it over my shoulder. The beast fell to the ground behind me. I turned around and straddled its back, kneeling on the creature's arms to keep it from getting up. From beneath me, the Nightmare squirmed and squealed, and in one quick movement, I wrapped my arms around its head and twisted, snapping the monster's neck.

"God, Daniel. A dagger would've done the trick," Samantha said. She and Seth dragged the other dead Nightmares to where mine laid on the floor. I helped them pile the heavy bodies, then Seth took a lighter out of his pocket and lit the corpses on fire. Their demonic blood burned hot and fast. We stepped back to avoid any accidental burns.

"Daniel has a natural flare for the barbaric," Seth said.

"I do not."

"Then do you want to tell me what that was?" Samantha asked.

I didn't reply. I'd taken out my irritation on the Nightmares, transferring the anger mounting for myself toward them. Kayla had become an itch I couldn't scratch. Tomorrow I would tell Giovanni to take me off her protection. As much as I hated to admit, I was emotionally compromised.

"Will you guys be okay if I pop out? My shoulder's killing me," I lied. Bartholomew's serum had worked well, but I couldn't stay here anymore. They'd ring me if things got out of hand.

"Sure," Seth replied. He stared at me like he knew I was hiding something. Avoiding eye contact, I vanished.

I leaned against the side of the shower as hot water pounded my back. How long I'd been standing there, I didn't know. Somewhere along the way, I just stopped thinking altogether.

Turning around, I rinsed the shampoo out of my wavy hair—that now hung to the top of my ears—and turned off the water. When I stepped out, I wrapped a towel around my waist and stared at myself in the mirror. My blue eyes were framed with black circles. I looked as shitty as I felt.

When I opened the door and entered the living room, Seth sat on the sofa, staring at me.

"Blast," I said, jumping. "What the hell are you doing here?" The sun wouldn't come up for hours. He should be helping Samantha catch, especially now that I wasn't there.

"After we killed the round of Nightmares last night, no more showed up. Sam said she'd text if she needed help."

Shaking my head, I crossed through the living room, closing the bedroom door behind me. After throwing on gym shorts and a T-shirt, I reemerged. Seth stood against the sofa, facing the bedroom.

"This is getting awkward," I said.

"What's going on with you, man? I've never seen you fight like that."

Ignoring him, I grabbed a beer out of the fridge.

"Daniel, I'm not leavin' you alone until you spill."

I slammed the fridge door shut. "What do you want me to say?"

"I don't know. Try the truth, maybe?"

I chugged my beer. Seth crossed the room and slammed the fridge shut when I reached for another, prompting a glare from me.

"It's the girl, isn't it?" he asked. "Sam told me you'd been spending extra time watching her."

Raising my hands in exasperation, I pushed past him, running my hands through my hair.

"What do you want me to say? I've never had this problem before. I can't stop thinking about her. I can't stay away. Hell, I went corporeal by accident once!" He knew what happened when we revealed ourselves—our time as a Protector ended. Permanently. I continued, "I'm tired, Seth. Tomorrow I'm asking Giovanni to bench me before I do something stupid."

He walked into the living room, his hands extended out in front of him. "Now, wait. Don't go doin' that."

I crossed my arms over my chest and raised my eyebrows, asking him silently if he had a better idea.

Seth dropped his hands and sighed. "Look, don't give up yet. You won't last long if Giovanni puts you to work behind a desk. We'll figure somethin' out."

For minutes we stared at each other, then finally I nodded. I'd give him one more night.

Just one.

CHAPTER EIGHT

My fists beat the punching bag mercilessly. I'd tried to sleep after my conversation with Seth, but Kayla's hazel eyes taunted me, reminding me of my inability to do my job. I'd evaporated straight to our mansion's gym, knowing if I didn't start punching something soon, I was going to explode. As I expected, the room was completely empty. Protectors usually slept during the day, even when they were on leave from assignment.

I punched and kicked like my life depended on it, not bothering to wrap my hands or put on gloves. I wanted to feel the pain. No, I needed to feel the pain. When my shirt began to stick, I tore it off, and I didn't stop beating the bag until my arms felt like they were going to fall off.

I let myself take a break when my knuckles throbbed. They were raw, my hands having left bloody streaks on the bag. Then, I noticed I wasn't alone.

"What do you want, Sam?"

She stepped out of the shadows. "To talk to you. I know what you're going to do."

Ignoring her, I punched the bag again. Pain shot from my hands down my arms, but I didn't care. The pain kept me from thinking.

"After all these years, Daniel, you've never backed down from a challenge. Now, all the sudden, you want to be benched? I don't understand."

Damn it, Seth. I didn't answer her.

"Daniel, talk to me."

"No." I threw another punch.

"Would you just stop for one minute!"

Sweat dripped down my chest as I turned to face her. "Sam, I appreciate your concern. But it's done with. Let me be."

She shook her head. "No, Daniel. It's not done with." Her voice shook. "Because we—I—need you."

It didn't take me long to read her face. Seth was right. Samantha still hadn't moved on from our night. After I picked up my shirt from the floor, I walked around a weight machine to where she stood and placed my hands on her arms. "You've proven yourself to be a good friend and a great Catcher. I promise you'll do fine without me."

"But if Giovanni benches you, he'll remove you as my mentor."

"You don't need a mentor anymore. I've seen you fight. You're fierce on your own. You'll be okay."

Samantha paused, seeming to understand that she wasn't going to make me change my mind. Then, before I had a chance to evaporate, her hands pulled my face to hers, and her full lips pressed against mine.

A gentleman would've stepped away. But right now, I didn't care about being a gentleman. Samantha was a beautiful woman. Even though I'd never felt about her the way she felt about me, not noticing her beauty was impossible.

Dropping my shirt, I wrapped my arms around her, pulling her closer to me. I kissed her back and gently pressed her against the wall where she had been hiding in the shadows. Our lips opened and closed together. Her hands moved from my face down my chest to my stomach. They glided around to my back, pulling the lower half of my body against hers.

I jumped back like I had been zapped with a Taser. This wasn't right. I had no real feelings for her, and she didn't deserve to be treated like this.

Samantha's large, brown eyes followed my every movement. I ran my hand down my face. "I'm sorry. This isn't… I can't." I walked to where I'd left my shirt and picked it off the floor. Before I evaporated to my apartment, I turned to look at her. Samantha's lips were tight, and her hands gripped her pant legs.

"Please forgive me," I said before I disappeared.

At 8:55 p.m., I returned to Kayla's room. Seth and Samantha were already there. They eyed me with sadness, but neither said anything. I resumed my usual position and leaned against the back wall, crossing my arms over my chest.

Given Hendrik standing by Kayla's headboard, Bartholomew must not have cleared Tabbi for battle yet. All the better. It'd be too hard to say goodbye to her.

Kayla sat on her bed, reading, and at 8:58 p.m., the nurse provided Kayla her medicine. By 9:05 p.m., she was asleep, and Hendrik went to work. I closed my eyes and waited for the Nightmares to arrive.

Within thirty minutes the hairs on my arms rose, and I opened my eyes when sulfur filled my nose. Six Nightmares came from all directions. Before I had a chance to react, the Nightmare nearest me ran for the bed. I sprinted and caught the monster inches from the footboard, knocking it to the ground. The Nightmare thrashed in my arms, its elbow catching my nose. I swore as black lingered on the sides of my vision then punched the beast in the jaw. Its head bounced off the floor.

But the Nightmare was stronger than usual. It reacted quickly and kicked me off. The middle of my back hit the corner of Kayla's bed. I gasped for air, the wind knocked out of me. A blade flew over my head, hitting the Nightmare between the eyes. I jumped to my feet and spun around. Samantha had just saved my life.

"Not today, Daniel," she said before mule-kicking the Nightmare behind her.

After rolling my eyes, I flicked them around the room until I found Seth. He was battling two Nightmares simultaneously—and losing. Plucking Samantha's dagger out of my Nightmare's head and tucking it into my belt, I ran across the room to help my friend, a dagger in each hand.

Wrapping my arms around one of the Nightmares' necks from behind, I yanked the beast away from Seth. Its claws dug into my arm, trying to squirm away. I groaned in pain, but when I pulled the creature back far enough that it couldn't reach Seth, I let the Nightmare go and in the same motion sliced my dagger across its throat. The monster fell forward, slashing at whatever it could before collapsing on the ground. The Nightmare's scream was like a foghorn in my ear. I winced and turned away.

And that was when I saw the Nightmare on Kayla's bed dig his claws deep into Hendrik's chest and stomach. He screamed and the dream above Kayla's bed flickered to nothingness. I ran as hard as I could, leapt onto the bed and stabbed my dagger into the Nightmare's back. It screeched and dropped Hendrik. Hendrik fell off the bed, dead, into a ball on the floor. In one swift movement, the Nightmare turned around and backhanded me so hard I flew into the window. The back of my head smacked the glass and I fell to the ground. Blackness took over.

Kayla's screams woke me minutes later. Samantha and Seth stood back to back, fighting two of the remaining three Nightmares. The third, the large one that tossed me into the window like a stuffed animal, poised over Kayla's body. From where I laid on the ground, I saw for the first time how truly massive the beast was, like someone had pumped it full of steroids. I'd never seen one so large. No wonder my blade didn't kill it.

I pushed myself up, my body aching everywhere. Throwing a dagger was out, given the monster's proximity to Kayla, but I could charge it. Running and jumping on the bed, I threw my entire body weight into the Nightmare. The creature budged but didn't fall. I did the only thing I could and heaved backward, pulling the oversized beast with me to the floor.

The Nightmare landed on top of me, sending ripples of pain down my back and legs. I jammed my dagger into the side of its neck as hard as I could. Black blood squirted out of the wound, coating both the floor and me, but I hit my mark. The monster squealed then went silent.

"No! Please no! Help! Somebody help me!" Kayla thrashed around in the bed, fighting whatever she was seeing in her nightmare.

My eyes snapped toward the bed, and I shoved the dead Nightmare off me, groaning at the pain in my lower spine. I should go straight to Bartholomew, but I hadn't been able to protect her. Again. There was no way I was leaving her in this state.

Forcing myself up from the floor, I stumbled to the bed while Seth and Samantha disposed of the bodies. Kayla was still screaming when I sat down, and I put my hands on her shoulders. I didn't know what my words would do, considering she couldn't hear them, but I had to try. "Kayla, calm down. You're safe now." When I touched her cheek, her screaming quieted. "That's it. You're okay."

"Um, Daniel—"

"Not now, Sam."

Kayla's eyes opened. And stared right at me. Again, the screams started.

"Help!" She smacked my hand off her cheek and forced me away, scooting back on the bed. "Somebody help me!"

Oh, shit. I jumped off the bed and raised my hands in the air. "I'm sorry. I'm not here to hurt you, I swear."

"Get away from me!" Kayla threw her pillow at me, smacking me in the face.

Samantha grabbed my arm and evaporated us to Rome.

50

CHAPTER NINE

W e landed in Samantha's room.

"What the hell was that?" she screamed at me. "You went corporeal! And you *touched her*!"

"I know."

"You *broke the first law of Dreamcatching*!"

"I know!" Breathing deep, I tried to calm my voice. "Sam, please. Don't say anything to Giovanni."

She sighed. "You know I wouldn't. But tell me—what were you thinking?"

I ran my left hand through my hair. "I don't know. I screwed up, again, and she paid for it. I didn't want her to be afraid anymore."

"Yeah, and you showing up out of nowhere worked like a charm."

"I didn't know I'd gone corporeal."

Samantha crossed the room and grabbed a towel out of her bathroom. "Yeah, no shit. I tried to warn you, but you wouldn't listen. You're covered in blood, by the way. I don't want you staining my stuff." She threw the towel at me.

I caught the cloth and groaned. The sudden movement of my arms sent a shockwave of pain down my back.

"You really should let someone see that."

"Yeah, I know." After wiping my face and hands, I threw the towel in Samantha's rubbish, opened her door and went to find Bartholomew.

"This is going to hurt, but don't move," Bartholomew said. I held my breath when his hands rested on my spine. Then he pushed, and I gripped the end of the hospital bed as sharp pain blackened my vision. When Bartholomew drove the long needle into my spine, I swore, pressing my forehead into the mattress. Did he have to make this as painful as possible?

"There. That should help speed up the healing process. But I want you off your feet as much as possible. After a few days you should be able to move around without injuring yourself any further. Take the pain pills as needed and wear the back brace, including when you sleep. Understood?"

I nodded into the sheets and breathed slowly through clenched teeth. The stabbing in my lower back had only intensified with Bartholomew's adjustment, and the serum burned through my body.

"You're lucky you only twisted it. Now, go give Giovanni a full report and then go home and lie down. Swing your legs off the bed to stand up. Don't bend your back."

I followed his instructions, and when I was standing upright, he wrapped the brace around my waist. This was going to be so uncomfortable. Slipping on my T-shirt, I left the hospital room. Samantha waited for me outside the door.

"Everything okay?" she asked.

"Just great." Every step made me want to punch something. How soon until the damn shot started to work?

"Here—lean on me."

I held up my hand. "I'm good." When she frowned, I added, "Thanks, though."

By the time we reached Giovanni's office, I sweated through my shirt. The pain was unbearable, but I couldn't appear weak right now. Samantha opened the door, and we entered.

Giovanni sat at his desk, his forehead in his hands. Seth stood to the side, still wearing the same clothes he'd fought in. His dark eyes told me we were going to have a serious talk later. Great. He was as bad as Samantha.

I walked up to the desk and sat in one of the chairs. My sudden appearance startled Giovanni.

"Daniel. How's your back?" he asked.

"Just twisted, sir."

"That's good. Seth told me about the attack tonight. Six this time?"

"Yes, sir."

He shook his head. "I don't understand." Standing from his chair, he continued, "I expected you to have to fight every night. It's why I picked you. But *six*? Has she shown any signs of violence?"

"No, sir." *Well, not on purpose.*

Giovanni stared out the window. People were starting to pile into the streets. Somehow, people-watching had become a way for Giovanni to sort out his thoughts.

"Then I think we need to dig deeper. There must be something about this girl that has their attention. Bartholomew found nothing yet, but with Hendrik's death…" He paused to collect himself.

I must have underestimated how close he and Hendrik were.

He continued, "I feel it more important than ever to determine their cause for such interest. Continue to report to me daily. I want to know everything about this girl. Understood?"

"Yes, sir." I stood from my chair and left his office, unable to tell him I couldn't do this anymore. Samantha and Seth followed me out the door.

Seth wasted no time bombarding me as soon as we got back to our apartment. "Are you tryin' to get killed?"

"I don't want to talk about it." Tossing the pain meds on the counter, I plopped down on the couch, covering my eyes with my arm.

"Well, that's too bad because I'm fed up with your brooding shit. You gotta wake up and face the facts, man. You can't stay away from her, but she needs you. You're the best Giovanni's got. If you died or asked to be benched or whatever, Giovanni will pull her protection, and she'll be a Nightmare feast."

My chest tightened. Twice now I'd seen her thrashing about as Nightmares fed off her deepest fears. I couldn't leave her to that fate. Damn it. Why after all these years had I developed feelings for *her*?

Seth continued, "I also think you deserve a chance at happiness."

I dropped my arm. "What?"

"Kayla. Screw the first Law. You broke it anyway."

"You *want* me to pursue her? You're insane. Giovanni would have me 'terminated.'" Which was a nice way of saying he'd end my afterlife.

"I'm your best friend, and I'm looking out for you because I know you'll wish you *were* dead if you have to spend the next forty or fifty years watching her with some other dude. So, do you wanna take a chance at somethin' real?"

Something real? It'd never be real. Eventually she'd want something more—someone to grow old with, to start a family with. But Seth had a point. I *wouldn't* be able to stay away forever. Tonight had made that painfully obvious.

"Did I ever tell you how I died?" Seth asked.

"No. You said you were from Alabama. That's all."

"Yeah. I was at the bank. My girl worked there as a teller, and I was visiting before work. The bank got held up and the bastard put a gun at my girl's head. She starts crying, filling the bags with money and starin' at me like she wished I wasn't there to see this. But there I stood, watching her, knowing I couldn't stand by and see her be treated like that. I jumped him. Took a bullet to the chest, but damn it, I took him down. I wasn't letting him hurt the one girl I cared about most in the world."

To be a Catcher, one must have sacrificed his life for the sake of others. Seth's story made my chest tighten. He died to save the woman he loved. There was no sacrifice greater.

"Look, I know you ain't 'in love' yet or whatever, but you could be. And then all this"—he opened his dark arms wide—"would have meaning again."

For seconds I stared at him, lost for words. I doubted Kayla would do anything but scream her head off when she saw me again. Was she worth dying for?

I sighed. "What's the plan?"

This was a stupid plan.

Dressed in dark jeans and a blue dress shirt, I evaporated into Kayla's room. She lay on her bed, a book propped against her knees. After taking a deep breath, I walked through the wall to stand outside her room. Then I snuck down the hall, corporeal, and grabbed a "visitor" badge off the nurses' station when they weren't looking. I clipped the I.D. to the pocket of my shirt and returned to Kayla's doorway, letting out a deep sigh.

"I should never have let Seth talk me into this." I knocked once like the nurses did and opened the door.

Kayla jumped off her bed with a yelp, holding her pencil out toward me like a sword. "You! I thought I imagined you!"

I held my hands up. "My name's Daniel Graham. I'm not going to hurt you."

"Get out of my room right now before I call the nurses and have you arrested!" She moved toward the button on her bed.

"Kayla—"

She pressed the button. "Please, I think I'm seeing things. I need—"

Grabbing her wrist, I pulled her hand off the button before she could continue. "Hey, look at me. You're not seeing things." I put her hand on my cheek. "See? I'm real."

She snatched her hand away as the door opened. I forced myself to stay visible, not wanting Kayla to continue thinking she was imagining me. Maybe she'd believe I was real once the nurse verified my existence.

The nurse gasped. "Who are you? What are you doing here?"

Kayla's eyes widened. *Good.*

I held up my hands. "I'm a friend from high school. Just visiting. We pressed the button by accident. Sorry."

The nurse, seeing my visitor badge, calmed. She frowned at Kayla. "Well don't push it again unless you really need something." The nurse left the room with a scowl on her face.

Kayla stepped away from me. "But last night... last night you were here. I swear you were here." Her eyes glistened.

I pursed my lips together before speaking. "I was. But it's not what you're thinking."

She stepped away from me, her face pale. "So you *were* watching me while I slept? What kind of sick monster are you?"

My stomach tightened. This was going so badly. "No, nothing like that. I'm—" *Damn it. I might as well say it.* "I'm your Dreamcatcher. Everybody has one."

"My *what?*" She reached for the call button again.

"Dreamcatcher. Each of us is assigned to someone to watch over them while they sleep and protect them from Nightmares."

She gaped. "This is insane." Kayla sat on her bed with a whimper and closed her eyes. "Oh god, you're still there," she said when she opened them again.

"I promise I'm real. Even your nurse saw me."

A tear rolled down her face. I paused, racking my brain for a way I could get her to believe me. No matter what lie I could come up with today, eventually the complete truth would make itself known, and then I'd be in worse shape than I was now. Getting it all out on the table now was important, and either she'd believe me or she wouldn't.

"Okay, I'll show you. Does this building have Wi-Fi?"

"I don't know. Probably."

"Good. Don't move." I evaporated back to my flat, grabbed my laptop off my desk, and then evaporated again to her room. Kayla jumped when I re-appeared and clutched her stomach.

Okay, maybe disappearing and reappearing wasn't such a good idea.

"Here." I handed her the computer. She stared at the laptop like it was a bomb ready to explode. Sighing, I nodded toward the bed. "May I sit?"

When Kayla didn't say anything, I sat anyway. She stiffened but didn't move. *That's one step in the right direction, I suppose.* I typed in the address to my favorite ancestry site—a site I knew housed England's records—and pulled up my family's.

The page displayed both certificates of birth and certificates of death. And underneath was a family portrait, scanned in by whoever owned the painting now. When I turned the screen so she could see, Kayla's eyes scanned the picture until she found what I wanted her to see. Me.

She pointed at the portrait. "Wait, you're not… this isn't… is this you?"

I nodded. "That's me in 1812. It's the last family portrait we had painted before my brothers and I left for the war."

She pressed the back of her hand against her forehead. "Okay. So, now you're telling me not only are you real, but you're dead? And you were born in"—she looked at the screen—"1797?"

"Yes."

Kayla shot up and paced, her hands shaking at her sides. "Oh god. Ghosts are real."

"We're not ghosts. They're different. They don't still have their bodies."

She whimpered again. "That doesn't make me feel any better. Wait, does this mean there *are* other supernatural creatures out there?"

"I wouldn't worry about that." Just about every story about a supernatural creature was grounded in something real, but I wasn't going to tell her *that*.

She gripped her stomach. "So, you stand guard over me while I sleep and protect me from nightmares. Like, you invade my mind and stop them from happening?"

"No. They're actual creatures. Contrary to scientific belief, a Nightmare isn't developed in the human brain. They're the result of demonic creatures that grab hold of you while you sleep and force the images into your head."

Kayla stared at me, her eyes wide and her face pale. Then, to my surprise, she covered her mouth and laughed. "Oh my god. This is insane." She paced the room again. "I'm crazy. I have to be crazy."

"You're not crazy."

"Only crazy people have randomly appearing people telling them they're not crazy. I am definitely crazy."

"Stop saying that word."

Her eyes squinted, as if she was sizing me up. Then she grabbed a pastel off her rocking chair and chucked the crayon at me. I caught it, and her eyes widened again.

She held up her pointer finger, opening then closing her mouth. My eyebrow raised.

"First," she said, "you have freakishly good reflexes. Second, if I was imagining you, that would've gone through to the wall, right?"

"Yes." I set the pastel on the bed.

Slowly, she walked across the room and poked me, hard, in the chest. I rolled my eyes when hers widened. What would it take for her to believe me?

"Okay, let's say I believe you," she said, backing away. "Then, no offense, but you've done a pretty crappy job of protecting me."

"Well, I have only been your Catcher for a few days."

"Yeah, and last night was probably one of the worst ones I ever had." Her eyes flicked from me to the floor then back to me, filling with tears.

She might as well have kicked me in the stomach.

This had been a mistake. I never should've attempted to be anything other than I was—a spirit. "You're right. Last night was brutal, and I wasn't able to keep you safe. I simply wanted you to know that I was the one responsible and to apologize for the fright my misstep gave you. I promise you'll never hear from me again." I stood.

She stepped toward me before I had the chance to evaporate. "No, don't leave." Her face whitened. Was she afraid to be alone?

Kayla wiped her forehead with the back of her hand. "I'm sorry if I insulted you. I'm just not used to... you know."

"What?"

"Knowing that something I'd seen was actually real."

I shifted my weight, aching to tell her how she *had* burned her attacker alive and how she was not a loon, but the words wouldn't come out. It felt like too much after all I'd shared already.

Kayla watched me like she was trying to put together a puzzle. Her eyes framed with red, and I stared into them, lost in the sunlight glow of the gold around her pupils.

"So, you said *everyone* has one of you?" she asked.

I nodded, her voice breaking me out of my stupor. The really evil humans, like Jeffrey Dahmer didn't, but there was no point in getting into technicalities.

"And you're usually invisible?"

Again, I nodded. "We can choose to show ourselves, but our battles with the Nightmares are on the other side of the veil."

"On the other side of the what now?"

"The veil. It's like a curtain that separates the living world from the dead. If you have the power—like me—you can go from one side to the other."

Her eyes widened again. Any more talk of dead things and I was going to scare her away for sure.

"Look," I said, "I need to meet up with the other two Dreamcatchers who will be with me tonight. But, can I meet you for lunch tomorrow? Maybe we could eat in the garden?"

She bit her lip and gripped the hem of her shirt. "Um… yeah, I guess that would be okay."

I nodded once. "Cheers, then."

"But do me a favor and sign in at the desk downstairs as one of my friends from high school? I don't want word getting around that I sneak boys into my room." Then, to my surprise, she smiled.

I couldn't help but return the gesture. "As you wish."

CHAPTER TEN

Catching was easy that night. Bartholomew finally cleared Tabbi to return to work, and I watched her pull memories of *Veronica Mars* episodes out of Kayla's head. Tabbi weaved together Kayla's very own episode of sleuthing alongside Veronica, laughing at inside jokes and stopping a criminal mastermind. She looked so blissful.

Only two Nightmares came to visit, and Samantha and Seth easily disposed of them, wanting to keep me from fighting as much as possible, given my still-sore back. As soon as the sun peeked over the horizon, the four of us evaporated back to our flats.

Giovanni still hadn't managed to secure separate apartments for Seth or Samantha, so again Seth crashed on my sofa. I wouldn't have enough time to get much sleep, so after showering and dressing for lunch with Kayla, I spent an hour or so with my nose in a book, not wanting to wake Seth. Then at 11:45 a.m., I evaporated to Kayla's room.

Kayla had braided her hair over her left shoulder and was staring out her window at the courtyard below. A soft smile lit her face, and she looked happier than I'd seen in days. I warned myself not to botch this up.

Walking through her door, I took the lift to the first floor then went outside to take a good look at the building. Another point of reference was needed so I wouldn't have to pop in on Kayla every time I wanted to see her. Something about that stood out to me as stalker-ish. As if watching her sleep every night wasn't. I shook my head.

At the side of the building, I glanced around to make sure no one could see me and went corporeal. I adjusted the blazer I'd worn to cover up the bulkiness of the back brace then stepped around the corner of the building, entering the doors and walking to the front desk where a woman sat in pink, Hello Kitty scrubs.

"Can I help you?" she asked.

"I'm here to visit someone. Kayla Bartlett."

She typed a few things into her computer. "Sign in on the clipboard. You'll need to wear this the entire time you're in the building. Drop it off and sign out when you leave. Go to floor five and check in with the nurses' station." She handed me a familiar lanyard with a red "Visitor" badge attached. I slipped it over my neck, signed in and headed for the lift. When I reached the fifth floor, I did as the receptionist instructed and stopped at the nurses' station. The one in SpongeBob scrubs led me down the hall. She knocked on Kayla's door and opened it.

"Kayla, you have a visitor."

Kayla turned from the window and locked eyes with me. A huge grin spread across her face. "You came."

"You doubted me?"

Seeing that she was expecting me, the nurse left the room, leaving the door open.

Kayla fidgeted with her fingernails. "Well, did you want to go to lunch?" She motioned toward the door. "The food's not the best, but it's something. And it seems like a really nice day for June. We could still eat in the courtyard, if you want."

"Do we have to wait for a nurse or something?"

She pressed her hands together and bit her lip. I didn't expect her to be so nervous. "Probably."

As if on cue, SpongeBob came back. "Are you two going to lunch?"

Kayla nodded, and I followed her out the door.

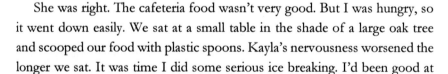

She was right. The cafeteria food wasn't very good. But I was hungry, so it went down easily. We sat at a small table in the shade of a large oak tree and scooped our food with plastic spoons. Kayla's nervousness worsened the longer we sat. It was time I did some serious ice breaking. I'd been good at this talking-to-girls thing once.

"Did you know that the first-ever shopping mall was built in Rome?"

Kayla covered her mouth as she let out a chuckle. "What?"

"It's true. The mall was built by Emperor Trajan and had more than one-hundred-and-fifty outlets. It was pretty impressive in its time."

"And what made you bring that up?"

"Well, I figured all girls like to shop. Seemed like a good random fact to pull out of the hat."

She smiled and swirled her mashed potatoes with her spoon. "Not all girls like to shop."

"I beg to differ. Seems to be inherent in their D.N.A."

Kayla laughed. "Okay, fine. I guess we all like to shop a little."

I couldn't help but smile. The sound of her laugh was intoxicating.

"What other random facts can you pull out of your 'hat?'" She took a bite of mashed potatoes.

"What do you want to know?"

She tapped her chin. "Okay, Mr. Smarty-Pants. What's the tallest building in Canada?"

"The C.N. Tower in downtown Toronto."

"The oldest castle in the world?"

"Well, if you're talking total area considered palace grounds, then the Palace of Versailles." I'd been to many of these places. The Palace of Versailles still impressed me.

She stared at me with a half-smile on her face. I wiggled my eyebrows, challenging her.

"Okay, fine. How about the oldest person, living, in the Northern Hemisphere to pick his nose under a full moon?"

I nearly spit the mashed potatoes out of my mouth and tipped my head back to laugh. "What kind of question was that?"

"A good one." She grinned.

"Well, then consider me stumped."

I took a drink from my water bottle as she moved peas around on her plate. Then she looked up at me. "Can I ask you a question?"

"Sure."

"How did you die?"

Damn, I knew this question was bound to come up. "I really don't want to talk about it."

She frowned. "Why? Were you a criminal or something?"

"No, nothing like that."

"Well, then what happened?"

I gave her the most roundabout answer I could. "Well, to become what I am, a Dreamcatcher, you have to have sacrificed yourself to save someone else."

"Another solider? You said you'd gone to war."

"Not exactly."

61

She stared me in the eyes. She wasn't going to back down until I gave her a straight answer. I sighed. "It was 1814. My brigade came over from England. We reached the mainland in August and from there marched toward Washington. It was ungodly hot. We were tired, thirsty, and hungry. A few times we passed through small villages, and one day, as I was leaning against a house, smoking on one of our stops, I heard women screaming from inside. I dropped my cig and ran in to find their skirts above their heads..."

I couldn't say the words, not with Kayla sitting right across from me. But the look on her face told me she knew where this was going. She was so pale. Still, I had to finish my story. "There were two girls, and one couldn't have been older than twelve. The same age as my sister at the time. I shot one of the men and fought off the other three. I saved the girls, but I was taken to the forest and killed for treason."

Kayla swallowed and nodded. Her eyes looked at the ground.

"I'm sorry. I didn't want to tell you."

She nodded, tears brimming in her eyes. "It's my fault. I shouldn't have forced you to answer."

I didn't speak for fear that I might cause her to shed the tears she was trying so hard to keep in. After what seemed like hours, she spoke again.

"Do you know why I'm in here?"

"Because you're depressed. And afraid you're seeing things."

She shook her head. "No. I'm in here because of what happened the day the visions started."

I might as well tell her I knew. To hide it from her longer would make the truth worse. "You mean what happened with your mum's boyfriend."

Her eyes found mine. They were wide with shock. "You knew?"

Nodding, I replied, "My partner, Tabbi, is a Dreamweaver. She reads your mind and uses your memories and interests to create pleasant dreams for you while you sleep. She's the one who told me what happened."

Her jaw clenched and unclenched before speaking. "Why didn't you tell me?"

"I didn't think bringing it up would be prudent."

"'Prudent?' Jeez, Daniel. How much *do* you know about me?"

"Enough."

We sat in silence. Kayla stared at her food, picking apart the carrot sticks with her fingers. Then her head popped up, and she looked right at me, her eyes tight. "Thank you for lunch, but I have to go."

She grabbed the edge of her tray and tried to stand, but I leaned forward and reached for her hand. "Wait." The sudden movement jarred my spine, and I sat back in my seat with a groan.

Kayla scrunched her eyebrows. "You're hurt?" She lowered herself into her chair.

Nodding, I took in a deep breath. "Comes with the job."

"Is this part of the 'job' then—eating lunch with me?" She clutched her tray tighter.

"No. This is… something I've never done before." I was going to say "illegal," but I figured that wouldn't go over well.

"Then why are you? I'm not exactly the type of person people want to be friends with anymore."

Her words brought a frown to my lips. Seth was right. I did care deeply for her. But did she really value herself so little? "Don't talk like that. We all have things about our past we wish we could erase."

"So you don't think I'm a freak?"

"Not at all. And anyone who thinks that way doesn't know what they're missing."

She held my gaze until a blush rose in her cheeks. She smiled softly as she looked down toward her plate. Out of nowhere, I felt a burning desire to lean across the table and kiss her. The sudden vigor surprised me, but my back brace was like a chastity belt. There was no way I'd be able to lean across an entire table.

Wanting some kind of connection, I rested my hand on hers. She flinched at my touch and blushed a brighter shade of red. Then, she gently moved her hand out from under mine and tucked a loose strand of hair behind her ear.

"We should probably be going. Lunch hour is up," she said.

A glance at the door showed patients filing into the building. My heart sank. I hadn't had enough time with her. But unless I wanted to push her away, I would need to move at a speed comfortable for her. That was the gentlemanly thing to do, anyhow. I hoped I hadn't forgotten how to be one.

Standing up from my chair, I piled her tray on top of mine and held out a hand to her. She smiled and, timidly, took it. I lifted her from her seat. My back didn't like the motion one bit, but I let out a deep breath to keep from showing the pain.

We walked side-by-side into the building, neither of us speaking, and dropped our trays off in the cafeteria. When we reached the part of the building where we had to go our separate ways, Kayla finally spoke.

"Thanks for, you know, visiting me today. It was nice to have some company other than the nurses for a change. Or Marcus."

Recalling the cafeteria scene where he'd freaked out and propelled her into the chair, I forced a smile. "My pleasure."

"Will I see you again?"

"I can visit you tomorrow for lunch, if you'd like."

Her face brightened. "I'd like that."

"Good. We'll call it a date, then."

She giggled. "Are you hitting on me, Mr. Graham?"

It'd been a long time since someone called me that. I didn't like the formality. But I wasn't going to ruin the moment. Instead, I continued to smile and played along. "Don't flatter yourself, Miss Bartlett. You'd know if I was hitting on you."

She giggled again. "See you tomorrow, Daniel."

"Bye, Kayla."

She turned to follow a nurse to her room. I signed out at the front desk and evaporated to my flat once I was sure no one could see me. Then I took a painkiller and fell face-first into my pillow. A grin never left my face.

CHAPTER ELEVEN

Someone shook me awake. I groaned, my face still pressed into my pillow. "Daniel, man, wake up. You gotta come with me to Rome," Seth said. Opening one eye, I looked up at him. Seth frowned, and he stared at me with sad eyes.

"What's going on?" I asked.

He shook his head. "Sorry, man. I can't say anything more."

Dread washed over me, my stomach churning like I'd eaten too much food. When I pushed myself up, pain streaked through my spine, and I took a deep breath before swinging my legs off the bed. I ran my hands through my hair and adjusted my shirt, still wearing the same clothes I'd worn to see Kayla. "All right. Lead the way."

Seth evaporated us to Giovanni's office where Tabbi and Samantha both stood, their eyes cast to the floor. Giovanni sat behind his desk, puffing hard on his cigar, and behind him stood Bartholomew. His expression was as upset as the girls'.

I walked toward the desk as stoically as I could. The nervousness running through me made me nauseous. "You called for me, sir?"

"Sit down, Daniel." He didn't look at me.

Obeying, I sat in the chair opposite his desk. Giovanni drew in a deep breath of smoke before pressing the lit end of his cigar into his ashtray, putting it out. He put his hands together on his desk in front of him. "How do you think I keep such close tabs on my Protectors?"

Oh crap. "I don't know, sir."

"I have spies, Daniel. Some Protectors, some humans. And I got the most interesting call from one of them earlier. Do you have any idea what it may have been about?"

I swallowed. "No, sir."

Giovanni smacked his hand on his desk. "Don't lie to me! I've been around for a long time. You think you are the first Catcher to be infatuated with a human?"

"Sir, I can explain—"

"You broke the first code, Daniel. You revealed yourself to her! You know it's absolutely essential the living world not know we exist."

My heart beat fast in my chest, like someone's fist hitting me again and again. Why had I been so naïve to think I could get away with this? Now my existence would be over, and all because I couldn't control myself. I forced myself to appear calm. "Sir, please, if you'd let me explain."

"No need to. I have no choice. Daniel, please follow Seth to your holding cell. You have been relieved of your position as a Protector of the Night."

"No!" Samantha and Tabbi yelled simultaneously. They leapt at me before Seth put his arms out, stopping them. Even with his dark skin, his face was pale. He knew what being relieved of your position meant—tomorrow, I'd be executed.

I gripped the armrests. My heart felt seconds from exploding. A week ago, I wouldn't have cared less about dying. But now…

No. I couldn't just cease to exist. But what could I say? Pleading for my life like a coward was out of the question.

My grip loosened on the chair. Giovanni might be taking my eternity, but I wouldn't take back what I did. I wouldn't give him the satisfaction of seeing me squirm.

As I was about to stand, Bartholomew stepped forward and held up a hand. "Giovanni, if I may, with the number of Nightmares we've seen with his charge, do you think it's wise to take one of your best Catchers off her case? I think it might be wiser to forgive his sentence."

"If I give him a pass, I will have to give everyone a pass. How do you think that makes me look?"

"*You're* not giving him a pass. I am."

Giovanni jumped up from his seat and stood inches from Bartholomew's face. "Who do you think you are? This is *my* call. *I'm* Daniel's superior. *I* make the call."

"And I'm technically your superior. If I'm giving Daniel a pass, so are you."

Bartholomew stared right at me then. As Keeper, he was the only Protector with authority over Giovanni. And he was saving my afterlife.

Giovanni flung his hands into the air. "Fine! Do whatever you want, Bartholomew. In fact, why don't you run the whole goddamn place?"

My eyes widened. Giovanni had a temper problem, but I didn't think he'd speak to the Keeper that way. My eyes widened even further when Bartholomew just rolled his eyes and stepped around the desk. "I feel there is more brewing than we're aware of yet, Daniel. The Angels are talking, though their words are not always open for me to hear. We cannot afford to lose you yet. Get close to Kayla and follow up with me on what you learn."

"Wait. You *want* me to break the code?"

"You've already broken the code. I'm trying to make something good come of it. Kayla's been receiving an abnormally large number of Nightmares in one night. I need you to figure out why they're so interested in her. Can you do this for me?"

Part of me felt like this was blackmail, but at the same time, Bartholomew was right. Nightmares didn't usually come out in such high numbers. And he was giving me a chance not only to get close to Kayla but to also figure out how to best protect her. This was an offer I couldn't refuse. "Yes, sir."

Bartholomew smiled. "Good. Then keep me updated." He smacked me on my shoulder—*ouch*—and leaned in to whisper as he walked around me. "Besides, I can't help but enjoy a good love story."

***

At 8:50 p.m., I evaporated to Kayla's room. Unable to remember the last time I really slept, I prayed it would be an easy night. I was going to be terrible in a fight.

Kayla's nurse flipped off the lights and left Kayla to crawl under her blankets. All four of us—me, Seth, Samantha and Tabbi—were very quiet as we waited for Kayla to fall asleep. After what happened in Giovanni's office, Samantha had wasted no time ripping into me about my "big mistake." Which led to Seth arguing with her about how they all would've done the same thing in my shoes. I'd tried to fall asleep on the sofa, but their yelling was incessant. Eventually, I'd given up and resorted to chugging a few energy drinks.

Kayla sat up in bed and looked around the room. "Daniel?"

Seth, Samantha and Tabbi all snapped their heads at me. Did they really not know what I was going to do?

Kayla startled when I went corporeal. "So, you actually do watch me sleep. Creep," she said.

A chill ran down my spine. "Yes—no—well, not exactly. I protect you *while* you sleep. I don't just stand there and stare."

Tabbi laughed from behind me. "Calm down, Daniel. She's just giving you a hard time."

I glared at Tabbi, who continued to wear a giddy smile.

"What are you looking at?" Kayla asked, unable to see the others.

"My team. They're... here."

"Oh." She gripped her comforter as her eyes flicked around the room.

I wanted to ease her nervousness, but I wasn't sure how. So, I did the only thing I could think of and prayed she wouldn't freak out. "Guys, you can stop hiding."

Tabbi and Seth went corporeal in seconds. Kayla gripped her comforter tighter. When I stared at Samantha, she rolled her eyes then obliged.

"Okay. This is not creepy at all," Kayla said.

"We're not that creepy," Tabbi replied. "We don't drink blood or eat people or anything."

Kayla's eyes grew baseball-sized.

"Really, Tabbi?" I said.

She shrugged as Seth chuckled. I shook my head.

"Trust me. They're just protecting you, that's all," I told Kayla, my hands outstretched in front of me.

Kayla's face paled, and she pointed at something behind me. "You mean from things like that?"

Spinning around and pulling my daggers into my hands, I swore as a Nightmare slithered through the wall behind Seth, reaching out to grab him. Seth turned and sliced through the Nightmare's neck. Behind me, Kayla screamed when black blood poured down the Nightmare's chest, and the beast fell back into the wall with a loud screech.

I glanced behind me. Kayla was pressed against her headboard, her knees up to her chin. Her hands trembled. Then it dawned on me—"You can see them?"

"What are they?" Kayla's voice shook.

Before I had the chance to answer, five more crawled through the walls. *Shit.*

"Oh my god, oh my god," Kayla repeated.

"Tabbi, get on the bed. Kayla, close your eyes."

I ran at the Nightmare nearest me and dodged as it slashed at me with long, black claws. It swung so hard that when I moved, the monster fell forward, unable to stop its momentum. The Nightmare squealed when I elbowed the back of its head. Using its stunned reaction to my advantage, I dug my blades into the beast's back, severing its spinal column. With an earsplitting scream, the Nightmare fell. It was silent by the time it hit the floor.

Samantha and Seth had each taken one down and now stood back-to-back, fighting the other two remaining nightmares. I threw a dagger into the skull of the Nightmare closest to me, then Seth and Samantha double-teamed the other and took it down in seconds. The three of us stood there, chests rising and falling, staring at each other.

Those Nightmares had not made a single move for Kayla. They'd come for us.

A Nightmare attacking a Protector unprovoked never happened. Usually, they were attracted to humans like moths to a street lamp, only fighting us when we got in the way. Tabbi sat on the bed, rubbing Kayla's back. Kayla's face was in her hands.

"She looked," Tabbi explained, frowning.

Grabbing my handkerchief out of my back pocket, I wiped my blades then stuck them back in their sheathes. Seth and Samantha evaporated from the room with the Nightmares in their arms. Burning the bodies in here was out of the question. Kayla was already freaked out enough.

"Tabbi, could you run and grab some bleach? We're going to need to clean the floor," I asked.

Tabbi nodded and disappeared. I sat on the bed next to Kayla and touched her arm. "Kayla—"

She jerked away and glared at me. "Don't touch me." Tears streaked her cheeks.

Frowning, I moved my hand away. "Are you all right?"

"No, I'm not all right! I just watched you three kill... whatever those things were."

"How can you see them?"

"I don't know! I don't even know what they are! What were those things?"

I paused, unsure if I wanted to tell her the truth. But I had no choice. "Nightmares."

"You mean *those* are the things that touch people—touch me—to give me bad dreams?"

There was no point in sugarcoating anything. She was much too smart for that. "Yes."

"Oh my god." She ran her hands through her hair. "What's happening to me?" Two more tears rolled down her cheek.

"Look at me." I touched her arm again. This time she didn't shrug me off. She looked into my eyes. "I've been fighting those things for two hundred years. As long as I'm here, you'll be safe. I won't let anything happen to you."

She wiped the tears from her cheeks and flicked her eyes over my face. I kept my gaze locked with hers, trying to show I was being sincere. She nodded, and I let out a sigh of relief. Then to my surprise, she leaned against me, resting her head on my shoulder. When I slipped my arm around her back, pulling her closer, she didn't object.

My heart raced. I liked the feeling of her in my arms, of her leaning on me for support. Now, knowing how it felt to hold her, keeping her out of my head would truly be impossible.

"Thank you," she whispered.

Leaning my head against the wall, I closed my eyes. Soon her breathing slowed, and I knew she had fallen asleep. I let myself do the same.

CHAPTER TWELVE

The sun had just peeked over the clouds when someone nudged me awake. I opened my eyes to find Tabbi standing next to the bed, a huge smile on her ivory face. She spoke in a hushed voice so as to not wake up Kayla. "Wakey, wakey."

"What time is it?" I whispered while glancing down at Kayla, still asleep on my shoulder. My arm was numb.

"Six forty-five. I figured you'd want to get out of here before the nurses came in to check on her. And then, you can change out of those nasty clothes before your lunch date."

I glowered at her through sleepy eyes.

"What? I only want to make sure your date goes well, *Mr. Graham*."

I pointed at her. "Don't call me that."

She laughed. "Why? It's funny."

"No, I only let Kayla get away with it because I didn't want to ruin the moment. Did you see the whole thing?"

Tabbi shrugged. "Pretty much. She was thinking about it as she fell asleep. I think she's pretty excited for today."

"Do me a favor?"

"What?"

"Next time Kayla starts reminiscing, find another human brain to focus on. I don't want to worry every time I'm near her that you're going to hear—and see—everything."

Tabbi laughed. "Why? What do you think I'm going to see? Kayla and Daniel sitting in a tree. K-I-S-S—"

"Stop that."

Tabbi evaporated, her giggling echoing after her. I reached over and tucked some of Kayla's hair behind her ear. She jerked awake and jumped off me.

"Sorry. I didn't mean to startle you," I said. Needles pricked my arm as the blood tried to flow again. I bent my elbow with a wince.

Kayla rubbed her face. "I'm so sorry. I didn't mean to fall asleep on you."

"Don't apologize. I passed out shortly after you did. Though I'm pretty sure the blood isn't going to return to my arm."

She blushed. "Sorry. My cheek's numb too. You could smack me in the face if you want. Maybe that'll wake it up. Your arm, too."

I smirked. "People usually only ask me to smack their face when they're drunk. Were you and Tabbi partying without me?"

"Not that I can remember, so if we were, I must've blacked out and forgotten everything."

"Well, next time, remember to invite me. A drunk Tabbi is always a sight to see."

"She drinks? She's like, ten."

With a chuckle, I stood up. "Twelve, actually. But for as long as she's been around, there comes a point when biological age doesn't matter anymore."

Kayla's smile softened as the silence between us grew. Then she bit her lip. "Will I see you for lunch?"

"Of course."

"Cool. Oh, and thanks for, you know, fighting those things last night." She tucked a strand of hair behind her ear.

Nodding my goodbye, I disappeared with a smile.

Kayla wasn't alone when I came to visit. SpongeBob was the nurse on duty again and when she opened the door, another woman sat on Kayla's bed—her mother. Kayla stood against the window, her arms crossed over her chest and her eyes swollen red.

"Oh, I'm sorry, Meredith," SpongeBob said. "I didn't know you were still here. I'll have Kayla's friend wait for her in the waiting room."

"No need. I was just on my way out." She stood up from the bed, grabbed her doctor's coat and hugged her daughter. Kayla didn't hug her back. "Think about it, okay Kayla-Bear?"

Kayla didn't respond. Dr. Bartlett—Meredith—glanced at me as she passed me on her way into the hall. I nodded a "hello," then she left without a word.

"Kayla, are you okay to accept your visitor?" SpongeBob asked.

She nodded.

"All right. Grab me if you two head down for lunch." SpongeBob left the door halfway open behind her on the way out. Silently, I thanked her for the privacy.

"I can go," I said.

Kayla shook her head, then her face dropped into her hands. Her shaking shoulders were enough to lasso my heart. I crossed the room in a few strides to embrace her. She wrapped her arms around my neck and cried into my chest as I rested my cheek on the top of her head. I stroked the ends of her hair.

"My mom wants me to come home. She thinks I can get the treatment I need there. But, she doesn't get it. That's not really why I'm here. I can't be in that house."

My jaw tightened as I recalled her attack. I couldn't blame Kayla for not wanting to go home.

For about two minutes, we stood without speaking. Then I felt her pull away and dropped my arms.

She wiped her cheeks with her hands. "Sorry."

"What for?"

"Crying. You came for lunch, not to stand here while I drench your shirt with snot and tears."

"I don't mind. Although, I could do without the snot. That's pretty gross."

She chuckled once. "Just give me a second." Kayla walked into her attached bath and closed the door. I heard her blow her nose a few times before she turned on the tap. A minute later, the water turned off and the bathroom door opened. "Okay, let's go."

We took a few steps toward the door, then I stopped. "Wait. Would anyone notice if you took off for a few hours?"

Kayla looked at me, her eyes scrunched. "I don't know. Why?"

"Did you want to go somewhere else for lunch?"

She bit her lip and fidgeted with the hem of her shirt. Was she afraid of me? I guess I should've expected that.

I continued. "I just thought you might like to get out of this place for a while. There's no pressure. If you'd rather eat here, we can."

She glanced at the half-open door then turned back to me. "How are you going to sneak me out?"

"The same way I go from my place to here every day. Think of it like teleportation."

Her foot tapped, but she quickly made her decision. "Okay, but they'll need to think I've decided not to go to lunch, or they'll come to check."

I nodded and waited for her to walk down the hall and notify the nurses. A minute later, she returned.

"Now what?" she asked.

"Give me your hands." She slowly lowered her hands into mine. My palms tingled at her touch. Her skin was so soft. "Okay, you're going to feel very disoriented. But, hold my hands and close your eyes. I'll tell you when to open them."

Kayla followed my instruction and squeezed my hands tight. I pictured my living room, blinked, and when I opened my eyes, we stood directly in front of the sofa where Seth sat.

"Holy shit!" Seth yelled, throwing the TV remote. "That was not cool, dude."

Stifling a laugh, I caught Kayla as she fell forward. "Open your eyes," I told her. Quickly, her eyes focused, and she looked around. Until I was sure she wouldn't fall—and because I didn't want to let go—I held onto her hands.

"Sorry. Not the most graceful," she said with a blush.

"You didn't tell me you were bringin' Kayla over," Seth said.

"We aren't staying long. Just wanted to swing by so she could pick up some clothes."

Kayla tilted her head. "Why? Where are we going?"

"Well, that's up to you. Where would you like to go?"

"Um… I can pick anywhere?"

"Sure. New York, Barcelona, Paris—"

Her eyes almost popped out of her head. "You can take me all the way to Paris?"

"Of course I can."

She smirked. "I forgot you were invincible. Do you always try to flatter girls with promises of French cuisine and the Eiffel Tower?"

Seth burst out laughing. "Oh man, I like her."

Ignoring him, I replied to Kayla, whose sense of humor continued to surprise me, "Only the stunners."

Her cheeks blushed. "Well, okay. I've always wanted to see the Eiffel Tower."

"Then let's steal something from Samantha's closet."

"Dude, she's gonna kill you," Seth said. He was right, but I still led Kayla out of my flat and knocked on Tabbi's door. When she answered, she stared at us with huge eyes.

"Hey, Tabbi," I said. "Is Samantha here?"

"Uh, no. Why?"

"Would you mind doing me a favor?"

CHAPTER THIRTEEN

A fter changing into dark jeans, a blue dress shirt, and a black jacket—and dealing with Seth's endless pleading to come along—I returned to Tabbi's apartment. It hadn't taken much to convince her to steal clothes from Samantha's closet. Tabbi always did enjoy giving someone a good makeover.

Whispers drifted from Tabbi's bedroom, so I sat on the sofa. Five minutes later, they emerged, and Tabbi's face beamed, like she'd received an Oscar. She turned around and held her hands out.

"Ta da!" Tabbi shouted.

When Kayla walked into the living room, I stood. She wore a pink, sleeveless dress that came down to her knees, with a wide, black belt wrapped around her waist, and on her feet, she wore shiny, black heels. Her dark hair curled over one shoulder, and Tabbi had even found makeup for Kayla to wear. She took my breath away.

The look on my face must've been hilarious because Tabbi burst out laughing.

"Well, I'd say my work here is done. You two have fun!"

I crossed the living room to where Kayla stood, her cheeks slowly matching the color of her dress. I held out my hands. "You look beautiful."

She looked away, fighting a smirk, and placed her hands in mine.

With a smile, I spoke. "Hang on tight."

We evaporated to Paris in the alley next to where I was taking her for dinner. Kayla fell into me when we landed. Luckily, she didn't weigh much. I caught her and helped her stand. "Did you forget to close your eyes?" I asked.

"Maybe." She stepped back and ran her hands down her dress. Her cheeks turned a brighter shade of red, and she mumbled, "Told you I wasn't graceful."

I chuckled and held out my arm for her to take. She slipped her arm through mine. "Come on. We're not far from the restaurant."

Given the time zone change, it was 9:30 p.m. in Paris when we arrived at the *Clair de Lune*, a small steakhouse near the Seine. I led her inside the dimly lit restaurant. Soft music played from a piano in the back corner near the bar, and all across the room, people sat at round tables with white tablecloths, conversing and eating by candlelight. We were seated at a table near the window that overlooked the river, and I waited for Kayla to look outside.

"Oh my god, no way. Is that the Eiffel Tower?" Kayla pointed across the river, her eyes wide with excitement, and her mouth open in surprise. Strategically placed lights lit up the monument, creating a beautiful painting against the dark, starry sky.

"Yep."

"Oh, this is so cool." She turned to look at me, a huge grin on her face. "Can we see it after we eat?"

"From a distance. It'll be too late to tour once we're done, but I'll get you as close as possible."

Before either of us could say anything else, the waiter stopped to fill our water goblets and take our orders. I ordered us both braised duck and chocolate custard for dessert.

The waiter nodded. *"Comme vous voudrez, monsieur."* He left our table without another word.

Kayla stared at me, her mouth open. "You speak French?"

"And a few others." I sipped on my water.

"You didn't order me anything gross, did you?"

"No. It's one of their specialties. You'll like it." Then a thought popped into my head. "You're not a vegetarian, right?"

Kayla shook her head, and my worry disappeared.

"Good. Sort of forgot to ask."

"Jeez, Daniel. So inconsiderate." She smiled.

I shook my head as a corner of my mouth rose. Kayla took a sip of her water and stared out the window again. She sat like that for a while, taking in the sights. But I had seen them a hundred times. Instead, I watched her—the way her eyes followed the people walking up and down the street; the way her lips seemed stuck in a peaceful smile; the way her hair fell over her shoulder into her breasts. But mostly, I watched the way she looked so happy. She was a totally different girl from the one I met in the asylum. Providing her with a chance to escape felt amazing.

When our food appeared, she turned her attention away from the sights of Paris. "So, tell me a little more about yourself, Daniel. I feel like you know everything about me, and I know nothing about you."

"What do you want to know?"

Kayla shrugged. "Did you play sports when you were a kid? An instrument? Did you have any brothers or sisters? A job?"

"That's a lot of questions," I replied with a smile.

"Well, then how about your brothers and sisters. Did you have any?"

I nodded. "Three brothers and two sisters. I was second born after my eldest brother, James."

"And, what did you do for a living? You know, before the war."

I took another bite before responding. "Well, first you must know that our lives back then were very different from how lives are today. I was an Earl's son. So my life consisted of a lot of lessons about politics, economics, languages… Really, we were all thought of as pawns in my father's game to gain wealth and friendship with the king, nothing more."

Kayla frowned. "I'm sorry."

"Don't be."

She took a bite of food before continuing. "And hobbies—did you have any?"

"Aside from playing War in the yard with my brothers, not really."

"Oh, come on. You had to have done something in your spare time." She took a bite of food and stared at me, waiting for an answer. But, what could I say when my entire life consisted of preparing to run the estate in the event Dad and James died, or wooing girls into my bedroom for one-night stands because "experience" was something society expected of a nobleman?

"When I was alive, there wasn't really such a thing as 'downtime.' There was always someone to impress or some lesson to complete—mathematics, Latin, sword fighting. Horseback riding I could maybe consider a pastime. But since I died, I've learned to play piano, and I've found books to be a great outlet. You play music, too, right?"

Kayla frowned. "I did." She played with the food on her plate.

I wasn't going to let her close up. "Tabbi said you play violin."

"Not for a while. I actually got recruited to Julliard last year, when I was fifteen. My father founded this music society for poor kids, and it was through a concert there that one of their scouts heard me. But I don't know if I'm going."

"Julliard's a great university. Though the life you live should be your own. If you don't want to go, then don't."

Kayla stared at me, her eyes wide with surprise.

"What?" I asked.

"You don't think I should go to *Julliard?*"

I shrugged. "Not if it wouldn't make you happy. I had no choice when I was growing up. My life was planned from the day I was born. Get a job in politics. Court a rich woman. I would've given anything to be something other than an Earl's son."

Kayla frowned. "So, you were married once?"

"Promised, but not married. My father had my marriage planned since I was ten. But then, when I was seventeen, I went away to war and, well, never came home."

She nodded as she took another bite of her duck. She tried to hide her feelings, but I saw the jealousy in her eyes. I couldn't make up my mind if it thrilled me or bothered me.

"I didn't love her, if that's what you're wondering."

Kayla bit her lip and set her fork on her plate to stare at me. "Am I really that obvious?"

"No. I'm just good at reading people."

"Well, quit." Her eyes flicked from me to her plate a few times before she stuck another bite of food into her mouth.

I smiled.

We finished our dinners, talking about our childhoods. I shared stories about my time as a Dreamcatcher, especially the hilarious ones that involved Seth or Tabbi, including the time Seth got so drunk, he'd popped in on the Pope, pretending to be the ghost of Christmas future. The Pope hadn't been very happy about that.

When we finished our desserts and I'd paid for our meals, I stood and held a hand out to Kayla. It was nearing eleven o'clock in Paris. "Want to get closer to the Eiffel Tower?"

She took my hand with a huge grin. "Yes, please."

Keeping her hand in mine, I led her from the restaurant and into the cool air. We walked a little further down the street until I was sure no one was watching, then I took both her hands in mine and evaporated us to a rooftop directly across from the Tower.

"Wow. It's so incredible up close," Kayla said.

"I came here a few times by myself whenever I needed to clear my head. There are few places on Earth better than this."

Kayla's eyes were wide with wonder as she looked around the city. I handed her my blazer when she began to shiver and waited for the clock to strike eleven. And when it did, I couldn't have imagined a better response. Kayla's mouth opened in awe as the lights on the Eiffel Tower blinked in different colors to the sound of music. She squeezed my hand tighter.

"Daniel, this is amazing! Oh my god, it's beautiful."

"I know," I said without taking my eyes off her. The lights sparkled in her hazel eyes, and her face was lit up in happiness, as bright as one of the lights on the Tower. Dimples formed in her cheeks, she was smiling so big. She really was the most beautiful girl I had ever seen.

Kayla looked at me, her eyes full of passion and wonder. I couldn't help myself and leaned toward her, slowly, expecting her to turn away. But instead, she kept her eyes locked with mine and lifted her chin. I cupped her cheek with my free hand and kissed her lips gently. Then I kissed her again, deeper this time. Electricity pulsed through me as Kayla grabbed hold of my arm with her free hand.

Stepping back, I looked into her eyes. "Thank you for an incredible evening."

"I think I'm the one that's supposed to be thanking you."

I smiled, but then the hairs rose on my arms. Out of the corner of my eye, a black blur flew past us to the other side of the roof, hidden behind the massive chimney. Whatever was out there, it was much too fast to be human. "Wait here."

Kayla's face paled as I stepped back from her. "Daniel?"

"I'll be right back." I held up a hand and walked slowly in the direction the blur had gone. Peeking around the side of the chimney, I froze when a black, wispy shape turned to face me. A wraith—a spirit that'd been around so long its connection to this world had completely severed, rendering it dangerous and evil. Wraiths sought out spirits—their touch was lethal, including to those with a virtuous purpose like Protectors—and destroyed everything, living or dead, in their path. I had seen one only once before, and then the wraith had been wandering aimlessly down the Rhine. This one stared right at me, as if targeting me.

Then, from the shadows stepped a man. He wore a black cloak, preventing me from seeing his face. He spoke in Latin. "*Occidere eum.*"

Kill him.

In a split second, the wraith charged toward me, its wispy body floating over the rooftop. *Oh shit.* Praying I was faster, I spun around and sprinted back to Kayla. Seeing what I was running from, she ran at me. "Daniel!"

I barreled into her, wrapping my arms around her, and evaporated to my apartment. We hit the floor with a thud, Kayla's body landing on top of mine. Any other time I would have enjoyed her lying on top of me, but right now, I needed to keep her safe. There was no doubt in my mind that man controlling the wraith was a warlock—and that wraith had latched onto my signal. We had minutes before the spirit tracked me back here, and only a few minutes more until the warlock arrived.

Expecting to see Seth, I swore when he wasn't here. His backup would've been great right now.

Kayla climbed off me. "What was that thing?"

I jumped up from the floor and dragged her to the bathroom. "I promise I will explain everything, but right now, you need to stay in here. Close the door and do not come out until I tell you to. Understand?"

She nodded, her arms wrapped around her stomach. I touched her cheek then ran to my bedroom and threw my dress shirt on the bed, leaving me in nothing but the brace, a T-shirt and jeans. I needed as much mobility as I could get.

After tying my weapon belt around my waist, I entered my living room and stood on high alert, waiting for the first sign that the wraith had followed my signal.

"Come on, come on."

A second later, the wraith popped out of the floor in the exact place we landed. I threw my dagger at the phantom, but it was too quick. The wraith jumped out of the way and crashed into my television. It used each piece of furniture like a stepping-stone to hop around my living room, knocking objects over in its path. I watched the spirit's pattern, trying to determine when to strike. When it was poised over my sofa, I threw my other blade.

The knife nicked its side. *Bugger.* The wraith hissed then charged. I dodged the phantom's attack just in time and ran around the sofa to grab my dagger. Our daggers were the only things that could kill spirits. With the blade in my hand, I turned around to strike back. But the wraith charged again before I had a chance to throw. I knew what I had to do if I was going to get Kayla out of here safely.

The second the wraith followed me here, the warlock would've performed a spell to determine our location. It wouldn't be long before the warlock found us, and I definitely didn't want to fight him. I needed to sever their connection now.

When the wraith closed the gap, I lunged. My blade found its mark, hitting the phantom in the very center of its body—but not without a price. In the mere seconds my arm was inside the wispy body, my skin melted like it had been drowned in acid. My shout of pain was muffled only by the cries of the wraith.

Letting the blade go, I snatched my arm out before falling to my knees. I tore off my T-shirt and, with a growl of pain, wrapped my forearm in the fabric, both to protect my wound and to keep Kayla from seeing it. Getting to Bartholomew was imperative—the wraith's poison was already moving fast within my veins. But first, I needed to get Kayla home.

I stood and sprinted to the bathroom door, knocking, then leaned against the frame. The pain in my arm was making me loopy, as was the wraith's poison.

"Kayla, you can open the door."

The door flung open, and Kayla appeared on the other side, her face red. "Care to tell me what's going on now? Because I'm freaked. All I hear is your apartment being destroyed, and then you scream."

"It was a wraith, but I killed it. You don't have anything to worry about." My knees shook and blackness framed my sight. I gripped the doorway.

Kayla looked me up and down, as if she could tell there was something off about me. "Oh my god. Daniel, your arm. You've lost so much blood." She tried reaching for my arm, but I pulled back.

"Give me your hands. I have to get you home."

Kayla took my face in her hands. "Daniel, no. You're hurt. I can take you to my mom. She can treat you."

I shook my head and pushed her hands away, trying to tell her I was fine, but the words didn't come out. Instead, my knees buckled, and I fell into her, blacking out before we hit the floor.

CHAPTER FOURTEEN

I awoke in one of Bartholomew's hospital beds and closed my eyes tight as bright lights above the bed blinded me. With gauze wrapped from fingertips to elbow, my right arm felt like it weighed one hundred pounds. I tried to sit up, but my head exploded with pain, like someone had set off dynamite in my skull. Lying back down, I covered my eyes with my good arm.

How had I gotten here? Did someone get Kayla home safely? God, she had to be terrified. What I had planned as a romantic evening to help her escape from her fears turned into something out of a blooming horror movie. I needed to find out what happened to her.

T.N.T. detonated in my head when I sat up. Gripping the edges of the bed, I inhaled deeply, trying not to vomit. The door to my room opened, and Bartholomew walked in carrying a large, glass jar full of dark, green liquid.

"Where do you think you're going?" he asked.

"Kayla. I need to make sure she's safe."

Bartholomew set the jar on the end table next to the bed and held up a hand. "She's fine. She's here. Tabbi is with her."

"She's here?"

He nodded. "She refused to leave. Was quite belligerent, to tell you the truth. But once I unwrapped your arm, she fainted. I had Tabbi take her to my study and keep her there until you woke."

I hated that she had to see me like this. But Kayla was safe. Bartholomew might as well finish his work before I went in search of her. I leaned against the wall behind me, and he removed the gauze from my arm. Though, he might as well have been ripping off my skin inch by inch. Only breathing through my nose kept me from crying out.

Bartholomew used a paintbrush to spread thick, green liquid on my burn, and the pain subsided in seconds. "You're lucky I had enough antidote prepared. What on earth possessed you to stick your arm through a wraith, Daniel?"

"It was set on me like an attack dog. I had to dispose of it before the guy controlling the thing could pinpoint its location. I had no choice."

"How do you know someone was controlling it? The wraith could've been just a rogue that felt threatened by you."

"Someone stepped out of the shadows right before the attack. He spoke Latin. *Occidere eum.*"

The paintbrush stopped moving. Bartholomew locked eyes with me. "A warlock?"

I nodded. "He was looking right at the wraith when he spoke."

"What did he look like?"

"I don't know. He was in a hooded cape, so I couldn't tell. But the wraith stared at me before it attacked. I'm certain the warlock set him on me."

"Where did this happen?"

"Paris. I was there with Kayla."

Bartholomew finished applying the salve in silence. He threw the paintbrush in the rubbish and closed the lid on the jar before rewrapping my forearm with fresh gauze. His quietness unnerved me.

"Is it common for a warlock to be able to command a wraith?" I knew they were capable of some pretty dark stuff, but I'd never seen this done before.

Bartholomew nodded. "A wraith has no ties to this world, no ties to the afterlife. They have no master to serve. Many warlocks would be capable of controlling them. But what I want to know is why a warlock would want you dead."

He did have a point. I'd never made a habit of associating with the Magus. Most of the time, witches and warlocks freaked me out. So why would one be interested in me?

Bartholomew gave me another shot of his painkiller-slash-healing-serum and handed me a shirt. "Daniel, I will ask you again, and I want you to be absolutely honest with me. This Kayla girl, are you sure you haven't noticed anything different about her?"

I frowned. Last time he'd asked, I hadn't known for sure. But now... "Actually, yeah. Tabbi believes Kayla really did burn her mother's boyfriend with her bare hands. And she can see through the veil."

Bartholomew's dark eyes grew so large, I thought they were going to pop out of his head. "Oh. Well." He scratched his black beard. "That's... very interesting. I will look into this."

I was about to ask him what Kayla had to do with any of this when he left me to stew in my thoughts. Again.

Tabbi and Kayla sat on the plaid sofa in Bartholomew's study when I entered. Both of their heads popped up at the sound of my boots clonking on the study's hardwood floor. The tense lines in their faces softened almost instantly.

"Daniel!" Kayla jumped off the sofa and ran to me. She flung her arms around my neck and hugged me. "I wanted to come see you, but Tabbi kept popping up in front of me when I tried to escape."

Wrapping my good arm around her, I pulled her tight, smiling softly at the mental picture of Tabbi hopping around the room, disappearing and reappearing with a grin on her face. Her personality always had matched the color of her red locks. When Tabbi reached us, I tousled her hair. "Thanks for staying with her."

She smacked my hand away. "It was like playing peek-a-boo with a two-year-old. Nothing I couldn't handle. I thought they taught you when we trained never to touch a wraith."

"Thanks for reminding me."

Tabbi grinned. "So, I guess I'm not needed anymore. I'll leave you two love birds alone. Keep the snoggin' to a minimum."

When Tabbi winked and disappeared, I shook my head then returned my attention to the girl in my arms.

Kayla still wore the pink dress Tabbi stole from Samantha's closet, but her shoes were missing. Between the bare feet, disheveled hair and smeared makeup, she looked like she'd had as rough of a night as I feared.

"I'm sorry about Paris."

She stepped back, far enough to look into my eyes but not so far that I couldn't keep my arms around her. She put her hands on my chest. "Forget about Paris. You almost died protecting me from, what, a wraith?"

I shook my head. "It was after me. I just didn't want to worry about you getting caught in the line of fire. The wraith can only kill what's already dead, but you saw what it did to my flat. When they're angry, they knock over everything in their path, living or not."

"Why was it after you?"

Sighing, I dropped my arms from around her and led her to the sofa. "Sit down. We need to talk."

Her lips tightened, but she did what I asked. I sat next to her and touched her bare knee. My mind wandered to the feel of her soft skin beneath my palm, and I removed my hand from her knee before my mind got carried away.

"Remember how I said there were other things out there—things that, as kids, we're told don't exist?"

Kayla nodded. She folded her hands in her lap.

"Well, one of those 'things' controlled that wraith tonight. I don't know why he wanted me dead, but we do know what he was. A warlock."

Her eyes widened in surprise. "You mean like a wizard?"

I nodded. "But not the wand-twirling kind. Warlocks are powerful, and the dark ones are extremely dangerous. They have a supernatural connection to the spirit world and harness its energy to perform their magic—or in this case, control the wraith."

"So, what can we do? How can we keep him from coming after you again?"

I would've laughed if the threat wasn't realistic. My stomach churned. If he had some vendetta against me, then fine. But I wasn't going to let Kayla get involved. Ever. "Bartholomew's looking for answers. But I don't want you being a part of this. It's my job to keep you safe. Which means 'we' are not—"

Kayla placed her hands on my chest. "I didn't say I was going to go snooping around. Besides, I know you won't let anything happen to me."

I sighed. "Your—not—lack of faith is disturbing."

"Did you really just try to apply a line from *Star Wars* to our relationship?"

"Maybe. But I like that you called this a 'relationship'. Takes the pressure off me to make it official." I chuckled when she play-smacked my chest.

"How about you take me home now, Darth?"

CHAPTER FIFTEEN

W e had to make a pit stop in Tabbi's apartment so Kayla could change into her hospital garb. I groaned when I looked at the clock—10:00 a.m.—which meant Kayla had been gone for a whole day. They definitely would've noticed her absence.

"This isn't good," I said, running my hand down my face. "I never should've taken you from that place."

"It's okay. I can say I took a bus downtown or something," Kayla said.

I frowned. She was putting on such a brave face for me, but the lines in her forehead told me she was worried.

She left me alone in Tabbi's living room to change back into her outfit. When she returned, I held out a hand to her. "As long as you keep your hand in mine, you'll stay invisible. When you're ready for people to see you, I'll let go."

She nodded, and we evaporated to the parking lot outside the asylum. Police cars were parked in front of the building, and I knew without a doubt they were here because of her.

Great. I turned to Kayla. "Remember, just because you can't see me, it doesn't mean I'm not here. I will be with you every step of the way, but you're going to have to put on one hell of a performance. You sure you're ready to do this?"

Kayla was pale, but she nodded. I squeezed her hand before letting go. At first she didn't move; she just stared at the building. *Come on, Kayla.* Then as if she could hear me, she took a deep breath and walked out of the shadows and through the front door. As I expected, the nurses sprung into action upon seeing her face. They called for the police and ran to her.

"Kayla! We've been searching everywhere for you. Your mother is terrified. Where have you been?" The nurse in the Hello Kitty scrubs grabbed her arm and led her toward the lift.

"I know. I'm sorry. I left after lunch yesterday. Just needed some new scenery. I took a bus downtown and saw a friend, but then we lost track of time. So, I stayed with her overnight. She dropped me off on her way to work."

Brilliant.

The nurse thumbed the button for the lift and took her upstairs. "You strictly disobeyed our rules and left the premises without an escort."

"I know. I'm sorry."

There was one officer talking with the nurses at the station on Kayla's floor. Another stood outside her door, conversing with someone inside her room. The policeman at the nurse's station spotted Kayla and spoke into his radio. His voice echoed from the radio attached to the other officer's shoulder.

From inside Kayla's room, her mother peeked her head out. Seeing her daughter, she sprinted down the hall and enveloped her in a hug. "Oh, thank god. I thought something terrible had happened to you."

"I'm all right, Mom." Kayla's voice was flat, emotionless. She told her mother the same reason she'd left.

Meredith nodded. "You shouldn't have been in this place anyway. I was just packing your things. We'll leave here soon."

Kayla froze. "Leave? Why are we leaving?"

"I only agreed to this because you were so adamant about it. But now that you're clearly not as stricken with terror or whatever, I'm taking you home." She left Kayla standing in the hall without waiting for a rebuttal.

Kayla marched in after her. "No. I won't go back there."

"I've had about enough. There is absolutely nothing wrong with the house. Now, put on these clothes while I finish packing." She threw Kayla's books into a duffel bag.

Kayla's bottom lip trembled and her eyes watered, but she held in the tears. She snatched the change of clothes off the bed and stormed into the bathroom to dress, much to my chagrin. I pushed the mental image of her nakedness out of my head.

Dr. Malcolm entered the room as Kayla exited the loo. "Kayla, I will need you and your mother to sign the discharge papers before I can allow you to leave. I would like to continue to see you, if that's okay."

Kayla nodded, and she and her mother signed the forms. After Dr. Malcolm shook hands with them and left, Kayla followed her mother to the car. I sat in the back next to the duffel bag.

"Did you want to get food?" Meredith asked while she drove.

"I'm not hungry," Kayla replied.

"You've gotten so skinny. You should eat something."

Kayla didn't respond.

Meredith tapped the steering wheel with her fingers. "I took the night off. Did you maybe want to order pizza and watch a movie or something?"

"Not really."

I gripped the handle on the car door. All this tension was suffocating.

We drove for fifteen more minutes before pulling through a large gate and up a long drive to a three-story, brick house. I knew they had money, given both Kayla's parents had been surgeons, but I was shocked by just how much. Their driveway curved in a semi-circle in front of the house, and on their front lawn was an oversized, stone fountain. We drove past the front door to a small drive along the left side of the house and into a three-car garage.

I followed Kayla and her mother inside. The same staircase Kayla had walked down in one of her dreams sat straight across from the door, then the foyer split off in three directions—left to a gold dining room with a table that sat twenty; straight ahead to the kitchen that sent a chill down my spine remembering Kayla's nightmare; and right, past the stairs, into a sitting area with a television and a black, grand piano in the front window.

Kayla frowned. "I'm going to go lie down."

"All right, Kayla-Bear. Let me know if you change your mind about the pizza, okay?"

Kayla ran up the stairs, two at a time. I followed her down a long hallway to a bedroom at the far end. The details of the room were clearer now that I wasn't seeing the place through Kayla's eyes. The walls were a light blue, and opposite her bed sat a large easel with an unfinished painting on it. A bookcase was positioned in the back corner, filled from top to bottom, and on a desk—*the* desk—were picture frames, figurines and stuffed animals. Lots of memories were stored in this room. Not all of them good.

Kayla closed the door behind her, dropped the duffel bag and stared at her desk. Then, in a few short strides, she crossed her bedroom, grabbed the pictures off her desk and threw them across the room with a scream. Glass flew everywhere.

I snapped out of my invisible state and ran to her, grabbing her shoulders. "Kayla, calm down."

She pounded my chest as sobs took over. "She promised she got rid of it. She promised! But it's still here. She always wanted to pretend nothing happened."

I'd understood her mother couldn't easily move them from this house. But not remodeling the room—or at least removing the desk—not giving Kayla a chance to move on… I wanted to go downstairs and smack Meredith into next year.

When no sound of footsteps came from the hall, I gathered Kayla into my arms. "I can get rid of the desk for you. Won't take more than a minute." Her sobs quieted, but she continued to grip me tight. I kissed the top of her head and held her, wanting to make sure she knew she was safe.

After a few minutes, she leaned back to look at me. Her hazel eyes were so gold, so beautiful; if I stared too long I would get lost in them. Cupping her face with my good hand, I stroked her cheek with my thumb, contemplating kissing her. Hell, I *wanted* to kiss her, but I didn't want to come on too strong. I didn't want to frighten her.

Then, as if she had read my mind, Kayla wrapped her arms around my neck and planted her lips on mine. She tugged on the ends of my hair, kissing me again with ferocity, and her touch woke me up, like a burst of adrenaline running through my body.

Placing my injured arm on her lower back, I pulled her hips against mine and slid my good hand up the bottom of her shirt to stroke her side. The feeling of her soft skin sent waves of excitement through my body, and my breath caught, imagining what she would look like without her blouse. Then I felt the scar, a thin, two-inch line of raised skin right above her hip bone, and the fire in me died.

Against every urge, I gently pushed her back and placed a kiss on her forehead. "Let's slow down, okay?"

Her eyes brimmed with tears. "But I thought… am I not…"

"No, no." I kept my injured arm on her lower back and held tight. It didn't matter how much it hurt; I wasn't going to let her out of my arms right now. "You are absolutely good enough. God, you're so beautiful it pains me to stop. But do you really want to do this right now, right here?"

My words registered. She shook her head and fell against me as a tear broke free. "I'm sorry. I just wanted you to make me forget. I don't know why—"

"It's all right. I understand." I kissed the side of her head and stroked her back. After a minute or so, I eased away and brushed the hair off her face. "Why don't you take your mum up on that offer to watch a movie? I can get rid of the desk while you're downstairs."

"I don't want to have anything to do with her. When they took me to the hospital, she stood up for him, asked me what I'd done to lead him on…" She wiped her tears with her fingertips.

Again, I fought the urge to go downstairs and smack the woman. "But she's your mum, and someday you might wish you'd spent more time with her. I certainly wish I'd spent more time with mine."

Kayla's eyes locked with mine. She stared at me for a minute, then she sighed. "Fine. It's better than being in this room anyway." She slipped from my arms and grabbed pajamas out of a dresser. Looking away before she removed her trousers—that was the last thing I needed to see right now—I took the few remaining things off her desk and evaporated, taking the piece of shit with me.

CHAPTER SIXTEEN

By the time I finished cleaning Kayla's bedroom of all the broken glass, she sat downstairs on her sofa, chowing on pizza and watching *The Princess Bride*. I figured Kayla would cover for me if her mother noticed a couple missing slices, so I ate them in another room to avoid Meredith freaking out at a random guy appearing and disappearing in her kitchen. My hands would go through the pizza unless I went corporeal first to grab them.

With a full stomach, I returned to the living room in time to see the swordfight between Inigo and the six-fingered man. Meredith laughed at all the right places, but Kayla just stared. She curled up against an arm of the sofa, her elbow propped on the armrest and her cheek in her palm. I wanted to go to her, to let her curl up against me, but that would mean revealing myself to Meredith, and that was the last thing Kayla needed right now. Resolved, I stood, invisible, near a white, high-backed chair that faced the emerald green sofa.

Before I even had a chance to get into the movie, Samantha, Seth and Tabbi appeared. I swore in surprise.

"Nice to see you, too. We have to talk," Samantha said.

The three of them walked into the kitchen, invisible to Kayla and her mother, and I followed.

"Seth overheard Bartholomew and Giovanni talking about your trip to Paris," Samantha continued. "They believe there's something darker going on than we're aware of."

"What do you mean?"

"Well, for starters, Bartholomew doesn't think you were the ultimate target in Paris—Kayla was," Seth replied.

My stomach dropped to my knees. "Did he say why he thinks it was her?"

Seth shook his head. "No, man. Sorry. But he seemed pretty certain."

I stared at the gray, marble countertop, unable to think straight. Bartholomew had been around for a long time. He'd seen a lot of things, met a lot of people. He had allies in the "otherworld" who provided him with information on the happenings in the supernatural realm. If he believed Kayla was in danger, one of his allies must've talked. I had no choice but to believe him. He never relayed information to Giovanni unless he was absolutely certain of its authenticity.

Tabbi patted my hand. "We'll help you look out for her. Don't worry."

I nodded and stood up straight. "Her movie will be over soon. Do me a favor and keep a watch outside until she falls asleep."

Seth, Samantha and Tabbi all nodded in agreement and went their separate ways through the walls of the house. With a sigh, I returned to the living room as the old man in the movie said goodnight to his grandson and the credits rolled.

Meredith turned to her daughter. "Well, that was fun. Did you want any more pizza?"

Kayla shook her head and sat up straight in her seat. "I'm good, thanks."

Meredith stood and grabbed their plates. "Kayla, you're home now. You don't have to be so polite. I'm not your nurse." She entered the kitchen to clean up the food.

I stood in the living room, watching Kayla. She moved from the sofa to the grand piano and ran her fingertips along the keys. She eyed the music that sat in a wicker basket next to it. Part of me hoped she would sit down and play, but I knew she wouldn't.

Thirty seconds later, Meredith walked back in, purse in hand and her doctor's coat tossed over her arm. "I'm sorry, honey, but one of my patients woke up unable to move half of his face. I'm going to need to run to the hospital for a couple of hours. Are you going to be okay here alone?"

Kayla nodded "yes" to her mother.

"Are you sure? Because if you're not, I can see if Doctor—"

"I'm fine, Mom." Kayla's voice was cold.

With a frown, her mother stepped toward the door. "Call me if you need anything." As soon as her car peeled out of the driveway, I revealed myself. Kayla walked into my arms.

"I hate it here," she said.

"I know." I changed the subject right away. "I saw you eyeballing the piano music. Do you play?"

She shrugged and stepped back, tucking her hair behind her ears. "Not since my dad died. He was the pianist in the family."

"Well, what if I played with you? Do you know the harmony for 'Heart and Soul?'"

The corners of her eyes rose in a smile. "You seriously want me to duet with you playing *that* song?"

"Hey, now what's wrong with that song? It's a classic."

She laughed. "Yeah, if you also call 'Mary Had a Little Lamb' a classic."

Grabbing her hand, I dragged her to the piano bench with a smile. "Sit."

She rolled her eyes and sat.

I joined her on the other side of the bench and elbowed her. "Now play."

She sighed and placed her right hand on the keys. Then she pressed them, providing the familiar melody. I joined her in the duet, jazzing up the baseline at the right spots. She laughed and changed the melody to throw me off.

"Hey, now that's not fair," I said.

"Keep up!" She smiled.

We continued to play, trying to outsmart each other until Samantha appeared, the sound of her voice startling me. "Daniel, you need to see this."

Kayla stopped playing, my jumpiness shocking her too. "There's someone else here, isn't there?"

I nodded. "I'll be right back." I followed Samantha out the front door. The sky was dark, so dark I couldn't see the moon. That alone struck me as odd. But then, something stirred out of the corner of my eye. Squinting, I stared off into the distance, waiting for the slightest movement. When I caught it, the blood drained from my face.

There were Nightmares everywhere, waiting to strike, like soldiers preparing to battle. I'd never seen anything like this in my two hundred years. We'd be lucky to all get out of here alive.

Samantha, Seth and Tabbi watched my face for a sign of what to do. I jumped through the options in my head. But only one of them seemed safe.

"Tabbi, go ahead of us and let Bartholomew know we're coming. Seth, Samantha, I want you to follow me into the house right now. We need to get Kayla to Rome."

CHAPTER SEVENTEEN

Kayla leapt off the piano bench when I re-entered the room with Samantha and Seth behind me. "What's going on?"

"We're leaving," I replied.

"What do you mean 'we're leaving?'"

"I need you to trust me. Go upstairs and pack whatever you need, but we need to leave now."

"Not until you tell me what's going on."

Scaring her was not my intent, but I didn't know what else to do. She *had* to stay safe. I grabbed her hand. "Kayla—"

She snatched her hand out of my grasp. "No, don't 'Kayla' me. I want to know what's going on!"

I snapped, more out of fear for her than anger, and pointed to the front door. "There are Nightmares floating around your house right now, waiting to strike the moment you close your eyes. If I don't get you somewhere safe, we won't be able to stop them all. We will get hurt, and you will have the worst night of your life. I can't let that happen. So, either you go upstairs right now and pack, or I will take you to Rome without your things."

Her eyes filled with tears, but she stormed out of the room before any of them had a chance to fall. I sighed and scolded myself, then followed her up the stairs. When I entered her bedroom, she was tossing clothes into a suitcase. Her cheeks were streaked with tears.

"I'm sorry," I said. "I didn't mean for that to come off so harsh."

She ignored me and piled books and art supplies into her suitcase.

I walked over to her and grabbed her arm. "Kayla, look at me."

She turned and slapped me across the face. I grunted at the impact and the stinging pain that lingered.

"I'm not a child, Daniel."

Before I had a chance to respond, a loud bang sounded from downstairs. Then Samantha yelled, "Daniel! Get out of here, now!"

Kayla looked at me, her eyes wide with fear. I grabbed her hand, planning to evaporate, but before I had a chance, I was slammed from behind. My body ricocheted off the wall, and I yelped when I landed on my injured arm.

"Daniel!" Kayla yelled.

Out of the corner of my eye, I saw her running for me, but I pointed to the bed. She needed to hide herself from the crossfire. "Get under your bed!" I jumped up from the floor, ready to fight. My arm throbbed, but I couldn't stop for a second.

When I turned around, a Nightmare stood in the middle of the room, facing Kayla and blocking her way to the bed. I leapt at the beast, grabbing its arm and jerking back. We fell to the ground, my knees in its spine. The Nightmare screeched when I yanked its shoulder out of its socket. Kayla, seeing her opening, ran for cover.

Reaching to my waist to grab my dagger, I swore under my breath when I remembered I hadn't slipped on my weapon belt after waking up in Rome. With no other choice, I wrapped my injured arm around the hellion's neck and leaned back with my knees planted firmly under its shoulder blades. The Nightmare's body thrashed under me as I crushed its windpipe, and when the hellion finally died, I took a deep breath. The pain in my arm was agonizing.

Then Kayla's piercing scream shook me to my core.

I flipped my head around to see her ripped out from under the bed by another Nightmare. The beast dug its claws into her ankle, leaving behind a smear of blood as it dragged her across the floor. My heart stopped in my chest. Never before had a Nightmare approached a conscious human, let alone attacked one. This wasn't right, wasn't natural. Something—or someone—had to be controlling them, forcing them to do more than feed off people's fears.

I panicked momentarily, uncertain how to get the monster off Kayla without hurting her, then snapped into action. If I didn't do something now, she would slip through my fingers. My heart pounded in my chest, and I jumped off the dead Nightmare. "Stop fighting or you'll bleed out," I warned Kayla.

She stopped squirming and covered her face with her hands, sobs shaking her body. On Kayla's bed, from when I had emptied her desk, was a heavy, metal award. The same one she'd tried to use on Matt. I sprinted to the bed, grabbed the statue and swung.

The medal's stone platform smacked the beast in the side of its chin. The Nightmare let go of Kayla, its claws slicing deep gashes into her ankle, and fell backward. Kayla screamed as blood poured out of her body. *Shit.*

I didn't have time to kill the Nightmare. I dropped to my knees, digging my arms under Kayla, and evaporated us to Rome.

We landed with a thud in Bartholomew's office. He and Tabbi ran to us, Kayla in my arms as I knelt on the floor. I moved my arm out from under her knees to brush the hair off her face.

"I got you. You're going to be okay." The words were as much for my benefit as for hers. She shook her head and cried out in pain.

Tabbi dropped to her knees and placed Kayla's foot in her lap. She slid up the leg of Kayla's pajamas to expose the wound and gagged. My jaw clenched. The Nightmare had cut clean through to the bone. Her artery was severed.

"Daniel, I'm sorry I didn't listen. I should've listened," Kayla said. Her words came out staggered between sobs and hyperventilating.

"Don't talk like that. You're going to be fine."

Bartholomew grabbed a blanket off the back of one of his office chairs. "Tabbi, wrap this around the wound and put as much pressure on it as you can. I need supplies." He disappeared.

Tabbi did as he instructed, her hands shaking.

"Samantha and Seth—did they come back?" I asked.

Tabbi nodded. "They ran to Giovanni as soon as they saw you weren't here."

Kayla grabbed my wrist, pulling my attention back to her. Her eyes stared into mine, the silent words of affection passing from her mind to mine. Then her eyelids fluttered closed—whether from pain or blood loss, I didn't know—and her grip slipped from my wrist.

"No, no, no. Kayla, keep your eyes open. Look at me. You can't go to sleep. Hey, look at me." I shook her head gently.

Her eyes opened.

"That's it. Keep your eyes open. Hey, look at me. I need you to fight. Stay awake."

She opened her mouth to speak, but instead a single tear rolled down her cheek. I wiped it away with my thumb.

"I know, I know. Please hang on just a few more minutes." A lump formed in my throat, and I swallowed. *Damn you, Daniel. Keep it together.*

A second later Bartholomew appeared with Trishna—the same witch who'd healed Tabbi—in one hand and an IV stand in the other. A bag of O

Negative blood hung on the stand. Bartholomew dropped the witch's hand and leaned over Kayla to stick an IV needle in her arm. He attached one end of a rubber cord to the needle and the other to the blood bag. Then he unclipped the bag and let the blood flow. Red liquid ran through the tube and into her body.

"Did you rob a hospital?" Tabbi asked.

"They won't miss these," he replied. "Tabbi, switch spots with Trishna. She can save Kayla."

Trishna slipped under Kayla's ankle. She spoke with a strong, Indian accent. "I can't replace the blood she lost, but I can heal her. This will hurt, so you must keep a firm grasp on her. Do not permit her to fight me."

I nodded and moved my hand from Kayla's cheek to her arm, prepared to hold her still while Trishna did her work. She plucked a smooth, white stone out of a leather bag and held it in both hands over Kayla's ankle. She closed her eyes and spoke Latin.

"Spirituum, te invoco. Cinis est pulvis ex ossibus, da mihi potestatem curandi saxo."

The creamy swirls in the rock spun, and the stone glowed. Trishna kept her eyes shut and repeated her spell. The skin on Kayla's ankle began to close.

Kayla whimpered, and then the whimpers turned into groans. The muscles in her arms tightened, and her hands clenched into fists. With my injured arm still under her shoulders and my good hand gripping her arm, I pinned her against my body.

As the skin around her ankle tightened further, her groans turned into cries. She gripped my arm and dug her nails into my skin. "Daniel, please. Let me go. Make it stop!"

"I will soon. Hang in there." My eyes burned as her screams intensified and she fought against my grasp. Since my youngest sister died in 1869, I hadn't shed a tear. There would be no crying now. Kayla needed me to be strong.

After what felt like hours, her cries softened and her struggles weakened, and Kayla's eyes closed, her face relaxing. Trishna wiped her brow, pushing loose strands of black hair from her forehead, and answered my question before I could ask.

"She's asleep. Her ankle is healed. She may be tired when she wakes, but there should be no pain when she stands."

Loosening my grip on Kayla, I touched her cheek. "Thank you," I replied to Trishna.

"The wound she carried was laced with dark magic. You're lucky I got here in time. How did you say she got injured?" Trishna asked.

"A Nightmare. A swarm of them attacked. I thought they came for us Protectors, but then one attacked her while she was fully conscious."

Bartholomew's gaping mouth confirmed I wasn't the only one who'd never heard of such a thing.

"Like someone was controlling them?" Trishna asked.

My eyes tightened. "Actually, yeah. I'd had the same thought."

Trishna sighed. "Then it's as I feared. A warlock is behind this. Just like last time."

CHAPTER EIGHTEEN

I laid Kayla on the sofa and covered her with a clean blanket while Bartholomew ran around his study like a hamster in its wheel. Tabbi and Trishna stood back and watched as he took book after book off his shelves. Seth and Samantha burst through the large, oak double doors of the study, both of them spotted from head to toe in black blood, and their faces lined with fear. Samantha's eyes caught mine and softened, then Seth noticed Kayla lying on the sofa, the IV still hooked up to her arm.

"Please tell me she's okay," he said.

I nodded, though I was sure the emotional damage was far from healed.

"Where's Giovanni?" Bartholomew asked, continuing to rummage through his books.

"Damage control," Samantha replied. "They're trying to stage the house like Kayla ran away so her disappearance doesn't end up on the six o'clock news."

"Ah, here it is," Bartholomew said.

We approached his desk to see what had him running around like a headless chicken. He slammed a thick, black book on his desk and flipped through pages until he stopped on the one he wanted. "Only once in history has a warlock been able to harness the Nightmares. He used them like attack dogs and destroyed multiple villages in Wales."

Samantha, Seth and I moved closer to peer over his shoulder.

"No way. I thought that story was a myth," Seth said.

Bartholomew shook his head and read from the book. "'In the fourteen hundreds, a warlock by the name of Tamesis attempted to harness demons to attack humans in an effort to destroy the human race. But instead of demons, his powers latched onto the Nightmares. He thought he had failed—until he discovered what Nightmares could do. At least four villages suffered from insanity and began killing each other, and when Tamesis realized the Nightmares could also physically harm humans, complete towns were destroyed within days.'"

"But why would he turn on his own kind? I mean, witches and warlocks are human, right?" Tabbi asked.

Trishna shook her head. "Not exactly. The Magus, as you call us, were created when a human was tricked by a demon into producing a living heir. Since then, whenever a witch or warlock procreates with a human, their child is also Magus. Half demon, half human. That's why black magic is easier for us to tap into, though many of us choose light."

"And Tamesis was as dark as they come," Bartholomew added.

"So then what happened? We know he didn't succeed in destroying Wales," I said.

"We interceded," Bartholomew replied. "By Law, Protectors cannot kill what isn't already dead, but we can kill the Nightmares. And since humans cannot see Nightmares and couldn't protect themselves, the Angels sent us into battle. We wiped out his entire army, and Tamesis fled."

I turned to Trishna. "So you think this Tamesis guy is still alive?"

"Someone claimed to have seen him ten years ago in Philadelphia. If he was powerful enough to have controlled these Nightmares, he may have found a way to sustain his life."

"And you did nothing?" Samantha asked. "I would've hunted him down."

Trishna glared at her through thick, black eyelashes. "And what do you think would happen if the Magus turned against one another? It would end badly, not just for us, but for thousands. Destruction everywhere."

"So, why Kayla?" Seth asked. "The Nightmares hovered around her house for at least ten minutes before they attacked. If a warlock is controlling them, what does he want with her?"

We stood silent, staring at each other until finally Bartholomew raised a finger. "Not just Kayla." He searched through his books again. "Trishna, you say Tamesis was supposedly spotted ten years ago?"

"Yes. Why?"

He picked two very fat, white books. *2000—2010* was written on one cover. On the other: *2011—*. "Because that's when the numbers started to rise." He dropped them on the desk and flipped through the one marked *2011—*.

"These are logs of all the times humans received more than three visits from Nightmares in a single night, usually appearing just one at a time. But starting in two-thousand-three, the pattern shifted. Daniel, when you told me that Kayla was receiving visits from five at a time, I went back and looked at the records. In this past year, there are three others who

100

have been visited by five or more Nightmares simultaneously and more than once."

My stomach churned. "Well, then the question still stands. Why is he targeting these four?"

Bartholomew looked up from his book and frowned. "That I don't know."

I ground my teeth. We needed answers soon before more people got hurt. And when Kayla woke, I wanted more to go on than "we don't know." Then Bartholomew's comment came back to me about "normal" humans.

"The other three—are they like her?" I asked.

Bartholomew squinted. "What do you mean?"

"Well, Kayla burned her attacker alive with her own hands. I was in her head. I felt it."

Trishna held up a hand. "Wait, you mean she's a witch?"

I'd never thought about the possibility, but now that Trishna mentioned it... I ran my hand down my face. "Maybe... yeah, I think so."

Both Samantha and Seth stiffened. Bartholomew looked down at his book.

Trishna raised her hands. "This changes things. Bartholomew, I must apologize, but I have to be going. If the warlock is going after his own kind, then we are all in extreme danger. I will learn what I can, but you must be prepared."

"For what?" Samantha asked.

Trishna frowned and disappeared without saying another word.

Tabbi worked on readying a room for Kayla in the mansion while Seth, Samantha, Bartholomew and I relayed to Giovanni everything we'd learned. He was none too happy about housing a witch, but he couldn't deny that something evil was stirring in the otherworld. If her protection meant throwing a wrench into the warlock's plans, then it needed to be done. In the meantime, he would call on the Catchers overseeing the care of the other three humans receiving over five Nightmares a night to determine if they, too, possessed magic.

After carrying Kayla to the room Tabbi prepared, I laid her on the white-and-lavender, flowered comforter of the bed positioned in the far corner of the room.

She woke two hours later. "Daniel?"

I jumped out of an oversized armchair and set down my book. Sitting next to her on the bed, I took her hand in mine. "Hey, how do you feel?"

"Like I got hit by a truck. What happened? My ankle—"

"Is fine." I squeezed her hand. "You lost a lot of blood, but Bartholomew found someone to heal you. You'll be fine."

"Like that warlock who was after you?"

"Not all witches are bad." *Why do I feel like I'm saying that for my own benefit?*

Kayla sat up and looked around at the pale yellow walls and the white bookshelf on the other side of the window from the bed. Next to it was a matching, white desk and the white, plush armchair I'd read in. A large, white armoire had been placed next to the entrance to her bathroom, and an oversized easel stood across from the window.

"Where am I?"

"You're in Rome. Tabbi fixed up a room to make you feel a little more at home."

"Rome?"

I nodded. "This is where the Protectors, like me, live. You're safe here."

She frowned. "How long will we be here?"

I stared at her, unsure how to tell her what I'd learned from Trishna and Bartholomew. She'd already been through so much, seen too much of the supernatural world. Now wasn't the time for big revelations. She needed to feel at ease, safe.

"I'm sorry, Kayla. But, until we figure out why you were targeted last night, it's best we keep you here under our protection."

"Targeted? You mean that freaking Nightmare was *set* on me?"

I nodded. "When that warlock tried to kill me in Paris, we think his ultimate target was you. And when he failed to get you that night… well, we think that's why he sent those Nightmares after you."

Kayla stared at the wall next to her and bit her bottom lip. She wrapped her arms around her stomach.

I touched her leg. "Hey, you're going to be okay."

She nodded. Then she shook her head and the tears overflowed. She covered her face with her hands.

Scooting closer to her, I pulled her to me, and she buried her face in my neck. I kissed the top of her head and stroked her arm with my thumb, trying to soothe her as best I could.

"Is my mom…?" She didn't finish her sentence.

"She's safe. Her Protectors have been alerted and will let us know if anything happens."

"God, she must be so terrified, thinking I've gone missing."

"We staged the house so it looks like you left of your own accord. Your mother will be fine. Once we're positive you're safe, we'll take you home."

Kayla nodded and wiped at her nose.

"Hey, how would you like to see the city?" I asked.

She looked up at me and spoke with a shaky voice. "But isn't that dangerous? I mean, with the warlock out there and everything."

I shook my head. "This is our home city. There are Catchers and Weavers all over the place. There isn't a safer place on Earth for you."

When she nodded, I kissed her and left to shower and change. After the attack, she needed something to lift her spirits.

CHAPTER NINETEEN

An hour later, we met outside her room. When Kayla emerged, her long, dark hair fell in waves down her back, and she donned a light blue, spaghetti-strap dress. Her eyelids were covered in a shimmery, gold shadow that made her irises pop. She looked just as radiant as she had the night I took her to Paris. I smiled, silently thanking Tabbi for stocking the room with girly things, and held out my hand for Kayla to take.

Kayla was only on the eighth floor out of the total twelve stories, but I gave her a quick tour of the lower levels as we passed through each of them. And when we reached the grand foyer, her jaw slacked. I chuckled, leading her out the front door.

We walked hand-in-hand past the pink, orange, yellow and cream-colored buildings of the city. Every now and then she'd trip on one of the road's cobblestones, and I'd grip her hand tighter to support her. A few times we had to dodge a car, but we mostly kept to the side streets.

On one of the corners stood a short man dressed in an elf costume, begging for tips, and twice we had to duck underneath clotheslines that hung low, weighed down by all the drying shirts. A smile was plastered to Kayla's face, and her eyes took in every sight, jumping from one side of the street to the other like a video camera trying to capture every moment.

The closer we got to the piazza, the more people we ran into. Everywhere, people from all nationalities filled the streets, and finally, we crossed into a large, open courtyard. A grandiose fountain sat in the very center with stairs that led up to each edge of the base. People visited along the steps, chatting and marveling at their purchases.

All around the piazza, vendors sold various products, from jewelry to food to pottery and plants. The smells of baking bread and spices flooded my nose, and across the square, a musician sat on the ground, playing sitar.

Doorways to different restaurants and shops stood between the vendors' displays. People walked through the piazza with smiles.

"This is amazing," Kayla said. She turned in a full circle, looking at every vendor, every store.

"This is the *Piazza dei Sogni Eterni*, or Plaza of Eternal Dreams. It's been here for at least a hundred years, if not longer. You won't find the piazza on travel sites or brochures, but it's one of my favorite places in Rome. See that restaurant over there?" I pointed across the square. "They make the best lasagna I've ever tasted. And that little ice cream place has the best chocolate gelato. And over here is a bookstore that carries original copies of the most famous works in history."

I led her to the bookstore, a place I had frequented quite often over the years, and walked through the open, arched doorway into a two-story building that housed books from floor to ceiling. In the back, a coffee shop sold pastries and newspapers.

The storekeeper noticed me immediately. He was a short, pudgy man with black hair that wrapped around the back of his head. The top of his head was so bald you could use his scalp as a mirror. He clapped his hands and limped over. "Daniel! *Cosi felice di vederti! Dove sei nascosto?*"

"What did he say?" Kayla asked.

"He's glad to see me and wants to know where I've been." I turned to the storekeeper, Signore Derci. "*Ciao, amico. Il lavoro mantiene un occupato. Vi present la mia ragazza*, Kayla." I hoped Kayla wouldn't mind me calling her my girlfriend. But I'd begun to think of her that way. Then again, she wouldn't have understood my words anyway.

Signore Derci approached her, took her hand and kissed her fingertips. He spoke with a very thick accent. "Miss Kayla. Very happy to meet you. You are beautiful girl."

She blushed. "Thank you."

Nudging her gently toward the coffee shop, I smiled. "Okay, I think I better separate you two. Good to see you, Signore Derci."

He laughed and waddled away to help a customer at the register. I pulled out a chair at a round table in the back of the store for Kayla to sit. "Coffee or tea?"

"Black coffee, please." She smiled.

I touched her cheek then ordered our coffees, grabbing a pastry for us to share. The plan was to take her to dinner, but I didn't want her to be starving by the time we got there. We'd eaten the pizza hours ago.

"Black coffee, huh? Would've taken you for a cream and sugar girl," I said when I sat down, breaking the flaky dessert in half and handing some to her.

"Nope. I'm easy to please."

"Well, that's good, considering today's outing doesn't include a sparkling Eiffel Tower. But I remember you saying something about all girls liking to shop?"

Kayla laughed. "You don't need to spend your money on me, Daniel."

"I'm not. It's Giovanni's. And we get our money from the Vatican. So really, it's the Pope's money."

"The Pope knows about you?"

"He's one of the only humans on the planet who does, and he's sworn to secrecy. But being 'God's appointed' or whatnot, he's entitled to know what's going on behind the veil."

"Oh. Well, I'll try not to buy everything in the city, then." She smiled.

Once we finished our coffees, we spent a few minutes in the bookstore. Having left all of her books in Columbus, I convinced Kayla to pick up a few copies to fill part of the bookshelf in her room. Then we stopped at different vendors. We sniffed perfumes—which made me sneeze—had our caricatures drawn, and tried on different hats and scarves like kids playing dress up. Kayla posed with the scarves and hats, each time in a different position with a different look on her face, like a model during a photo shoot. I couldn't remember the last time I laughed so hard. I loved seeing this side of her.

We passed a man painting a watercolor landscape of the villa. Kayla yanked on my hand when she stopped to watch, her excitement mirroring the night we'd been in Paris. Her eyes creased at the corners, and her lips turned up in a soft smile. I couldn't help but grin, seeing her so peaceful.

When the sun started to go down, we sat on the steps of the fountain, listening to one of the musicians singing and playing a soft, romantic waltz on his sitar.

"What's he saying?" Kayla asked.

I listened to the man singing in Italian and translated for her. "'The red rose whispers of desire; the white rose breathes of love. Forever I will treasure you. Each day, a rose to you I will send, now until the end.'"

She scrunched her nose. "That's cheesy."

"It sounds better in Italian."

"Yeah, I should've left it alone." She smiled as her hair blew over her sun-kissed shoulders in the evening breeze. "Thank you for today, Daniel. I don't remember the last time I had this much fun. And after yesterday..." Her eyes fell to the ground.

"I know. It's been a good day for me, too." Usually, I came to this place alone and was in and out of one or two shops before heading back to the mansion. It was great being here with her, building memories I never thought I would. Taking her hand, I lifted her to her feet. "Come with me."

"Where are we going?"

"I want to get you something." I led her across the piazza to a small jewelry shop.

"Daniel, no. You already bought me a few books. That's enough."

"Oh, please. What girl doesn't like to receive jewelry?"

Kayla bit her lip and peeked through the doorway at the different displays. Then she pointed at me. "Okay, but nothing expensive."

Smiling, I led her through the door, and together, we picked out a yellow gold necklace with a charm in the shape of a rose. I clasped the pendant around her neck when we left the shop.

"So, do I have the Pope to thank for this, too?"

"No, I used part of my inheritance."

"Wow. How rich were you?"

"Rich enough."

"Well, thank you. I shan't take it off," Kayla said in her best British impression.

I shook my head at her attempt to mimic my accent. "Do me a favor and don't do that again."

She laughed. "Sorry."

Slipping my hand into hers, I smiled. "Peckish?"

"Didn't you just tell me I couldn't speak British-ese?"

I chuckled. "Are you hungry?"

"Starving."

"How does lasagna sound?"

After spending dinner talking and chowing on lasagna and cheesecake—and drinking one too many glasses of wine—we walked back to the mansion in the moonlight. We laughed the entire way up the stairs to the eighth floor and kissed outside her bedroom like we were at the back of a movie theater. I had to let her go when my resolve to drop her off like a gentleman dissolved. By the time I got to my room, I was blissful and exhausted and barely got my clothes off before passing out.

A loud knock on my door woke me. Rolling out of bed, I opened it, still feeling the grogginess from a little too much Moscato. Seth stood on the other side.

"Hey, man. Sorry to catch you like this, but Giovanni wants to see us all right away. Don't bring Kayla."

"What's going on?"

He looked down at the ground. "I can't tell you. Get dressed and come upstairs." He left without another word.

I stared after him, nausea building in my stomach. I closed the door, dressed, then ran up the stairs to Giovanni's office.

Bartholomew, Giovanni and six other Protectors were present, as were Seth, Samantha and Tabbi. Every face was tense. Given what I knew already, the haste with which Seth called us up here meant some new piece of information was uncovered. My heart pounded as I stood next to Tabbi and waited for Giovanni to begin.

"Last night, the team watching over Adelynn Rudolf was attacked. One of the three, Ivan, was able to escape. He's downstairs in Bartholomew's medical center recovering."

After our bar brawl, I could've cared less that Ivan was injured. But my gut told me this was somehow connected to Kayla, so my knees locked. I waited for Giovanni to continue, my body stiff.

"But we lost Alektor and Adelynn's Weaver, Josefine. From what Ivan said, they were attacked by fifteen Nightmares at one time, and before he left, screams came from the parents' room. We have not heard from the parents' Protectors." He picked up the controller to his TV. "And then this news report ran this morning."

Giovanni flipped on the TV and changed the channel to the news station in Seattle.

"The search for sixteen-year-old Adelynn Rudolf is still under way," the reporter said. "Both parents were found dead in their beds when their maid came for her regularly scheduled cleaning. There are no suspects yet."

Giovanni flicked off the television and turned to my group. "The attack happened within an hour of Kayla's. Bartholomew and I both agree—we believe the warlock may have Adelynn."

My heart stopped.

Everyone spoke at once. "What do you mean a warlock has her?"

"There was another attack?"

"What aren't you telling us?"

Giovanni raised his hands. "Okay, everybody *silenzio*. You're giving me a headache. We only put the pieces together last night. After Daniel brought Kayla to Rome, we researched the attacks a little further. Kayla and Adelynn were both receiving regular visits of five or more Nightmares."

He turned to the other six Protectors. "As were your charges, Margaret Tucker and Alex Sheffield. But what we then discovered was that all of you had reported your humans to be 'abnormal.' They were all capable of some kind of... power. Like this Adelynn girl—Ivan told me she touched her boyfriend, and he was electrocuted."

Bartholomew jumped in. "All of your charges, we discovered, are not human at all. They're Magus. And they all carry a specific characteristic: They were all born sixteen years ago on October thirty-first, exactly at midnight."

I gripped the bookshelf behind me to keep from falling. Kayla wasn't just a witch—she was born on the Magus' holiest night. This was why the warlock wanted them. They all had dark, powerful blood running through their veins, more than an average witch or warlock.

Bartholomew continued, "I've spoken with Trishna, our primary contact in the supernatural realm. She too agrees there is something bigger going on than we were aware of, and given this warlock's possible identity... well, let's just say, it's imperative this man not get the other three Magus."

"So what do we do?" one of the Weavers, Cindy, asked.

Giovanni replied, "Well, the good news is, one of them is already within our walls. Kayla Bartlett is here and safe. The bad news is, two are still out there, and from what we can tell, this warlock is moving quickly. We must bring them to Rome immediately."

"You mean kidnap them?" Cindy asked.

"What other choice do we have? If we don't, he could attack another one of them tonight, and then he'll be one step closer to getting all the pieces he needs. He is capable of controlling Nightmares, creatures as bound to the Underworld as we are to the Heavens, and forcing them to attack while our humans are awake. If he is successful in capturing all four Magus, his power will quadruple and an apocalypse will rain on this earth.

"I will call for a meeting at lunch hour. All who can be there will be, and those who can't I'm sure will hear the news through the grapevine. Our orders have come from Above. We're going to war."

CHAPTER TWENTY

I couldn't get Giovanni's news out of my mind. He refused to give us more specifics until everyone could hear, but our orders had come from Above. *Above.* That never happened. Sure, the Angels gave us our positions in our afterlives, but that was the only time a Protector ever had communication with the Heavens. For them to send us a direct order for war meant something catastrophic was happening.

And Kayla was right damn smack in the middle of it.

"You're awfully quiet today," Kayla said.

"Yeah, sorry. Rough morning. Did you want a Coke or something?" Jumping up, I crossed the room to the small fridge next to my desk.

"Um, sure. Is everything okay?"

I grabbed two cans of Coke, handed one to her and plopped back on the bed. "Just a meeting with Giovanni. You'll hear soon enough."

"Does it have to do with the warlock?"

I sighed, not really wanting to have this conversation with her. But I also didn't want her to have a panic attack in front of hundreds, maybe thousands, of Protectors. Turning off the TV, I tried to calm my turbulent stomach.

"There was another attack last night. We're certain the warlock was involved. Giovanni's holding a meeting at lunch today to relay everything we've uncovered."

Kayla gripped her can so hard I thought her fingers were going to burst through the metal. I slipped the Coke out of her hand before she hurt herself.

"Why is he going after us? What could he possibly want?"

I paused, not sure how I wanted to answer her question. How does someone tell another they're not fully human? I scratched the back of my neck. "I don't know how to say this. It's not going to be easy to hear."

Kayla's face paled. "Daniel, you're scaring me."

"I know. I'm sorry. Just... that night when your mom's boyfriend went

110

up in flames…" I couldn't seem to find the words, so I spoke as quickly as I could. "You weren't seeing things. It really happened."

Her eyes filled with tears. "What do you mean?"

I shifted in my seat, not wanting to continue. But I knew I had to. "You're different, Kayla." I ran my hand down my face. *Why was this so bloody hard?* "You're a witch."

She jumped off the bed and glared at me like I'd told her I just ran over her puppy. "What? No. No, you're wrong. I'm normal, just like everyone else. I am not a… a *witch*."

"Kayla—"

"I can't be." Her hands shook, and she paced.

Standing, I grabbed her shoulders and forced her to look at me. "I told you it wasn't going to be easy to hear. But people don't explode into flames for no reason. Think about it. Did you feel anything before it happened, like a tingling sensation or something?"

I knew she had, but I didn't want to scare her more by telling her I'd felt the prickling, too. While being in her head.

She let out a soft whimper and nodded.

"And after everything, do you really think I'd tell you something like this if I wasn't certain?"

Kayla shook her head. A tear fell from her eye. "Is that why he wants me—the warlock?"

"We think so. But I promise I will keep you safe. No matter what happens, I will not let anyone hurt you."

Kayla nodded, but the fear never left her eyes. Before I could say anything else, the loud gong in the cafeteria shook the house. Giovanni's meeting was about to start.

Kayla and I walked hand-in-hand through the crowded hallways and filed into the cafeteria on the second floor. Protectors from across the globe had been summoned to the meeting and the room was filling quickly. Kayla gripped my hand tighter.

The usual tables had been removed and replaced by benches. The only other piece of furniture in the entire room was the podium at the far end where Giovanni would stand. I grabbed seats in the middle of the room. Tabbi, Seth and Samantha joined us soon after, and by the time everyone had arrived, we were packed wall-to-wall.

Giovanni stepped up to the podium, dressed in a black suit I'd only seen him wear at funerals. Again, his black hair was slicked back like Dracula, and his olive skin had a sheen to it. He spoke into a microphone, his thick, Italian accent filling the room. "It is with anxiety and sadness that I call you all here today. I trust you will share what I have to say with those who are not here. Our world, my friends, is under attack. Last night, Alektor and Josephine fell at the hands of a very powerful warlock."

He paused briefly to let the Protectors take in the news. "This warlock is capable of summoning the Nightmares to do his bidding—a feat that only one other warlock in existence has ever achieved. Many died at that man's hand, and unless *this* warlock is stopped, many more will die. The Angels have seen, have heard. And they have spoken to us. Humans cannot see the creatures that haunt their dreams and now attack them while they're awake. We can. As of this moment, we are at war."

Gasps and whispers filled the room. "War" was not a word we were accustomed to. We were the peacekeepers.

Giovanni continued, "Those of you who are currently overseeing the care of your charge will continue to do so. It's important that you remain in your position. But for the rest of you, the time for relaxation is over. At dawn tomorrow, you will be given specific instructions as to where you will be sent. There, we expect you to seek out and bring to us any creature with knowledge of this warlock and his plans.

"In addition, we will play host to three Magus—individuals this warlock intends to use for malicious purposes. You are responsible for their safety. If any of you determine the whereabouts of this warlock, report to me immediately. I will have a team on standby to follow through with your intel.

"These are your instructions. If you have any further questions, you will find me in my office. On behalf of the Angels we serve, I thank you for your dedication and wish you the best of luck."

Catchers and Weavers stood and filed out of the room or evaporated to their locations across the globe. A tap on my shoulder made me jump, and I turned my head to see Bartholomew sitting behind me.

"I need you and Kayla to come with me." He disappeared without another word.

Giovanni was waiting for us when we appeared in Bartholomew's study. *So much for being in his office.* Seeing Kayla, he walked up to her and took her hand.

"Miss Bartlett, I presume. Nice to finally meet you. I trust you are enjoying your stay?"

I raised my eyebrows. He spoke as if this place was a luxury hotel, not a safe haven.

"Yes, thank you." She replied with grace, but her other hand gripped mine tighter, and I gave it a squeeze.

"Good. Daniel, we need to talk. I want you to lead the task force assigned to destroying this warlock when his location is uncovered."

The fact that he felt me capable of such a feat was flattering. But I had Kayla to worry about. I couldn't be responsible for training a strike team. "Surely there's someone more qualified, sir."

Giovanni shook his head. "On the contrary. You are one of the best Catchers we have ever had, and your ability to strategize far exceeds those who have been in the field longer. Even Samantha, your understudy, has benefitted from your training. She's stronger, more agile than many four hundred years older than her. I know you can lead a team to follow the three Magus into the warlock's den."

I held up my hand. "Wait a minute. You want to involve Kayla and the other two? No way."

"Daniel, we need them. This is a *warlock* we are chasing after. We have swords and guns, but he has magic, charms and spells. If you go up against him, you're going to need individuals capable of taking him on at his level. To go in without them would be suicide."

I pinched the bridge of my nose. What he said made sense, but I *did not* want to get Kayla involved. I promised I would keep her safe, not lead her to right to the enemy.

To my surprise, Kayla spoke. "If we help him, do we have a chance?"

"Kayla—"

Bartholomew cut me off. "Yes. He is much older and much stronger than you individually. But when combined, you three could be as strong as him. Trishna is ready to come work with you three, to ensure you're prepared."

"Then I'm in."

"Kayla, no. I'm not letting you risk your life for this," I said.

She turned to me with narrowed eyes. "My life is already in danger, Daniel. And besides, it's *my* life, not yours. If this is what it takes to get my life back, then I'm doing it. And you can't stop me."

Wanting to argue, I ground my teeth, but her jaw was set and her gaze unfaltering. There would be no talking her out of this decision. There was no choice. I turned to Giovanni. "Then count me in, too. We'll start training tomorrow."

As soon as we got back to my room, I closed the door and turned to Kayla. "You shouldn't be doing this."

"This isn't just about me anymore! Two of your kind died protecting another girl"—she took a deep breath—"*witch* like me. How many more are going to die because of us? I won't stand back and let you walk into that warlock's hideout knowing I might never see you again. I won't let you die for me." Her fists clenched at her sides, and her eyes filled with tears, her lips tight.

With a sigh, I pulled her into my arms. Her unfaltering courage was both unnerving and impressive. "All right. But tomorrow, I want you to join us at training. And I want to be there with you when you work with Trishna. If you're going to fight alongside me, I want to know you can protect yourself. We'll do this together, okay?"

She looked up at me. "Does that mean I get to fight you?" Her face split into a mischievous grin.

"Probably. But don't worry. I'll go easy on you."

She shoved me away from her with a smile.

CHAPTER TWENTY-ONE

O ur training room was in the basement of the mansion. It was the entire width and length of the building and could fit upwards of five hundred people at one time. The walls and floors were covered with wrestling mats, and different stations were set up for different purposes—weight training, cardio training, hand-to-hand combat, etcetera. There were even shooting ranges for guns and bows. For the longest time, we'd only trained to fight off the dark spirits of the world. Now we were going to be taking on creatures completely different—*living* creatures. The training center took on an anxious feel when I entered the room.

It had been so long since I was here, I almost didn't recognize the place. Our old machines had been replaced with newer ones, and the weaponry at the back had been freshly stocked. All around, Protectors trained. Catchers instructed Weavers how to protect themselves, and they prepared to take down creatures we'd only read about in lore. We knew how to fight the Magus, but we'd never had a reason to—until now.

Seth carried long, wooden poles across the room. With my right arm clean of gauze, I jogged to him. "Training's not for another thirty minutes. You don't have to help me set up, mate."

Seth handed me half the stack. "I know, but if I'm not down here helping, I'm up there thinking. And I don't want to be thinkin' right now, man."

Couldn't blame him. I didn't want to think about our reason for training either. Together, we carried the poles to an open area in the center of the room and paired them. After a few more trips of carrying sheathed daggers, as well as ankle and wrist weights, we were set.

Soon after, Samantha and Tabbi led Kayla into the room. Kayla had styled her hair into a ponytail, and she wore workout clothes that hugged her curves. I took a moment to stare at her body—her tank top stretched slightly over her breasts, and her gym shorts stopped halfway down her thighs.

"Quit staring," Seth said. "You look like a drooling ape."

I coughed, the heat rising in my cheeks, and elbowed him in the arm. He laughed.

Eight Catchers followed them through the door, and Seth waved them over to us. Four of them had been in Giovanni's office earlier—Lian, Lucca, Vasin and Hakan were overseeing the protection of the other two witches. Lian was a Chinese girl, about seventeen, and was the best martial artist we had in our entire ranks. Her sixteen-year-old understudy, Lucca, was Italian and had been raised in a farming village. I remembered him from Samantha's training. He was incredibly strong.

Vasin, an Indian born in the 1700s, was Hakan's mentor and the oldest of the group at twenty-one. Hakan, a fifteen-year-old Native American, also had trained with Samantha. Besides the fact they had Protected one of the other witches, they were a fierce pair. I was glad to see Giovanni had pieced together a strong team.

The others introduced themselves as Lizzie, nineteen and from Germany, and her understudy, Brian, from America; Irene, eighteen, from England; and, to my chagrin, Ivan, also seventeen, like me. Though, given he was the remaining Protector from Adelynn's team, I wasn't surprised Giovanni had assigned him to the group.

"You're all on the strike team Giovanni assembled, correct?"

"What do you think, *debil*," Ivan replied.

Great. This was going to be fun. "Then, I'm sure you're all aware of Giovanni's plan for us. Once the location of the warlock is determined, we will accompany the three Magus to take him out. Therefore, it is extremely important that we're all able to trust that we'll have each other's backs." I made a point to stare down Ivan. He glared at me.

I continued, "That's what these training exercises are for. Not only will we be practicing and perfecting our fighting skills, but we'll learn how to work as a unit so there's no weak spot. I'll also use what I see to name my second-in-command. This person would take my place if I were to fall."

Kayla watched my every movement, hanging on every word. At the mention of my possible death, her face fell into a deep frown. I looked away from her before I lost my momentum.

"There are wooden poles on the floor. Grab one and pair up with someone, preferably someone whose fighting skills you do not already know. I want to see quick response time, endurance. I want to see your ability to pay attention to the tiniest detail, so avoid hitting each other's hands. Take a moment to stretch, and then we'll begin."

I walked over to Kayla and Tabbi. "Tabbi, you're not on the strike team, are you?"

She shook her head. "No, but I want to be able to protect myself."

"Then, stay here with Kayla. Take it easy today, yeah? Watch the fights. Try to absorb some of what they do. Tomorrow when they're training in their teams, I'll work with you two. Sound good?"

They nodded, and I took Kayla's hand in mine, giving her fingers a squeeze. I leaned in to whisper in her ear, "You look great in workout gear, by the way."

She shoved me playfully and blushed. I smirked and turned to my team. "All right guys. Take a stance. And, go!"

The room filled with loud clicks from my Catchers' fights, and I watched from a distance, waiting a few minutes for them to tire a bit. Seth hit Vasin's hand with his pole. "Watch the hands, guys. You need to see everything and strike only where appropriate."

Circling the group, I first observed Ivan and Lucca's battle. Ivan had helped me train Lucca and Samantha's group before we'd all been assigned our understudies. Ivan had taken him down pretty easily at the time, but now they were both strong, fast and agile. Lucca held his own. In fact, he was a little faster than Ivan given his smaller size, and he managed to land the first blow. Ivan winced when Lucca's pole smacked him in the side of the thigh.

"Well done, Lucca," I said with a smile. Ivan needed to be knocked down a peg.

I left the two of them to center in on another pair—Lian and Irene. Neither of them I knew very well, but Lian moved with grace and speed. Irene was a powerhouse and swung at Lian's legs with a strength that, had she hit Lian, would've left a large welt in seconds. But Lian was quick and jumped before the pole could hit her. She smacked the back of Irene's shoulder.

Nodding in approval, I moved on. Hakan battled against Lizzie. The two of them taunted each other like players in an American football game. I laughed when Lizzie stabbed her pole into Hakan's stomach like a sword and stepped back with a cheer.

Finally, I focused on Samantha and Brian, a blue-eyed, blond-haired boy who sounded like he was from Chicago. He couldn't have been older than

Tabbi. He'd had the least training of anyone in the group, and it showed. Samantha was kicking his ass. Every time he swung or lunged at her, Samantha spun out of the way and landed a blow somewhere on his body. He was the first to hit the floor. He tried to jab Samantha like Lizzie did to Hakan, but Samantha stepped out of the way and swung at the back of Brian's knees. He crashed to the ground.

I returned to where Kayla and Tabbi stood, watching and keeping track of points. For another twenty minutes, my team fought, then I called time. Every chest rose and fell in deep breaths of exhaustion.

"Well done," I said. "Take a break for lunch. We meet at two o' clock for round two."

I spent lunch in the dining hall for the first time in years. Tabbi, Kayla and I joined Seth and Samantha. Seth devoured his turkey sandwich like a bear after hibernation.

"You both did well today," I said as I sat down.

Seth mumbled a response, while Samantha turned to Tabbi. "Why are you training? You're a Weaver. You shouldn't have to fight."

"I want to learn how to protect myself. And I think Giovanni wants me to oversee the care of the witches. You know, in case they need anything."

"Speaking of, what is Kayla's purpose in this, exactly? I mean, she can't fight. Have you ever thrown a punch?" Samantha asked.

Whoa. What the hell got up her nose?

Kayla's cheeks reddened. "I'm sure Daniel will show me how."

"Right." Samantha waved a carrot back and forth between Kayla and me as she spoke. "And is that before or after he beds you and pretends like nothing ever happened?"

"Sam, that's enough," I said. Samantha had her bitch tendencies, but I'd never known her to lash out at people. Especially about something that happened *twenty years ago.*

"No, really. I want to know. Can she do anything other than stand there and look all mopey? I saw the way she watched us. She couldn't hurt a damn fly. She's going to walk into that warlock's den and get herself killed."

Kayla set down her fork, stood and left the room without a word.

I glared at Samantha, and the corners of her mouth turned up in an arrogant smile.

"Tabbi, can you go make sure Kayla's okay?" I asked. "I'll be right behind you." When Tabbi disappeared, I narrowed my gaze at Samantha and lowered my voice. "What the hell is your problem?"

"Nothing." Samantha bit into her carrot and swiped a loose strand of blonde hair out of her face. "Just making sure your little *girlfriend* knows what she's getting herself into."

I ground my teeth and kept my voice low for Samantha's sake. "What happened between us was twenty years ago. I have already apologized for the *mistake* I made, being with you. You really need to grow up and move on. Clear off, or I will make sure you never have another opportunity to even breathe the same air as her. Is that clear?"

Seth stared at me, slack jawed. Samantha's face reddened, and her eyes glistened. In one swift motion, she grabbed her glass of water and threw the liquid in my face. She stormed out of the cafeteria before I could respond.

"Man, I do not want to be you right now," Seth said.

I rolled my eyes, wiped my face with my hand and evaporated to Kayla's room.

Kayla sat on her bed with her knees up to her chin. Her eyes were red. Tabbi was nowhere in sight. I joined Kayla on the bed and touched her cheek. She leaned away from me, and her rejection forced a pang in my chest.

"I'm sorry. Sam had no right—"

"Did you sleep with her?"

My heart raced. "What?"

"Did you sleep with her?"

I swallowed. "Yes."

Kayla pushed me. "Samantha, really? God, Daniel. You have your ex-girlfriend looking out for your new one? Are you insane?"

My palms sweat. "First, she was never my girlfriend."

"Oh, great. So you just screwed her and threw her to the curb. That's so much better."

"That's not how—" I pinched the bridge of my nose. "I'd lost my mentor, my closest friend, and she was there. I was loaded. It just… happened."

Kayla's lips pursed in a tight line. When she spoke, her eyes remained hard. "I'm sorry about your mentor. I know what it's like to lose someone you care about. But you could've at least told me. And now every time I look at her, I'm going to picture you two—"

I grabbed her hand. "I'm sorry for what Samantha said, what happened between us. But that was twenty years ago, and I let her know right away it'd been a mistake. She's just jealous because for the first time, I've found someone I truly care about."

Kayla stared at me like she was afraid of who I might say that person was. If my heart hadn't been racing in my chest, I might've laughed. "You, Kayla. She doesn't even hold a candle compared to you."

Her face softened. Then she leaned into me and wrapped her arms around my stomach. "I'm so sorry. I shouldn't have said what I did about throwing Samantha to the curb. I was just jealous and she's so pretty, like model-pretty, with her blonde hair and blue eyes and big boobs, and I thought maybe—"

I lifted her chin, looking into her eyes. "Stop talking." And then I kissed her. She let out a soft whimper and held me tighter. I kissed her again, deeper this time, and laid her back so her head rested on her pillows. The fabric of her gym shorts slid up her legs, leaving her thighs exposed. My hands wandered down them. They were so soft and feminine, and my excitement grew as goose pimples rose on her skin.

Kayla's breathing became heavier as my lips moved from her mouth, down her chin and neck. They wandered over her collarbone to her shoulders, nibbling gently. She moaned and grabbed my face, bringing my mouth back to hers.

I was about to strip off my shirt when Tabbi popped into the room. Kayla yelped, and I jumped off the bed.

"Jesus, Tabbi! We still knock on doors, you know," I said.

"I know, I'm sorry. This is as awkward for me as it is for you."

Not likely.

"But I need you to come quick," she continued. "Alex is trying to kill Bartholomew."

Tabbi, Kayla and I popped into Bartholomew's study. I ducked just in time to avoid a book smacking me in the face. A small, African-American girl crouched in a corner and covered her head with her arms. Bartholomew was pinned to a wall by a hat rack. A tall boy with sandy hair and green eyes stood in the middle of the room, his arms waving around his head as he threw objects at Bartholomew—and now us. I could only assume this was Alex, one of the other Magus.

Again, I ducked just in time to avoid injury.

"Go away! I didn't ask for this! If one of you doesn't take me home now, I will kill him!" Alex yelled.

Holding my hands up, I walked toward him. "Calm down. We aren't going to hurt you."

"Bullshit you're not!"

Another book flew at my head. I ducked and checked behind me to make sure Kayla and Tabbi were still unharmed. Then I turned back to Alex. "I promise. We're on your side. Please let Bartholomew go."

Alex glared at me. My heart raced. I couldn't hurt him, and I couldn't stop him. I was powerless.

Kayla appeared at my side, her own hands held out in front of her. "Alex, right? Look, I know you're scared. I was pretty freaked too when I found out what they were and why they brought me here. But Daniel is right. They're on our side. They won't hurt you."

"You're not one of them?" Alex asked. He eyed Kayla with as much fear as he had me. The hair on my arms bristled. I stood on the balls of my feet, ready to jump in the way if he tried to strike her down.

Kayla shook her head, keeping eye contact. "No, I'm like you. I have powers too. And you're right. This sucks. But there's someone out there who wants to hurt us. All they're trying to do is protect us, keep us safe and teach us how to fight back."

"They want us to kill someone, did you know that? I'm not a killer!"

Kayla nodded. "I know that. Neither am I. But maybe we won't have to. We're gifted, Alex. If we can get them close enough to this guy, they can take care of him for us. And then we can go back to living relatively normal lives. Please put Bartholomew down."

She was incredible. Her hands were steady, her voice didn't shake, and her eyes never left Alex. Maybe it was because they had something in common, or maybe it was the same compassion I'd seen in her that first day in the asylum, but she handled Alex like a pro. My heart swelled with pride.

Alex dropped his hands, and Bartholomew crashed to the ground. Stepping slowly past Alex with my hands still in front of me, I ran to Bartholomew. He was unconscious, but alive.

Alex fell to his knees. "I'm sorry. I'm so sorry."

"It's all right, Alex," I replied. "Tabbi, would you mind taking the other girl to her room?"

Tabbi nodded and helped the girl—she had to be Margaret, the other Magus—to her feet. They evaporated.

"Kayla, I need you to find Giovanni. He should be on the twelfth floor in his office. Turn right at the top of the stairs and walk straight ahead through the double doors. Alex, help me carry Bartholomew down the hall. He's too heavy to lift on my own."

Alex looked at Kayla who nodded. When he stood, Kayla ran out of the room. Alex took Bartholomew's legs while I carried him by his shoulders. Evaporating with him to the medical room would've been easier, but the last thing I wanted to do was take my eyes off the boy.

After a few stops, we reached one of the "hospital rooms." I grabbed the sheet off the bed, and together, we rolled him onto it. Alex lifted one side of the sheet while I lifted the other, and, after a lot of effort, we managed to get him on the bed. Good thing Bartholomew was a small man.

The silence was awkward as we waited, so I had to speak. "We really are on your side, mate."

Alex nodded and looked at the floor. "Yeah. Sorry I threw the book at your head."

"I've faced worse than killer novels."

Alex looked up at me and forced a smile. Moments later, Kayla returned with Giovanni. I explained to him what happened, and when Tabbi returned from settling Margaret down, she took Alex to his room.

Having calmed the storm, I grabbed Kayla's hand and walked her to her bedroom. "You were brilliant with Alex."

She shrugged. "I could see how scared he was, and he was going to hurt you. I couldn't let him."

"Well, it's good to know you have my back."

Standing in the hall, she smiled mischievously. Her golden eyes stared into mine. "But what if he hadn't listened to me? Maybe tomorrow you can show me how to fight? You know, like arms and legs around each other, pinning each other to the floor, that sort of thing." Her voice dropped, and she ran a fingertip down my chest.

Wow. Where that boldness came from, I didn't know, but holy shit, it was hot. I leaned closer to her and brought my lips to her ear. "Only if you wear this outfit again."

"Well, I suppose I have to wear something." She smirked.

The mental picture of her wrestling in the nude made my breath quicken. Pinning her against the door, I kissed her hard and fumbled with the doorknob. I needed to get her inside the room now or clothes were going to start coming off in the hallway. But before I could turn the doorknob, Seth appeared.

"Whoa, man! Sorry!" Seth covered his eyes and pretended to run into a wall.

I jumped off Kayla like a scared cat and kept my back to Seth until I could compose myself.

"What is it?" I asked, my voice gruff. How many times could we be interrupted in one day?

"Um, just wondering if we were going to train again today. You had us all come back at two…"

Damn, how could I forget? Well, I knew how. But that was beside the point. "Yeah. I'll be right there."

"Okay," Seth replied. "Uh, sorry, Kayla… about this."

Kayla covered her mouth as a smile burst free. Her cheeks were so red they were purple, but she giggled.

"Is he gone?" I asked.

She nodded and finally laughed.

"That was not funny," I said and grinned. Seeing her laugh made me want to kiss her all over again. She was so beautiful when she smiled.

"Oh, yes it was. You are blushing so bad."

"Yeah, well, enjoy it while you can."

She wrapped her arms around my neck. "Oh, I am."

I tickled her before playfully shoving her aside. Then I grabbed her hand and evaporated us to the gym.

CHAPTER TWENTY-TWO

Kayla, Samantha and Seth stayed to help me clean up after I'd dismissed my team, then the four of us walked to the cafeteria to grab what was left of the supper we'd missed, thanks to Alex delaying me. And maybe Kayla.

Tabbi waited at one of the tables when we entered the room. "Jeez, you guys took forever. You do realize you've missed supper."

"We're aware," I replied. "Is there nothing left?"

Tabbi shook her head. "I tried to save you some, but Thing One and Thing Two over there," she pointed to two of the humans in charge of prepping the food, "wouldn't let me."

"That's stupid. Don't they know they work for us?" Samantha asked.

"It's fine, Sam," I said. "We'll just—"

Seth interrupted me. "Have to go out! What about *L'alce*? They have bar food. We haven't been there for a while."

The last time we were there was the night Seth decided to pop in on the Pope. We all had had way too much to drink and stumbled back into the mansion, annoying everyone within earshot of the staircase.

"What about somewhere else that isn't quite so... insane?" I asked.

"Oh, come on. Don't be such a prude," Samantha said, crossing her toned arms over her large chest.

"I'm not being—"

"What's *L'alce*?" Kayla asked.

"A *dance club*. Which Daniel apparently thinks is too *crazy* for him," Samantha replied, rolling her brown eyes.

"No, I just don't think right now's the best time to—"

"I'd kind of like to go," Kayla interrupted. "I've never been to a club."

"Please, Daniel. I want to go, too!" Tabbi bounced in her chair.

"All right, fine. But don't forget we have to wake up early tomorrow." I pointed my finger at Seth, the person I knew would be responsible for encouraging drunkenness all night.

"Okay, Dad." Seth laughed, and I smacked him round the head as we exited the room.

At nine o'clock, Seth and I waited in the foyer. We'd all decided to take showers—and the girls wanted to dress up—so, we'd separated after we left the cafeteria. I hadn't seen Kayla until now.

And, *my god*.

Kayla descended the stairs in a silver, strapless gown that stopped mid-thigh and hugged every curve. Her dark hair had been tied in a loose bun, though a few strands hung into her face. On her feet were blood-red heels, and the only jewelry she wore was the necklace I'd bought her in the piazza. Lightheadedness hit me, and I had to take a deep breath to keep from falling backward.

"Wearing that dress is cruel," I whispered in her ear when she took my arm.

Her cheeks blushed as she smirked, and we followed the other three out into the night.

The club, a two-story building in downtown Rome, wasn't far from the mansion. The first floor was a bar and restaurant, with the club above. Tabbi shared a story with Kayla about the time she'd landed in *L'alce*'s toilet as they evaporated into the building, her Irish accent fading into the background as they disappeared. After flashing the fake I.D.s that made the rest of us eighteen, we met them in the restaurant.

We ate fast then jogged up the stairs to the club. The bass pounded in my chest before we even entered the dim room. The only lights were the ones at the bar and the strobe light over the dance floor. Seth immediately bought us a round of shots, and I held Kayla's in my hand.

"You don't have to drink. I'm sure Seth wouldn't mind putting this down," I said.

Kayla held out her hand. "I said I hadn't been to a club. I never said I hadn't drunk alcohol before."

With a raised eyebrow, I smiled and handed her the shot glass. She downed the whiskey like a pro. Seth cheered as I followed suit.

"Well, come on, you two! Let's get this party started!" Tabbi yelled and dragged both of us onto the dance floor.

Seth and Samantha wasted no time grinding against each other, both of them with drink in hand. Kayla closed her eyes and raised her arms above her head. The reds, blues and greens of the strobe light bounced off her dress as her hips moved from side to side with the music. My body warmed at the sight of her in that dress, and the way she moved…

I jumped when someone tapped my arm.

"You don't have to dance by yourself for my sake," Tabbi said. "I can take care of myself if some jerk tries to pinch my butt again."

I laughed, remembering how Tabbi had kneed the last guy in the crotch so hard he'd had to call an ambulance. "I bet it took a surgeon to get that bloke's goolies back into place."

She smiled. I tousled her hair, which made her swear at me, then I stepped toward Kayla. Sliding my hands around her waist from behind, I pulled her against me. Together, we danced to the beat, our hips moving in sync, and my hands wandered her body. I'd forgotten how arousing dancing could be.

When Kayla turned to face me, I pictured my hands unzipping her dress, the fabric falling from her body, her in nothing but lingerie and heels. I glided my hand down her back to rest on her bum and gave it a gentle squeeze.

Kayla leaned into me and lifted her lips to speak into my ear. "We can sneak off to the bathroom, if you want."

The air caught in my throat, and I coughed. Again, her boldness shocked me, but definitely not in a bad way. It *would* be easy to simply lift the dress, and that was something I'd never tried before. I was about to grab her hand and lead her to the bathroom when a loud scream from behind me shook me out of my daydream.

My hands dropped from Kayla's body, and I turned to see what had happened. The scream had come from Samantha—and Seth was lying on the ground.

I moved Samantha out of the way and dropped next to Seth. My fingertips pressed the side of his neck for a pulse. His heart beat slowly. People surrounded us, staring and whispering.

"He's alive," I said to Samantha. "Get Kayla back to the mansion. I'll take him to Bartholomew."

Samantha nodded then grabbed Kayla's hand. Tabbi followed them to a place where they could evaporate unseen. I held up Seth's head, ready to disappear right there, when his eyes opened—black, and shiny like marbles. Sweat formed on his brow, and he gripped my forearm. "Daniel, I can't hold him. He wants—" Seth shook, closed his eyes and cried out in pain.

"Hey! Who's 'he?' Who can't you hold?"

Seth's eyes reopened and stared at me. No, more like *into* me. As if he could read my soul. "Bring me the girl. Tomorrow. Midnight. The rooftop in Paris. Fail me, and all you know will suffer."

Seth's eyes closed, and I evaporated us to one of Bartholomew's hospital rooms as ice ran down my spine.

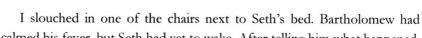

I slouched in one of the chairs next to Seth's bed. Bartholomew had calmed his fever, but Seth had yet to wake. After telling him what happened, Bartholomew had only been able to come to one conclusion—the warlock was getting creative. And he knew where Kayla was. Would he come for her when I didn't deliver her to him? Leaning forward, my elbows on my knees, I dropped my forehead into my hands.

"How is he?" Kayla asked from behind me.

I raised my head. She still wore her silver dress. "Alive. We won't know any more until he wakes."

"What happened?"

I turned away so she couldn't see the truth in my eyes. She *could not* know what the warlock really said. "We think the warlock attacked Seth to get to us."

The room was silent for at least a minute. Then finally, Kayla spoke. "I'm sorry, Daniel."

"Don't be."

"But the warlock is after me, and you guys are protecting me."

I looked at her again. Her bottom lip trembled, and I held my hand out to her. "Come here." When she took my hand, I pulled her into my lap and tucked a loose strand of hair behind her ear. "Don't take the blame for this. You cannot help that you're the center of this warlock's attention. You didn't ask for it, and you certainly didn't encourage him. Besides, we're not just harboring you, love."

She shrugged and leaned against me to rest her head on my shoulder. I rubbed her arm with the side of my thumb. For minutes, we sat in silence, then Seth stirred, and we both jumped off the chair. I raced to my friend's bedside before turning to Kayla. "Go find Bartholomew. Tell him Seth's waking."

Kayla nodded and sprinted from the room.

Seth's eyes fluttered open. They were no longer the color of coal, like they had been at the club, but instead their normal shade of dark brown.

"Where am I? This isn't another trick, is it?" He tried to sit up, but his breathing labored.

"Calm down." I pressed my hands to his chest, pushing him down on the mattress. "You're in one of Bartholomew's hospital rooms."

"Where's Kayla? Tell me you didn't take her to Paris."

"Why would Daniel take me to Paris?" Kayla asked.

I closed my eyes. *Damn, she was quick.*

"You didn't tell her?" Seth asked.

Bartholomew stood on the other side of the bed when I opened my eyes, watching me and anticipating my answer.

"Didn't tell me what?" Kayla asked.

I swallowed. "Seth wasn't just attacked by the warlock. He was possessed. The warlock gave me an ultimatum. Hand you over to him, or he would make everyone I know suffer."

Bartholomew scowled then started gathering medical supplies. But when I turned to look at Kayla, her face was ashen, and her hazel eyes glared at me. She stormed from the room before I had a chance to speak.

CHAPTER TWENTY-THREE

After I'd made sure Seth would be okay, I knocked on Kayla's door. When she didn't answer, nervousness bit at me. She wouldn't have tried to get to Paris on her own, would she? I pictured her in my mind and evaporated to wherever she was, sighing with relief when I stood in her room.

Kayla threw a book, catching me square in the face.

"Ow! God, Kayla. What the hell?"

"You lied to me!"

I touched my cheek where the corner of the book had hit. My fingertips were coated with blood. Grabbing a washcloth out of her bathroom, I held the rag to my face. "I didn't lie to you. Seth *was* attacked."

"Yeah, and *possessed* because of me! Why didn't you tell me?"

"Because I didn't want this reaction." My voice was louder than I expected. Kayla shrunk back on her bed. I sighed and dropped my hand. "I'm sorry. That's not what I meant."

Her bottom lip quivered. "You think I'm some porcelain doll, but I'm not. I'd hoped, by now, you'd see that. You should've told me."

"I know. And I know you can take care of yourself." I pointed to my split cheekbone.

Seconds passed, and we just stared at each other. Then Kayla slid off her bed and walked to me. She reached up to where I still held the cloth to my cheek and gently removed it from my face.

"I'm sorry. I didn't mean to hurt you," she said.

"I know."

"At least you won't need stitches."

"Always a plus."

"Daniel—"

I stepped back from her. "Please don't make me take you to Paris. I won't do it."

Kayla frowned. "That's not what I was going to say. I was going to ask you to train me tomorrow. I want to make that bastard pay." Her lips tightened, and her hands balled into fists at her sides. I'd never seen such a reaction from her, and, if I was being honest, I was a little terrified.

Stepping toward her, I placed a hand on each shoulder. "I promise, Kayla. We will make him pay."

She nodded and wrapped her arms around my neck, then her lips met mine. My breath caught when she pressed her body against mine and slipped her tongue into my mouth. I eased away. I couldn't do this right now, not after watching my enemy speak through the mouth of my best mate, and definitely not after just agreeing to train my girlfriend to fight the most powerful warlock in existence—to the death.

"What's wrong?" Her eyes searched my face.

I pressed my forehead to hers. "I don't think I can do this tonight."

Kayla looked at me like a mother assessing if her child was sick. Then she nodded. "Will you at least stay with me? We don't have to do anything. Just sleep."

I forced a smile. "Of course."

I fell asleep that night with Kayla in my arms.

A knock woke me the next morning. I tugged my arm out from under Kayla and slipped trousers on over my boxers before answering the door. An African-American girl stood on the other side, the same one who'd crouched under Bartholomew's table while Alex went bonkers.

"Um, I'm supposed to pick up Kayla. I thought I had the right room." She spoke in a very quiet voice.

My cheeks warmed. The last thing this girl needed to see was me answering Kayla's door. Shirtless. "You do. She's still asleep. I'll wake her. Where is she supposed to meet you?"

"Bartholomew's office. Trishna's come to train us today."

"Thank you. Margaret, right?"

She nodded and looked at her feet.

"Okay. Thank you, Margaret. She should be there soon." I closed the door as Margaret disappeared down the hall and leaned against it, sucking in a deep breath. At least I'd remembered to put on trousers.

"Blushing again?" Kayla asked. She was propped up on one elbow, looking at me with a smirk on her face.

"Yeah, yeah. Get up. You're wanted in Bartholomew's office."

"I heard. Come with me?"

I was supposed to train my team this morning, but if they split into teams like they did yesterday, I could spend the first half of the day watching the Magus practice. It'd be good to know what they were capable of anyway.

I nodded. "I'll meet you down there." Crossing the room, I kissed her forehead before leaving to change and attend to my Catchers.

When I arrived in Bartholomew's office, Alex, Margaret and Kayla had formed a half-circle in front of Trishna. Her black hair was braided down her back, and she wore a black vest over her blouse and jeans. With their eyes closed, the three Magus stood with their hands out, palms facing up. Trishna walked back and forth in front of them.

"Do you feel the energy inside you?" she asked in her thick, Indian accent.

The three nodded. I grabbed a seat on the far side of the room, next to Bartholomew, and watched.

"Good. Now draw it to you, like you're trying to roll it into a ball. Condense it."

I remembered the way Kayla's energy had felt the day she lit her mother's boyfriend on fire—like her entire body had been asleep and was waking up. Controlling that intense tingling energy had to be awkward.

"Now, when you're ready," Trishna continued, "I want you to open your eyes. Focus your energy on me. Turn your palms to face me, and then push the energy from your body. This vest will protect me, and I have a shield up, so hit me with everything you've got."

Margaret was the first to let her energy fly. Water spouted from her hands into Trishna's shield. The invisible force field swallowed the water like a sponge. My eyebrows rose.

"Good. You favor water. Very powerful," Trishna said. "Alex, you next."

Alex followed Margaret with a burst of air. Except, instead of hitting Trishna's shield, Bartholomew's papers flew around the room. Apparently his ability to move objects didn't mean he'd be able to control his energy.

"Okay. That was a good try. Seems like air will be your strongest element. Start over and see what you can produce. Kayla, your turn."

Kayla's eyes had remained closed while the other two took their turns. But now, she opened them and pointed her palms at Trishna. A circle of gold formed around her pupils, then a sharp *crack*, like the sound of a whip, filled the room as Kayla let go of her energy. Bartholomew and I jumped out of our chairs as a ball of fire hit Trishna's shield so hard, she flew into the desk.

Kayla's face whitened. She stepped back, placing a hand over her heart. Both Alex and Margaret slunk away from her as Bartholomew ran to Trishna.

Kayla's chest rose and fell rapidly, and her eyes filled with tears. "Is she hurt? Oh god, I didn't mean to hurt her."

"I'm okay, Kayla," Trishna said as Bartholomew helped her up from the floor.

I sighed in relief. The last thing Kayla needed was for Trishna to be injured on account of her.

"I'm so sorry," Kayla said.

Trishna smiled and nodded. "I know. Was not expecting that, or I would've put up a stronger shield. Fire it is, then. You are powerful. Now please, let's try again. And, this time, I will be prepared." She winked at Kayla.

The blood returned to Kayla's cheeks, and her posture relaxed. Sitting down again, I observed as Trishna had the three of them go through the same exercise again and again until each was comfortable enough to produce the element they wanted—even the ones that weren't instinctive. After hours, Trishna let them break.

"Well done. I must return to my coven now, but if Giovanni approves, I would like to see you again tomorrow."

"Of course he will," Bartholomew replied. He held his tanned hand out to Trishna.

"Until then," Trishna said and took Bartholomew's hand. They disappeared.

Alex and Margaret nodded their goodbyes to Kayla, their faces tight with exhaustion. Then Kayla turned to me.

"I think that went okay?"

I nodded. "You all did well."

"Trishna said once we've mastered being able to control our energy, we could pretty much harness it to do whatever we want. Even produce charms and spells."

I pulled her into my arms. "Well, that's good, considering I'm not letting you walk into that warlock's den until I know you can take him down."

Bartholomew returned, carrying a book.

"Kayla, Trishna asked me to give you this." He handed it to her.

I let go of Kayla so she could take the thick, black book with severely worn pages. She ran her hand along the cover. "What is it?"

"Trishna's Book of Spells. She figures you'll get a lot more use out of it than she will, considering she knows them all by heart now. She wants you to study the spells and go to her with any questions."

"But, why give this to me? I mean, shouldn't the others see this, too?"

Bartholomew shook his head. "Not yet. She says she senses something in you, something more powerful than the others. It won't take you as long to control your energy. She thinks you could master some of these spells within days."

"But how? Doesn't it take weeks—months—for witches to fully harness their power, more than simply being able to control elements?" I chimed in.

Bartholomew shrugged. "Not always. Especially when a traumatic event forces the witch's energy to rise to the surface."

He was talking about Kayla's near-rape.

"Trishna had a similar event happen to her. And then there was Tamesis. They say he mastered his energy within a day."

"Don't compare her to him."

"I'm not comparing them, Daniel. I'm simply stating that Trishna and Tamesis both are more powerful than the average witch or warlock."

Kayla nodded, but I could see the fear in her eyes. I squeezed the hand that wasn't latched onto the spell book.

"Well, tell Trishna thanks," Kayla said.

Bartholomew nodded. "Of course."

Kayla clasped my hand tight and dragged me out of the room.

CHAPTER TWENTY-FOUR

B ack in her room, Kayla stared at the spell book, which now rested on her bed.

"It's not an animal you have to be afraid of. Open it," I said.

She gripped the sides of her shorts and spoke barely loud enough for me to hear. "But what if my powers, you know, make me evil? Like him."

"Just because you have magic, it doesn't mean you will be evil. What you do with your magic is what makes you who you are."

Kayla nodded then took a deep breath. She crossed the room in three big steps and opened the book to the first page. I peeked over her shoulder. The first spell was how to create light when there is nothing but dark.

"See? Not evil," I said.

Kayla's posture relaxed, and she let out her breath. "Don't you have another training session?"

"Samantha will run it. I can stay here with you."

Kayla turned to me and forced a smile. "I'm okay, really."

"You sure?"

"Yes."

I touched her cheek. "All right. Well, you know where I'll be if you need me."

Kayla leaned in for a quick kiss before I evaporated to the training room.

When I arrived, my team was already split into two groups. I took turns joining the two teams, watching everyone fight. They were training like gladiators. Two people stood back-to-back, defending themselves while the other three circled and attacked. Everyone wore gloves, but every now and then, someone would get punched or kicked and they would shout in pain. Joining in on the offensive side, I paid attention to everyone's defensive tactics and gave pointers or compliments.

For two hours we trained, then, when I was about to call for a break, a Catcher I'd seen only once before in my life appeared. "Daniel! You and your team are needed immediately."

The eleven of us loaded our belts with real weapons and ran up the narrow flight of stairs to the lobby where five Catchers slumped on the floor. One held his hands over a wound in his gut, dark red blood pouring through his fingers. Bartholomew pressed a towel to the side of another's face, and a third lay on the ground, his throat slit. His girlfriend knelt on the ground next to him, her forehead pressed against his chest and her arm draped across his stomach. Her shoulders shook with sobs.

The fifth, Aran, one of the Catchers I'd trained with two hundred years ago, sat on the floor, talking to Giovanni while Trishna used her stone to heal a huge gash in his leg. His face was streaked with sweat and blood—red, not black.

They hadn't been fighting Nightmares.

Catchers and Weavers stood in a big circle around the room, their hands over their mouths—some in tears and others pale as ghosts.

Giovanni approached me. "Aran and his team were attacked by a coven at a plantation in Kansas. That's where I need you to follow up. Check for clues. See if they're involved with this warlock we're hunting. And if any are still there, make sure you bring at least one back alive."

We landed in a cornfield in Kansas. The dark sky was illuminated only by the full moon, clouds covering most of the stars. My eyes needed a second to adjust to the sudden change, and when they did, I counted off my team to make sure we were all present.

"We need to see if anyone stayed after the battle. Stay invisible until you need to interact with the other side." Trishna waited on standby at the mansion in what was now being converted into a dungeon area to bind the Magus as soon as we arrived.

We walked with assault rifles in our hands, prepared to shoot if need be. Our invisible bodies moved quickly through the ears of corn, not a single one affected by our presence. We stopped when we'd passed out of the edge of the field. The house in front of us was a large, white plantation home that needed a good painting. Dark green shutters framed the windows, and on the side of the house nearest us, a pentagram had been spray-painted on the wood siding, the color of blood.

"Wait here," I said, wanting to get a better idea if anyone was home. I walked along the edge of the cornfield until I faced the front of the house. A light was on in the far left window, but a white curtain covered the pane, making it impossible to see into the room.

As I was about to return to my team without a solid lead, the curtain moved and a head peeked out—a girl, no older than Kayla. Short, auburn hair was styled in a pixie cut, accentuating her thin face. Large eyes roamed back and forth across the yard. When the curtain closed and the girl stepped away from the window, I jogged back to the team.

"There's at least one in there. We need to get in that house." I pointed to a single-pane window at the back corner of the house. "I will peek through there to give us a point of reference, then we can evaporate inside and take down however many witches there are."

"Are you sure that's safe?" Lucca asked. "I mean, didn't the other five do the same thing and come back in pieces?"

"It's our best option, and there are ten of us this time. Trust me."

Everyone nodded, and I sprinted to the edge of the house, peeking through the window. An old bed sat in the middle with an ugly filigree duvet on top. It was a design I was sure I wouldn't forget. But to be safe, I took in the sight of the rest of the room, ensuring that we wouldn't accidentally appear in another house with the same duvet. When I was positive I could draw up the image of the room in my mind, I sprinted back to the cornfield where my team waited.

"All right. Everyone link hands. I'll evaporate us in there."

When we were joined together, I closed my eyes and pictured the room. But when I opened my eyes, we still stood in the cornfield.

"Um, nothing happened," Brian said.

"Yes, I know," I replied, my voice sharp. Closing my eyes again, I focused hard on the ten of us vaporizing to the coven's bedroom. Yet, when I opened my eyes again, we still stood in the cornfield. "Blast."

"Maybe we can't evaporate in there," Lizzie said, adjusting her blonde ponytail. "Maybe they put up some type of shield or something after the other Protectors left."

"Maybe." I sighed. "We'll have to get in another way. I can try walking through the wall, but if that doesn't work, we can easily slide a knife into that old window and unlatch it."

"I'm small," Lian said. "You won't have to open the window as far for me. Let me go. If there are too many, I'll signal for backup. But, I should be able to go corporeal and get a hand on the one witch without being discovered."

She *was* light on her feet. And she was quick. I'd watched her at practice. "All right," I said, "but I'm coming with you. The rest of you, keep your eyes on me. If something happens and you can't get to Rome safely, our rendezvous point is *Las Lajas* in Columbia."

My team nodded in agreement, then Lian and I took a breath and made a break for the house. We sprinted through the side yard to the window nearest the pentacle and pressed our bodies against the wall. Neither of us went through.

Knowing we had no other choice, I went corporeal, grabbed a dagger out of my belt and glided it in between the windowpanes. I slid the blade over until it caught on the metal latch then tipped the knife sideways, unlocking the window. Pulling the dagger back out, I stuck it in my belt and carefully wiggled the window until my fingertips fit underneath the bottom.

Again, I listened for a sign that our cover was blown, but nothing happened, so I wiggled the window up, slowing down whenever the slightest squeak rang out. When the opening was large enough for Lian to crawl through, I twined my fingers together into a toehold for her. She placed a foot in it, and I boosted her onto the ledge and through the window. There was no sound of her landing, which was a good sign.

Invisible again, I stood like a statue, listening. My heartbeat was louder than anything else in the world. Then a head popped out the window. I turned, poised to attack until I realized who it was.

"There are four of them. I need backup," Lian said.

Nodding, I held up two fingers to my team. Samantha and Lucca sprinted across the yard. We paused to make sure the coast was clear, then I opened the window a little further to make sure we could all fit. After helping Samantha through the window, Lucca pulled himself up, and I followed.

The four of us stood, invisible, in the dark bedroom that smelled like it hadn't been used, or cleaned, in years. I scrunched my nose at the stench and followed Lian into the hall. Straight ahead past two other doors, two witches sat in a living room, whispering.

We stepped back into the shadows in case anyone's nerves forced them to accidentally go corporeal. Our visible state was natural. Staying invisible took effort. In the middle of the night when your charge is sleeping, no big deal if you went corporeal for a minute or two. But when trying to take down a coven of witches—different story.

"What do we do?" Lucca asked, his dark hair falling into his face.

"We'll have to sneak up on them," I replied. "Luckily, they can't see us, so only go corporeal when you're close enough to take them down. And remember, one of them needs to get back to Giovanni. Are we ready?"

They nodded, and we snuck back down the hall. But when we got close to the living room, both witches were gone. *Great.*

"Cover me," I mouthed to Lian and crept around the corner—and into the line of sight of one of the four. "Shit," I said as the witch threw a bag of powder on me. My skin burned, and I groaned. The sack must've been infused with magic.

"We can feel you, dumbass," the witch said and slammed me into the wall before I had a chance to react. I looked at my arms when I fell to the ground. My skin glowed.

Lian turned the corner, going corporeal, and shot the witch between the eyes. I swore when the loud *boom* from the gun shook the room. *So much for being stealthy.* From the kitchen came the other three Magus—the young witch I had seen in the window, and two others, a warlock and another witch.

Lian tried to shoot them, but the warlock flung her into the wall opposite me before she had the chance to squeeze the trigger. Her head hit the wall, and she fell to the floor, unconscious. I jumped up to fight, but he was too strong. His hand pointed in my direction, and white-hot pain covered me from head to toe, like I'd stepped into a furnace. I fell to my knees.

Before I had the chance to warn him not to, Lucca threw a blade, revealing his location. The older witch stopped the knife in midair, and with a twist of her hand, the dagger spun around and landed in Lucca's stomach.

"No!" Samantha screamed, her resolve to stay invisible breaking. The older witch blasted her with a burst of air. Samantha flew down the hall until I could no longer see her.

"You people just don't know when to quit," the warlock said. "Here we were, enjoying a nice summer night, when five of you stained our floors with magic blood. I thought I made it very clear when I let those Protectors return that our fight was not with your kind. And yet, a few hours later, four more show up. Do you have any idea how insulting that is?"

"You made it your fight when you used Nightmares to attack humans," I replied. The pain in my body intensified. I bent forward and gasped. With every ounce of energy I could muster, I placed my finger on my gun's trigger as he spoke and tipped the gun upward.

"So, that's what this is about?" he teased. "You think we're the ones running the show?" He laughed. "You fools. You have no idea how deep the pool of shit is you've stepped into. Not just Nightmares are on his side. And as soon as he gets his hands on the three Magus you're harboring, you're going to wish you'd followed him when you had the chance."

"We'll see about that." I pressed my gun's trigger. The bullet went straight through the warlock's head.

The older witch screamed and held her hands out to attack, but from behind me, another shot rang out and a bullet hole smoked between the witch's eyes. I snapped my head around. Samantha stared straight ahead, her eyes hard.

Alone now, the young witch I'd seen in the window ran.

I nodded Samantha my thanks and pointed at Lian. "Get her and Lucca back to Rome. I'm going after the girl."

I jumped up from the floor, the pain in my body gone with the death of the warlock, and sprinted through the house. The front door swung open as I rounded the corner from the kitchen into the front room. The girl ran across the porch and down the steps. She stopped when my team stepped out of the cornfield, corporeal, guns pointed at her head.

"Please, don't hurt me!" she screamed when I barreled out the front door. She sobbed. "They kidnapped me and brought me here. I swear I'm not one of them."

I crossed the front yard to where she stood, but when I got closer, I stopped cold. Finally, I recognized her face. Adelynn Rudolf, the witch who had been taken from her bed in Seattle.

Dropping my gun, I walked toward her slowly. "Adelynn, yeah? I saw your picture on the news. I'm a friend. I won't hurt you. But, I need you to come with me. We have someone who can help you."

She nodded and walked toward me, her gloved hands outstretched like she wanted a hug. Then, I remembered what Bartholomew said about her abilities—her touch killed her boyfriend.

Standing perfectly still, I watched her every movement. If I grabbed her clothes instead of her skin, I could get us both back to Rome. But if I slipped and touched her skin, I was going to die.

When Adelynn closed in on me, her eyes squinted. "You really should've let me go." She leapt on me, knocking me to the ground. I flipped her over, careful to avoid skin-to-skin contact. With a leg on each side of her and my hands pinned to her upper arms, I evaporated to Rome.

We landed on the floor in the room designated as her holding cell where Trishna waited.

"*Manus in manu tua alligo!*" Trishna yelled. And just in time. Adelynn kneed me between the legs. My arms weakened beneath me, and I sucked in air, the throbbing pain radiating from my groin to my stomach. Adelynn grabbed my face and smashed her lips against mine.

But nothing happened.

Adelynn jostled me off her with a scream. I squeezed my eyes closed and winced. Any further movement, I would vomit on the floor.

"No! You should be dead!" Adelynn turned around to Trishna. "What did you do to me?" She ran at her, poised to attack, but Trishna held up her hands, freezing Adelynn.

"Sit." She moved a hand to her left, forcing Adelynn into a chair. "Daniel, can you move? I have to put a gate over the doorway, and you need to be on the other side."

Nodding, I turned onto my stomach and pushed myself up with a grunt. I bent over, nauseous, and then walked out the door.

CHAPTER TWENTY-FIVE

By the time I reached the grand foyer, the pain in my stomach and groin had mostly subsided, but the shock hit me at how easily Adelynn could've taken my life. I should've known better than to leave myself open to attack like that. If Trishna had waited one more second to perform her spell, I'd be floating in eternal blackness. Never another thought, another smell, another sound—never another anything.

Kayla's voice was the first thing I heard when I stepped into the foyer, and I turned to her just in time to catch her in my arms as she flung herself at me. I held her tight, burying my face in her hair, taking in the strawberry smell of her shampoo and the feel of her body in my arms. After a minute, I pulled away and lifted her face, staring into her beautiful, hazel eyes. The bottoms of them were filled with tears. I kissed her forehead, her nose, her lips. The others were watching, but I didn't care.

"When Sam came back with Lian and Lucca, I was worried. But then when Seth appeared and told us Adelynn attacked you, I thought that meant she touched you, that you were dead. Daniel, I don't know what I would do—" Her words turned into cries, and she gripped the back of my shirt.

It wasn't surprising that Kayla knew what Adelynn was capable of. I squeezed her tight and kissed the top of her head. "I'm all right. There was a moment where I thought I was in trouble, but Trishna saved my life."

Kayla nodded and looked up at me. "Seems she's good at that."

I tried to smile, but I couldn't. Behind her, a body was covered with a blanket, and Samantha stood with a hand over her mouth. Lian sat on the ground next to the body, her hand on his chest. Her eyes were red, and her black hair fell in wisps around her round face. Lucca had been her understudy, her partner.

After kissing Kayla's forehead, I stepped away. "Give me a second."

Kayla nodded and squeezed my hand before I walked over to Samantha and Lian. "You both all right?" I asked.

Lian nodded but didn't look at me. Samantha shook her head.

I glanced down at the body of my comrade who had come so far—from an Italian farm boy to one of the Protectors' best Catchers. Going up against witches was nothing like fighting Nightmares, and we'd been unprepared. Before we even went in the house, I should've warned him not to throw his dagger. I'd seen Alex in Bartholomew's office, and I knew what they were capable of. Yet, I'd neglected it. I was his leader, and I failed him. My fists clenched.

"Where's Giovanni?" I asked.

"He and the others went to search the house. He asked me to send you as soon as you had handled Adelynn," Samantha replied.

I nodded. "Thank you both for your hard work today. Tell the others tomorrow's practice is not mandatory."

Leaving the two of them, my chest aching, I returned to Kayla. "I'm sorry. I have to go back to clean up our mess. I'll come find you as soon as I get home, okay?"

She nodded. "Be careful."

·I touched her cheek then evaporated to the house.

My team wandered through the rooms, collecting everything they felt could be evidence in finding this warlock. Tonight had been our first real breakthrough. We weren't leaving anything behind.

In what appeared to be a study, I sat at their computer. The screen was black, like it hadn't been used in hours. Yet, when I moved the mouse, the monitor sprung to life. I nearly laughed when I saw it wasn't password protected. With as many people as there were in the house, I understood. But still… *idiots.*

Their home screen was as normal as any other—icons for their web browser, one of those role-playing games, and other things like that. But in their Documents, I noticed something weird. There were no folders. I adjusted the settings until all the hidden folders were forced to show. My pulse raced.

There was security footage, visitor logs, background checks and more. I tried opening a file and, when it turned out to be encrypted, searched frantically through the desk for some way to save all of this information without pulling out the hard drive. Eventually, I had to resort to returning to my room in Rome to grab my own USB drive.

When I returned to the coven's house, Giovanni sat at the desk.

"What are you doing?" I asked.

He jumped out of the chair and spun around to look at me. "Oh, I was just looking to see what was on here."

"The files are encrypted."

Giovanni's eyes stayed locked with mine. "*Sì*, I figured that out right before you walked in. So, get what you can, and let me know what you find." He ran from the room without another word.

I stared after him. Was he being dodgy? If I didn't know better, I'd think he was hiding something. Forcing down the unease in my stomach, I zipped all the files into one massive folder and transferred the documents onto my flash drive. Then I joined the others in the living room. Each Catcher held a box full of books, papers and other trinkets that might be of value to our cause.

"Where's Giovanni?" I asked.

Ivan shrugged. "Who knows. He left us ten minutes ago. Said to come back when we were done."

With a frown, I nodded that it was time to go. We evaporated to Rome.

When I re-appeared in the foyer, Lian was on the bottom step of the staircase. I tucked the flash drive into my pocket and joined her. She wiped her almond eyes.

"They took his body to be burned. I can't believe he's gone."

"I'm sorry."

She sniffed. "It's not your fault. I should've warned him not to throw that dagger."

My heart squeezed like someone trying to burst a water balloon. "Don't blame yourself. I'm your leader. I should've been the one to warn everyone about using weapons against them."

Lian dropped her face into her hands and spoke into her palms. "I hope Kayla and the other two can figure out what they're doing. Because if they can't, we're all dead."

My lungs forgot how to breathe. "Forgive me, Lian," I said before disappearing.

In the artillery in the basement, I stared at our weapons. We had guns, knives, swords, maces, spears—a hundred different types of weapons collected over the centuries. And none of them would truly be safe against magic. We got lucky in Kansas with the guns, for with a flick of their hand, a witch could turn even our own guns against us. The only safe way to take down a witch was with another witch.

Which meant I couldn't protect Kayla.

Hot bile rose in my throat. I glared at the weapons as the room blurred. My hands shook in anger, and my jaw clenched. Finally, the rage took over.

I flipped the tables of guns, sending them crashing to the floor, the sound of metal on concrete deafening. I knocked over the display of spears and swords, and overturned the table of daggers. One of them sliced my arm, but I didn't care. For two hundred years, I'd protected humans. My record was flawless. And now I couldn't protect the *one* person I cared about most in this world. I'd never felt so weak.

Blood ran down my forearm, dripping off my fingertips into a small puddle on the floor. My chest rose and fell as I tried to catch my breath.

"Daniel?" Kayla said from behind me.

I hung my head, not wanting her to see me like this. Hearing her voice was a reminder of how hopeless I felt—how much I didn't want to lose her. Gripping the edge of one of the remaining tables, I focused on my breathing.

"Tabbi said I might find you down here. Did you do this?"

I sighed, picking up one of the tables, and started to put the daggers back. Giovanni would be annoyed if I left the room in shambles. Besides, it gave me something to do other than think about how much I wanted to hide her away to keep her safe.

Kayla quietly approached and helped pick up the tables and the weapons. She didn't quite put things back the way they were supposed to go, but I doubted anyone would care. Together, we worked in silence until the room was tidy, then I dug my hands in my pockets and looked straight ahead.

She gingerly touched my wounded arm. "You should get this looked at."

I glanced at the wound. The blood had clotted. "It's fine. I'll clean it later."

We stood there for a minute or so, until finally Kayla had had enough. "Talk to me."

"I don't have anything to say." My voice came out colder than intended.

She dropped her hand, nodded and stepped back. "Well, I'll be in my room if you change your mind."

I closed my eyes and sighed. Turning, I grabbed her wrist before she had a chance to leave. "Wait. I'm sorry. I just… can't."

"Why? Because you're afraid you'll look weak?"

"More or less."

She placed a hand on my chest, her eyes glassy. "Daniel, you don't have to be all macho around me. I already know that you're strong and courageous.

You've done nothing but fight for me, protect me, comfort me. But we're in this together, which means I want to be here for you, too. So don't put up a wall between us, please."

Her words filled me with warmth from head to toe. She had so much faith in me.

I was still angry, still scared for her future. But pushing her away was not going to make things any easier. She had dug herself into my heart. I wasn't going to let her go. Not now. Not ever. God help me—she was not going to die while I existed.

Wanting to be close to her, to feel her, I placed my hands on her lower back and pulled her to me. I kissed her like it was the last chance I'd ever get. She returned my advances with such passion that my heart ricocheted in my chest. Her arms linked around my neck as our mouths opened and closed in insatiable hunger. Her touch, her want for me, was enough to push me over the edge. Holding her tight in my arms, I evaporated us to my room.

As soon as we landed, Kayla grabbed the bottom of my shirt and, breathing heavily, lifted it over my head. I raised her lips back to mine and slipped my tongue into her mouth. Running her fingertips down my chest to my stomach and around my back, she let them linger just under the top of my trousers. The way she caressed my body sent a shiver down my spine. I wanted to touch her, to kiss her body, to feel her every surface. Gently, I pushed her against the wall. Again and again, we'd been interrupted. It was not going to happen this time.

Holding her hands against the wall so she couldn't reach out, I nuzzled her neck, nibbling softly until she began to moan. Then I kissed down her chest to where her breasts peeked out the top of her tank top. She whimpered and fought to get her hands out of mine.

Aching for her, my hands released hers to tear off her shirt. I returned my lips to her mouth and ran my hands down her back, stopping only to pull her sports bra over her head. Her chest naked, she arched her back, and her breasts pressed against me. I shuddered and moved my hands down the back of her gym shorts, giving her bum a squeeze. Then I pulled her hips against mine, and she moaned into my mouth.

God, I wasn't going to make it much longer.

I carried her to my bed, laying her down on her back, and undid my trousers, sliding them off with my boxers in a single motion. Her cheeks flushed as I joined her on the bed. I fought the insecurity that wormed its way into my stomach. I'd never felt more vulnerable with a woman than I did right now.

I kissed her stomach, up between her breasts to her neck. Goose pimples rose on her warm skin, and her entire body shook. I smiled at her involuntary reaction and took her breasts in my hands. Her pulse raced in her neck beneath my lips as she dug her fingertips into my back and moaned loudly.

Pulling off her gym shorts and underwear, I took in the sight of her lying naked on my bed. My heart jumped in my chest. *Holy shit.* She was so beautiful, so curvy, so perfectly sculpted. I swallowed, my throat dry. Never had I wanted so badly to make someone happy.

"Do we need, you know?" she asked.

Protection? I shook my head. "Catchers can't procreate."

She grabbed my face and kissed me hard, and I lost myself in ecstasy.

CHAPTER TWENTY-SIX

A knock on my door startled me awake. Kayla hid under the covers. The TV was on in the background.

"Did I fall asleep?" I asked.

Kayla nodded. "We were talking and the next thing I knew, you were snoring."

Burying my face in my pillow, I tried to apologize, but the words came out muffled. "Smrwy."

She squeezed my arm and laughed. "Yeah, you should be."

Someone knocked on the door again.

"You gonna get that?" she asked.

I rolled off the bed, putting on my trousers, and opened the door just enough to see who was there. Seth.

"Hey, man. I need to talk to you."

"All right?" The last thing I wanted was for him to come in when there was a sexy, naked girl in my bed. I also didn't want that sexy, naked girl to put any clothes back on. Hopefully this would be quick.

"It's about Giovanni. Can I come in?" he asked. "I don't wanna talk in the hall."

I sighed. "Yeah, hang on a minute." Closing the door in Seth's face, I shot Kayla an apologetic look. "Put your clothes on." I grabbed a clean shirt out of my dresser while she dressed. When she was ready, I opened the door and ushered him inside.

"Did I interrupt something?" Seth smirked.

I closed the door, clearing my throat and fighting the heat in my cheeks. "What about Giovanni?"

Seth looked at Kayla, whose cheeks had also reddened, and chuckled. "I can come back later."

"Seth, just talk."

He held up his hands. "All right. Look, when we were in the house searchin' for clues, Giovanni seemed like he was nervous being there. I think he's hidin' something."

I held out a hand to stop him. "Wait a minute. You thought he was dodgy, too?"

Seth's eyes widened. "You mean—"

"Yeah, I saw it."

"No way. And you weren't there when Bartholomew figured out Kayla was the real target in Paris. It was like he was annoyed. And then, when we found out about the other three, he rushed us out the door because he needed 'to think,' but it was like he wanted us to get away before we figured anything else out. You don't think he's in league with this warlock dude?"

I shook my head and ran a hand through my dirty blond hair. "I don't know. Maybe? But then why would he send us all to war against the warlock?"

"To cover his tracks," Kayla replied.

I turned around to face her. "What?"

She stood and walked over to us. "Tabbi was talking to me this morning about this warlock—how he's controlling the Nightmares, how he wants the four of us to help him murder people, how a war between the Magus could be catastrophic. If Seth is right and Giovanni really is in league with this guy, wouldn't he want to make it look like he was on your side?"

"Yeah, I guess. But why would Giovanni make a deal with the guy in the first place? Doesn't that violate what he is, the oath he took?" Seth asked.

"If he is in league with this warlock, then we're in deeper shit than we thought," I replied. "Giovanni's clever. He could convince thousands of Protectors to follow him under false pretense. Seth, do you have access to his office when he's not there?"

He shook his head. "No, Giovanni's the only one with access. He also turns on an alarm system that freaks out at the slightest movement. As soon as we go corporeal to touch something, the thing will go off."

"Then you need to think of a way to distract him so he doesn't turn it on. Samantha and I can break in and search through his things. Until then, pay close attention to what he's doing, where he's going, who he's speaking to. If he is a traitor, we need to figure out who else in these walls is working with him."

The Magus in that house in Kansas said we had no idea who was loyal to this warlock. If he got under the skin of Giovanni, there was no telling who else was involved. Until then, I needed to be on guard. We couldn't afford to have our walls destroyed from within.

Seth nodded. "I'll do what I can."

I plucked the USB drive out of my trouser pocket and handed it to him. "Also, see if you can find someone who can decrypt these files. And don't tell Giovanni you have this."

"I'll let you know as soon as I got somethin'."

Four hours later, there was a knock on my door. Kayla slept on the bed next to me, having passed out halfway through *Gladiator*, and I got off the bed as gently as I could to avoid waking her. Seth and Irene stood on the other side of the door.

"Man, you need to see this," Seth said, pushing his way into the room.

"Keep it down, mate," I whispered. "What do you need to show me?"

"What I found on the USB drive Seth asked me to hack." Irene pulled it out of her pocket and slipped the small piece of plastic into my laptop. Seth and I stood behind her and watched as she decrypted the files. I paid close attention to what keys she pressed.

"I couldn't decrypt much, but I was able to get into a couple files," Irene said. "This is from a week ago."

Irene brought up security footage from a small warehouse or storage unit. Someone parked a black B.M.W. in front of the building, and the passenger door opened. Giovanni stepped out of the car. I gripped the back of the desk chair. He *was* in league with this bastard. Bugger. Seth had been right.

A man stepped out of the building and shook hands with Giovanni. He had dark hair and wore black clothing, but from this angle I couldn't make out his face. Giovanni's smile, though, told me they'd known each other for a while—a smile you'd reserve not for a business partnership but for a friend. Then, the man turned to lead Giovanni into the building, and I got a good look at his face. I'd seen him before, the first night I'd watched over Kayla in the asylum. With a gasp, I stepped back from the desk.

The warlock was Richard Bartlett—Kayla's father.

"You know who that is?" Seth asked.

No, this couldn't be happening. My palms sweat.

Right then, screams filled the halls. Loud *booms* rang out and a bell alarm sounded. Seth and I stared at each other, our eyes wide. Irene ran out the door without another glance at either of us.

"Daniel, what's going on?" Kayla asked, having been woken by the noise.

Snapping into action, I shoved the USB drive into my pocket before she could see the screen. "I don't know." I grabbed my weapon belt out of my closet and wrapped it around my waist. "Seth, get her to the rendezvous point. I'll meet you there as soon as I can."

"No!" Kayla yelled. "I'm not leaving without you."

I grabbed her shoulders and looked her in the eye. "I will be right behind you. I promise."

She nodded, though her face paled. I kissed her forehead then ran out the door.

The halls were already filled with corpses of Catchers and Weavers. My heart stopped. We were being ambushed. With weak legs, I evaporated to the artillery, filled my belt with as many weapons as I could carry and ran up the narrow stairs to the lobby.

Everywhere, Catchers battled Nightmares—and we were severely outnumbered. Right and left, Catchers fell as claws ripped through their bodies. Soon they began to evaporate, leaving more and more Catchers to fight on their own. I looked around the room until my eye caught the person I was looking for.

A man dressed in a long, black cape marched up the stairs. Richard.

Sprinting through the lobby, I dodged the swipes of the Nightmares all around me. Then halfway across the room, a Nightmare blocked my way, swinging at my face. The beast's scaly, humanoid body was much bigger than the one that had attacked Hendrik in Kayla's psychiatric room. I ducked just in time and sliced at its gut. Black blood oozed out of the hellion onto the floor, but it didn't fall. The Nightmare swung at me again, and I dodged its attack as quickly as I could. The monster's claws found my arm. I swore as my flesh tore and blood soaked through my sleeve.

Again, it swung. I sliced off the Nightmare's hand before claws could make contact with my body. Then, as the beast leaned back to roar in pain, I leapt and stabbed my blade clear through its neck. The creature fell to the ground without another sound.

I sprinted again for the staircase, determined to reach the warlock, and threw a blade between the eyes of the last Nightmare in my way. For only a second, I stopped to pull the knife out of the beast's head—Catchers' blades were priceless—and then, finally, I reached the stairs. Up eight flights I ran, glancing right and left for any sign of Richard. When I was on the eighth floor, a scream caught my attention—Kayla.

No! She wasn't supposed to be here.

I turned right and ran down the hall. Across the hall from Kayla's door was Seth, lying unconscious on the ground.

No, no, no! When I kicked open Kayla's door, Richard stood across from me, one of his hands wrapped around her wrist. She struggled to get free, but he was too strong.

"Daniel!" Kayla screamed as an invisible force grabbed me and threw me across the room. My head smacked the corner of her bookshelf, and I crashed to the floor.

CHAPTER TWENTY-SEVEN

Will he wake soon?" a feminine voice asked, sounding far away. Was I dreaming?

"I don't know. He split his head open, Samantha. Given the amount of blood on her floor, we're lucky he didn't crack his skull," a woman responded with a German accent.

Hearing about hitting my head, the memory of it smacking on Kayla's bookshelf came back—as did the pain. *Nope. Not dreaming.* And then I remembered being tossed like a rag doll. *Kayla.*

Opening my eyes, I sat up, nearly smacking Lizzie in the face. "Kayla— where is she?" I groaned at the nauseating pain in my head and fell backward.

Samantha placed her hands on my chest, keeping me from sitting up again. "Daniel, don't move. You hit your head."

"Kayla—"

"Would you lay still? I'm not done stitching your head," Lizzie replied. Her blonde hair was splotched with black blood.

"Somebody answer me! Where the hell is she?"

"Daniel." Seth's voice caught me off guard. Thank god he was okay. "She's gone. The warlock has her."

Someone may as well have dropped a bowling ball on my chest from ten stories up. I swallowed the lump in my throat and ground my teeth until they hurt.

"Why was she still there, Seth? I told you to get her out!"

"She was insistent on goin' back for something and wouldn't take my hand unless I promised to take her to her room first. I'm sorry, Daniel."

My hands gripped the edges of the wooden table until my knuckles whitened. I had to get up, to find her, to bring her home. As soon as the bell rang, I should've taken her from the mansion.

"Are you done yet?" I yelled at Lizzie.

"Just one more stitch! Be patient."

I felt the tugging and stitching of Lizzie's handiwork, but there was no pain. They must've numbed me.

"There. You can get up now," Lizzie said.

I smacked Samantha's hands off my chest, then teetered sideways when I stood. Someone was hitting me over the head again and again with a sledgehammer, and I blinked a few times until my eyes focused.

We were in some sort of classroom inside a church. A very old church with stone walls. Bibles filled a small bookcase near an old, wooden door, and above the door was a crucifix. A poster hung on the left side of the chalkboard, and on closer examination I noticed all the words were in Spanish. We were in *Las Lajas*—our rendezvous point.

I stormed down a long, stone hallway. Large, gothic windows provided light from the outside, and from where I stood, we were high above the *cascada* flowing through the deep canyon where *Las Lajas* sat. A short flight of stone stairs took me to the main floor were Tabbi stood amongst the other remaining members of my team—Lian, Ivan, Vasin, and Hakan.

This is all?

"Daniel!" Tabbi yelled. At her voice the others turned to stare. She ran up and hugged me. "I was so worried."

I patted her back and stepped out of her grasp to address the others. "Brian and Irene?" When Lian shook her head, I frowned. "Well, I'm glad you all are safe."

"Yeah. Though why you picked this hellhole of a place to meet up, I'll never know," Ivan said.

I ignored him, too scared and angry right now to deal with his shit. One of us would end up killing the other.

"The warlock has all three Magus?" I asked.

Seth nodded, and his eyes met the floor. "Sorry, man. There were just too many of them."

Balling my hands into fists, I sucked in a deep breath. "You all still willing to fight?" There were not enough people for war, but there were enough to scout. I knew who the warlock was now and could track him. He should've made sure he killed me when he had the chance.

They all nodded.

"Then wait here. I'm going to go find this bloke, see where he's hiding out."

"Do you know who he is?" Samantha asked.

I grimaced. My stomach ached thinking about how Kayla must be feeling right now. "His name is Richard Bartlett. He's Kayla's father."

The room was so quiet; I could hear the river flowing three hundred feet below. Only Tabbi managed to speak. "Then go find out where he took her. We'll wait here."

I nodded and closed my eyes.

When they opened, I still stood in the church. *What the hell?* I closed my eyes and evaporated to the other side of the room, making sure the blow to my head wasn't interfering. Then I tried to evaporate to Kayla, but like last time, I opened them to find myself standing in the same spot.

"What the hell?" I yelled. "I can't evaporate. Not to him, not to Kayla. *What the hell?*"

I paced around the room and ran my hands through my blond hair. This couldn't be happening. With the power to go anywhere in the entire world, why couldn't I nip to the *one place* I wanted—needed—to be? There was only one conclusion.

"He must've spelled his hiding place," I said.

"Or maybe you hit your head too hard and your mind's still trying to recover. Wherever she is, it's a lot farther than across the room," Samantha said.

"Then you try."

Samantha closed her eyes. And went nowhere. "Okay, maybe there's a spell blocking us."

"Bugger!" I punched the wall. Pain ran up my arm as my knuckles split, but I didn't care. My hand hadn't broken.

Everybody stared at me, their eyes wide, and a couple of them stepped back. Only Ivan enjoyed my turmoil. Finally, Tabbi stepped forward. "Daniel, there's another option. I can get into Kayla's head, remember? Maybe if we could see what she's seeing—"

"We could figure out where she is," I finished her sentence.

She walked to me and held out her hand. Taking it eagerly, I closed my eyes, waiting for her to pop us into Kayla's head.

At first I felt like I was floating—much different than last time when I popped right into Kayla's head. Was it because of the miles between us? A slight ache ran through my bones, then morphed into numbness. Finally, I was seeing through Kayla's eyes, feeling her emotions.

Kayla's thoughts entered my mind.

My father is supposed to be dead.

Kayla slid her shaking hands out from under her legs and stared at the wall in front of her, remembering how her father had dragged her to a Catcher who grabbed her arm and evaporated here.

He should've tossed me in a dungeon for all I really am, she thought. *A prisoner.*

Kayla gripped the rose pendant that hung around her neck.

Daniel... Did my father kill him? He'd been so limp when he hit the floor.

Kayla took a deep breath as a small whimper escaped her lips. *I never even told him I loved him.* She covered her mouth as tears fell from her eyes.

She jumped when the door to her room unlocked. A tall boy, maybe seventeen, entered the room. His brown hair sat in a spiky mess on top of his head, and his dark eyes pierced through her.

"Your father wants to see you," he said with an American accent. His voice was deep.

Kayla glared at him. "Tell him I'm not interested."

"I'm not above carrying you over my shoulder."

"You wouldn't dare."

He took a step toward her. Kayla jumped off the bed to stand on the other side. She held her hands out in front of her, trying to remember what Trishna taught her. *Feel the energy inside you. Call it. Grab and throw.*

He laughed. "I'd like to see you try." His dark eyes sparkled as his lips turned up in a mischievous grin.

Kayla ground her teeth and threw a ball of energy out of her hands. But he blocked her attack and threw the energy into the lamp next to him. The light crashed to the floor.

"Nice try, but the day you catch me off guard is the day I turn myself into a pumpkin for Cinderella's ball."

God, he's arrogant. "Or maybe I'll turn you into a toad and run over you with my car," she said.

Again, he laughed. "You have his wit, that's for sure. But seriously, Kayla, if I don't return with you, I very well might be turned into a frog. So, either you come with me willingly, or I make you."

Kayla dropped her hands. "Then you'll have to make me."

He shrugged. "Okay."

He crossed the room quicker than Kayla expected. She barely had enough time to leap onto the bed before he was right behind her. She tried running across the mattress to make a break for the open door, but his hands caught her feet, and she crashed to the bed.

Kayla squealed. "Let me go!" She kicked him in the chest, and a grunt escaped him. But then his hands tightened around her ankles, his fingers digging into her flesh. She cried out in pain.

"I told you I would make you," he said. He fell against her and scooped her into his arms, tossing her over his shoulder.

Kayla beat his back. "Put me down!"

He carried her out of the room with a laugh. Kayla fought against him, elbowing him in the back of the head, but he was too strong. Flashbacks of Matt's attack flooded her mind, and quickly her resolve weakened. Her heart raced, and her eyes flooded with tears.

"Okay, okay. I'll go with you. Just put me down," she pleaded, her voice shaking.

"Well, darn. This was very erotic." He stopped and set Kayla on the ground.

She scowled at him as blood rushed into her cheeks, and she gripped the bottom of her shirt with shaky hands.

He grabbed her arm. "Come on, then. Your father's waiting."

Kayla winced at his grip and tried to keep up. The gray walls and oak doors of the office-like building passed in a blur until they stopped at a door in the middle of the hall. The guy holding Kayla's arm knocked twice, then entered. Margaret and Alex sat in steel chairs, their hands tied behind their backs. They both stared at Kayla, their eyes full of fear. Kayla held her stomach as it churned.

Richard stood at the front of the room next to a thin girl with a pixie cut. She eyed Kayla like a lioness ready to attack her prey. *Adelynn.*

"Ah, Nolan. Thanks for bringing her, mate. I hope she wasn't too much trouble," Richard said to the boy holding Kayla's arm.

Kayla pulled in a deep breath. Since when had her father developed a British accent?

"Nothing I couldn't handle," Nolan replied.

Kayla snatched her arm out of his grasp. *Jerk.*

"Good. Kayla, come stand with me," Richard said.

She gripped the hem of her shirt, her legs shaking, and stared at her father. He still had the same comb-over she remembered, his cowlick forcing him to part his hair off center. However, his dark strands were now streaked through with gray, and he had a goatee, something she'd never before seen him wear. She wanted to run to him, to fall into his arms and cry and welcome him home and hear him call her Kayla-Bear. But the way he stared at her, like an obstacle he needed to overcome or destroy, terrified her. Not to mention he was responsible for the deaths of all those

Protectors who'd been nothing but kind to her—maybe even Daniel.

And, from what she'd been told, he wanted her to help him kill even more.

"Kayla, I will not ask you again. Come here."

She glared at him, daring him to make her.

And he did. Richard nodded to Nolan who pushed her, hard, right between her shoulder blades. She stumbled forward and bent over, winded.

Richard grabbed her arm and jerked her closer to him. "That's better. Now, tell me. How did you sleep?"

"What does it matter to you?"

"I love you. I want to know if you're comfortable. If you're not, I'm sure Nolan can find you a better room."

No way. I'd end up in the one next to him so he could cut a hole in the wall and peek in on me while I slept. Or changed.

"I'm fine." She snatched her arm out of Richard's grasp.

"Good. And the food? Did someone bring you breakfast?"

"I don't care about breakfast or whether or not my mattress is comfortable," Kayla shouted. "You let me cry over you for *years*, you forced me to leave Mom and my home, and now you have my friends tied up. Tell me right now what I'm doing here, or I'm walking out that door."

The kindness in Richard's eyes died. A chill ran down Kayla's spine. She tried to appear tough, though her heart raced, and any minute, she was going to throw up all over his shoes. Her dad stood in front of her, but she didn't even recognize him.

"Very well," he said. He shook his head, forcing his features to soften. "You're here because I want to make the world a better place for you. Kayla Bear, I've missed you for so long, and I'm sorry I didn't call. But I'm here now. Join me, love." Richard held out a hand to her, like he was escorting her to a ball.

Kayla rubbed her chest and closed her eyes. She pictured the way he'd been—a kind and gentle man, born and raised in Columbus, Ohio. Eyes that brightened when she entered a room, not squinted in hatred. This was wrong. This wasn't her father.

Kayla shook her head as she opened her eyes, glowering through teary eyes at the monster before her. "If you think I'm going to fight alongside you and kill people, you're crazier than I thought, old man."

Nolan chuckled behind her. Kayla's father shot a look at him that nearly brought *her* to her knees. Nolan quieted in seconds.

"Watch it, Kayla. I will not put up with disrespect."

She crossed her arms over her chest and raised an eyebrow. Her legs felt like jelly, but the last thing she wanted was to show a moment of weakness. After everything he'd done—and was planning to do—he didn't deserve the satisfaction of seeing her fear.

Richard's fists clenched at his sides, then he spoke. "I will ask you one more time, Kayla. Will you join me?"

Kayla stared right into his eyes, as gold as her own. "No."

Margaret's sudden scream made her jump. It took Kayla a second to realize what was going on. Then she saw the grin on Adelynn's face.

Adelynn was torturing Margaret.

"Stop! You're hurting her!" Kayla yelled as she stepped past her father to grab Adelynn's hands. But Richard held her back.

"Touch her, you die."

Kayla wobbled as Margaret continued to scream. She placed her hands over her ears. "Stop it, please!"

"Then say 'yes,' Kayla."

"Please. I know you loved me once. Please, for me, stop this!"

Richard stared into his daughter's eyes, and for a moment he looked like he wouldn't give in. But then he nodded at Adelynn. She dropped her hands, and Margaret's screams ceased.

He turned to Kayla. "Call this an act of mercy. Tomorrow, if you refuse me again, both of them will scream until you say yes."

I tore my hand out of Tabbi's grasp and paced back and forth across the room, trying to calm my racing heart. Crouching down, I stifled the gag that wanted to escape. Everything Kayla had felt, seen, or heard, I experienced... and this was all my fault. I left her alone. *I fucking left her alone.*

"Daniel—" Tabbi started to say.

Not ready to listen to anyone yet and needing to sort out everything that I'd just experienced, I held a hand up. That guy who touched her... God, if I ever got a chance to meet him, I would punch his jaw so hard it'd shatter. And her father, for what he was doing to Alex and Margaret—for what he was doing to *her*—I would make him suffer.

And Kayla, for the first time, said she loved me.

I cleared my throat before speaking. "They have Kayla in an office building. I'm not sure where. I didn't get to see much." My quivering hands ran down my face. "But, we need a new tactic. If we can't use our abilities to find them, then we do it the old-fashioned way. Everybody grab your things. We're checking into a hotel."

CHAPTER TWENTY-EIGHT

We arrived at a hotel in Alaska minutes later, having chosen the remote location to stay out of the peering eyes of Giovanni's spies. They could be anywhere. The fewer people who saw us, the better.

Samantha, Seth, Tabbi and I grabbed the room nearest the back exit then "shopped," having to resort to stealing the necessities and pre-paid mobile phones. Who knew if Giovanni watched our card transactions, and we needed to be able to stay in contact without worrying about him tapping into our calls. We couldn't always pop in on each other whenever we had a message to share.

When we were back in our room, we flicked on the TV. Graphic images of Rome flooded the screen. Buildings collapsed, people fought each other with knives and guns, cars exploded. Bodies lined the streets. Someone leapt from a tall building, covered in flames. Even the Coliseum was flattened. My stomach tightened when I saw when the destruction started happening—the same night our mansion was sieged.

Whatever apocalypse Richard had been planning had begun.

"How are you going to track him?" Seth asked, his voice spiritless.

I turned off the TV. "Using Giovanni."

"Daniel, if Giovanni was working with Kayla's dad, then do you really think we could just evaporate to wherever he is?" Samantha asked. "If it didn't work with Kayla or Richard, it won't work with him either."

"I don't plan to track *him* down. I want to return to Rome and search through his things."

Both of their heads tipped to the side, like I'd spoken in some alien language. The mansion was a war zone, and I wanted to go back.

"Can't you check the flash drive? There has to be more on there," Seth said.

"And what if we can't make sense of it? Look, right now, Giovanni is our best lead. Are you coming with me or not?"

Seth and Samantha nodded.

"Okay. Tabbi, you stay here. Seth, go rally the others. We leave as soon as everyone's ready."

Thirty minutes later, we stood in the middle of the mansion's grand foyer. The beautiful, crystal chandelier that once illuminated the ornate room now lay in pieces on the floor. Dead bodies of Nightmares and Protectors alike lined the marble. Red and black blood mixed together on the cream floor like a gothic painting.

But the eeriest thing about the mansion was the noise. There was none.

Gripping my daggers tighter in my hands, I swallowed the lump in my throat. This had been my home for two hundred years. Now it was a gravesite.

"Come on." I couldn't linger here any longer.

Through the decimated room we walked, stepping over and around the bodies. We jogged up the stairs, pausing at every landing to glance down each hall. The last thing we needed was for a swarm of Nightmares to catch us off guard. Or worse—Magus.

We reached the twelfth floor with no problem and entered Giovanni's office. Everything sat in perfect place, like this room had remained untouched. I scowled as the bile churned in my stomach. The rest of the building was destroyed and littered with the bodies of Protectors, yet Giovanni's office was pristine.

Well, we weren't going to leave the room so tidy.

"Search everywhere," I instructed my team. "I want everything uncovered. Grab anything that might help."

Vasin and Hakan stood guard at the entrance while the rest of us split up and ransacked the room. I tossed books off shelves, searching for secret compartments, ripped drawers out of his desk, and broke the pictures on his wall, hoping for some clue as to where Kayla might be held. But I came up empty. I cracked my knuckles as heat flushed through my body.

"Hey, I think I got something," Seth said. He held a navy blue book in his hands.

I looked over his shoulder. A day-planner.

Seth pointed to a letter 'R.' "This comes up a few times in here. But the first time it's written, two sets of numbers follow it, separated by a comma."

"Latitude and longitude," I replied.

Seth nodded and flipped through the pages. "Looks like he went there a lot."

"Good. Grab the book."

Hakan and Vasin burst into flames. Their screams were deafening and shook me to my core. I stepped back and shielded my face from the heat as my stomach dropped to my knees.

From the doorway came two Magus. The largest one, a dark-skinned man with a scar across his left eye, flung Lizzie across the room when she lunged at him, dagger in hand. She fell to the ground like a rag doll.

"Go, get out of here!" I yelled at my remaining teammates before running toward where Lizzie lay on the ground, unconscious. Holding out my hand, I planned to evaporate as soon as I touched her. When I'd about reached her, a blast of air slammed me against the wall. I grunted as I hit the floor hard, ass first, and tried to push myself up. But I was stuck in my seated position, like my back was super-glued to the wall.

"Hello, Daniel," the dark-skinned warlock said. "I've been looking everywhere for you."

I spat at his feet. His nostrils flared as he brought his hand up, his palm facing toward me. Pain shot through me like lightning. With a shout, I leaned my head back against the wall, breathing deep.

"Oh, Lord Bartlett will be pleased when I return with you," he said.

Lord Bartlett? Really? "Please, take me to him. I've been searching for him. You'll be doing me a favor."

The warlock stepped toward me. "You think you're so high and mighty, being one of the Angels' chosen. But really, you just have farther to fall. Let's see how you feel when Lord Bartlett carves into you."

"Never going to happen," Samantha said, appearing behind the warlock. Her knife dug straight through the back of his neck, the tip protruding below his Adam's apple. His eyes widened in surprise, then Samantha twisted the blade. The warlock fell into a pool of red blood on the ground.

The pressure against me disappeared. I jumped up, ready to fight, then saw the other Magus fall into a similar position on the ground, her throat slit. Standing over her body was Ivan.

"Are you all right?" Samantha asked me as Ivan checked on Lizzie.

"I'm fine," I lied. Truth was, I had wanted that warlock to take me to Richard. I would've been one step closer to finding Kayla.

And one step closer to killing him.

We'd lost Vasin, Hakan and Lizzie at the hands of the two Magus. Samantha had tried to resuscitate Lizzie, but her body had been too damaged from the blow she'd taken from the warlock. She never recovered.

Ivan and I worked together to dispose of Lizzie's body. It was my responsibility as their leader, and I was shocked when Ivan volunteered to help me. We'd been reduced to burying her, as a large fire would've been too noticeable, and I didn't want to use our mansion's crematory or sneak in somewhere with the threat of discovery looming over our heads. I hated not giving her a Catcher's funeral, but what other choice did I have? Giovanni's spies were everywhere.

The others stayed back, drained after watching two friends roast alive and another die on my hotel floor. Excluding Tabbi, we'd gone from a team of eleven to a team of five in mere days. My body had never felt so cold.

"I still hate you, you know," Ivan said in his thick, Russian accent.

"Yeah, I know." I tossed another pile of dirt over Lizzie's body.

"But… I will fight for you."

Pausing, I regarded him. He purposely avoided eye contact, but to even have said the words took a lot for someone like him, so hell-bent on being the top dog—the Alpha.

I nodded my thanks, then we finished burying Lizzie in silence.

When I returned to the hotel, Tabbi waited for me in the hall. Seeing Ivan and I walking toward her, she jumped up and looked me straight in the eye. Her small body was tense.

"Tabbi, what's wrong?" I asked.

"Seth and Sam wanted to sleep, but I had to check in on Kayla."

I waved at Ivan to go into the room without me. "What happened?" My heart pounded in my chest.

"It's that guy, Nolan. He says he's on Kayla's side, our side. He wants to help her escape. He's going to get her out tonight, at three a.m."

"What time is it now?"

"Two-fifty-five."

With a nod, I held my hand out to her. She didn't have to ask what I wanted her to do. I held my breath and closed my eyes as Tabbi popped me into Kayla's mind.

Kayla sat on her bed, ready to run as soon as Nolan appeared. She jumped when someone knocked on her door. Just once. The thump was followed by the sound of a key turning in the lock. Then nothing.

Is that Nolan? Is this my chance?

Not wanting to miss her opportunity, Kayla leapt off the bed and sprinted for the door. She grabbed the knob and turned.

It was unlocked.

Kayla opened the door just enough to peek into the hall. If Nolan had been letting her out, he was long gone. The hall was empty.

Okay. You can do this.

With shaking hands, she nudged the door open farther and dashed down the hall. She ran until she reached the stairwell, closing the door behind her as softly as she could. Then she sprinted down one set of stairs to the main level.

Kayla glanced at the numbers Nolan had written on her hand earlier— the code to turn off the rear door's alarm. She had almost reached the keypad when she tripped. Unable to stop herself, Kayla fell into the steel door's handle, pushing it open.

An alarm sounded throughout the building.

Oh no. Nausea filled her stomach. She forced herself to keep going, to not panic, and ran the rest of the way through the exit into the alley behind the building. Her heart raced in her chest. *Oh god, oh god, oh god.*

As Kayla was about to exit the alley onto the main road, two men in black outfits rounded the corner, blocking her. They stepped forward, their eyes fixated on her. Then a small ring around their pupils glowed.

Warlocks.

Kayla turned around and ran down the alley, praying there would be another exit, but she hadn't gone far when two more warlocks exited the same office building from which she had fled.

She spun around, trying to find an escape route. Tears filled her eyes and sweat ran down the back of her neck.

She was trapped.

Kayla held up her hands, trying to signal she meant no harm, but the four warlocks continued to close in. Unwilling to go back, Kayla shot waves of air from her hands at the two who'd rounded the corner, forcing one of the warlocks into the building next to him. The other blocked her attack and countered, sending her flying into the warlocks behind her.

One of them grabbed her arms and yanked them behind her back. Kayla squealed as the warlock cuffed her wrists together with a plastic tie.

"No, please," she begged. But he shoved her into the arms of another who dragged her back into the office building.

Kayla screamed and fought him the entire way up the stairs. When they dragged her through the entrance to the second floor, Nolan leaned against the wall. His body language portrayed a man who didn't give a rat's ass, but his eyes were sad and his jaw tight.

Kayla fought the urge to yell for him to help her. But the last thing she wanted was to get her ally killed. Especially when it had been her own fault she hadn't succeeded.

The warlocks dragged her into one of the rooms and tied her to a steel chair. Her legs shook, and she was going to vomit any minute. But she held her chin high and tried to appear strong.

Until her father entered the room, followed by two Nightmares.

He backhanded her so hard she jerked sideways. Kayla shrieked.

"How dare you disobey me!" Richard yelled. "I have done nothing but treat you with kindness, and this is how you repay me?"

"Treat me with kindness? Are you crazy? You tortured my friend right in front of me!"

"That was the price you paid for saying no to me. Her pain is on you."

Kayla scowled at him. Hatred filled her heart, and behind her back, her hands balled into fists.

"Now, because I am the loving father, I will give you one chance." Richard held up a finger. "Who helped you escape?"

"Go to hell."

Richard frowned, then snapped his fingers. The Nightmares pounced.

"Goddamnit!" I screamed as I yanked my hand out of Tabbi's. I'd tried to evaporate to Kayla as soon as she left the building, but nothing happened. Again.

I kicked the wall so hard a shock wave of pain ran into my hip. Then I punched the wall and kicked it again. My chest constricted and my eyes burned. Raising my fist to punch the wall again, Tabbi walked into my arms. She wrapped hers around my waist.

Tabbi said no words. She just hugged me like a little sister would. Embracing her back, I forced down the tears that wanted to explode. Crying wouldn't help Kayla. Only finding her would.

"I'm going to kill him, Tabbi."

"You better."

CHAPTER TWENTY-NINE

I didn't sleep when we returned to the room, no matter how exhausted my body felt. Kayla needed to be found now, before any more harm could come to her. I stole a laptop from a nearby store and, after setting it up, grabbed Giovanni's day-planner off Seth's nightstand. He must've spent an hour or so pouring through the details before falling asleep, considering he'd highlighted every time the same letter appeared in the book. Giovanni had visited Richard at least twenty times in the last two months.

I typed the latitude and longitude into a search engine and waited for the results. A map appeared with a pinpoint in Amarillo, Texas. After jotting down the address on a piece of paper, I zoomed in on the picture and froze. This place looked familiar.

Popping in the USB drive and remembering which keys Irene had pressed to decrypt the folders, I searched through the files until I found the image of Giovanni and Richard shaking hands.

The picture wasn't of a storage unit. It was a garage.

I jumped out of my chair and flipped on the overhead light. "Everybody up."

Samantha growled, Lian and Tabbi covered their eyes with their hands and Seth covered his face with his pillow. Ivan, having fallen asleep on our floor, swore at me.

"I'm serious. Get up. I have a lead."

They perked up. Samantha jumped out of bed and sat in front of the computer, fluffing her blonde hair. "A house in Texas? Are you sure?"

"Positive. When Seth and I looked at that image earlier, we'd thought it was a warehouse or a storage unit. But if you look at that image of the house in Amarillo, you can see a detached garage. Look." I zoomed in next to the garage door. "And they both share the same number—1031. It's the same building."

"Holy shit, man," Seth said. "You think he's holding them there?"

"No, Kayla's in some sort of office building. But this is the first lead we've had. Maybe we can find something there that'll tell us where he's holding her. We'll leave in an hour."

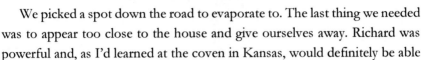

We picked a spot down the road to evaporate to. The last thing we needed was to appear too close to the house and give ourselves away. Richard was powerful and, as I'd learned at the coven in Kansas, would definitely be able to feel us, even if we were invisible. We needed to enter the house slowly to avoid detection as long as possible.

After we loaded our weapons onto our belts, the six of us evaporated to our destination, making sure to stay invisible. Then, without a word, I led my team down the street.

The house was a brick, two-story, colonial-style home, a style completely different from the white, detached garage at the side of the house. The front door and shutters were painted white, and the front lawn looked recently mowed.

I approached the house cautiously and peeked inside the windows. Expensive furniture and the latest gadgets filled each room, but there was no sign of anyone. Someone needed to get inside.

"Stay here." I evaporated into the entryway. The house was dark, but smelled of lemons, like it'd been freshly cleaned. When there was no sign of life, I opened the front door to let the others in.

"There's definitely no one here," Tabbi said. "I don't hear a single thought."

"Good," I said. "Let's look around. Seth, Lian, go upstairs and see what you can find. Sam, Ivan and I will search down here. Tabbi, stay near the door and let us know if anyone's coming."

I split off from the group and wandered until I found the study and walked slowly around the room, scrutinizing. If I were Richard, this is where I would hide my secrets. In one corner was a coat rack, and along that wall was a large bookshelf with cabinets underneath. I opened each cabinet and looked inside, but nothing appeared important. Then I peeked inside the wardrobe, moving coats around and pulling out boxes of old files for some sort of clue.

Frantically, I searched through every drawer of his desk and between every book on every shelf, but I couldn't find anything that might lead me to Kayla. With a roar, I threw books across the room.

Then I noticed a large globe in the back corner. From a distance, nothing seemed out of the ordinary. But when I stood at just the right angle, sunlight bounced off a pinhead. I walked over to it and examined closer. The pin was pressed into Paris, France.

I turned the globe around until the U.S. faced up. Pins of all colors were pressed into spots all over the country. There had to be at least fifty of them. He was definitely using the globe to track something, which meant he frequented the house.

Again, I ran around the room, trying to find some clue to Kayla's location. I tore the wardrobe to shreds, then looked through the cupboards under the bookshelves again, ripping everything out and feeling around for something out of the ordinary. When I was about to give up, I felt a small groove in the wood where there shouldn't have been one. Grabbing a dagger out of my belt, I forced it into the opening.

"Please," I muttered under my breath. My blade pried the wood until a piece popped out, then I stuck my hand in the hole. The secret compartment went back further than expected, but my fingertips touched plastic. "Yes."

Pulling the object out, I jumped for joy when I saw what had been hidden. A hard drive. I ran out of the room.

"Guys, I got something," I shouted, knowing we were alone.

From different directions came Samantha, Ivan, Seth, Lian and Tabbi.

"Daniel, this place is definitely lived in," Seth said. "And I don't think just by Richard."

"That doesn't matter." I held up the hard drive. "I found this, hidden in one of Richard's bookshelves. Whatever's on here has to be important."

I was about to tell them it was time to leave when Tabbi's eyes widened. "Guys, we have company. It's him. And he knows we're here. Daniel, you triggered some alarm when you opened the front door."

Blast. In my haste, I hadn't considered what types of protection might be in place. We all immediately went invisible.

"Okay. Everyone get out of here now." With the laptop tucked securely under my arm, I tried to evaporate. But nothing happened.

"Um, Daniel— " Samantha said.

"I know. I'm not going anywhere either."

"Are Magus always this powerful?" Ivan asked.

The front door burst open. Richard walked into the house, followed by four others.

"Feel that?" Richard said to his groupies. "Those Protectors always give off such a strong vibe."

Richard and the others walked through the house, their eyes searching for some clue to where we stood. They felt our energy, but our exact location was still hidden from them.

I prayed they didn't have any of that revealing powder with them and handed Tabbi the hard drive. It would stay invisible as long as she held it. "Do not let this out of your sight and stay far away from the warlocks. As soon as you can, evaporate back to the hotel. Got it?"

Tabbi nodded, grabbed the hard drive and stepped behind me.

I ran through the options in my head. Richard was mere feet away. If I could get a jump on him, I could kill him. But then we might die at the hands of the other Magus before we could find Kayla. Still, if I didn't take my shot now, the next time I faced him, we could be more severely outnumbered.

Before I could make my decision, Richard spoke again. "I know you're here, Daniel. Don't make me return without you. It wouldn't bode well for Kayla."

Samantha grabbed my arm before I could assault him. "Daniel, going up against him is suicide. We need to sneak out while we have the chance."

My pulse raced, and my fists were so tight that my knuckles hurt, but I nodded. She was right. We needed an attack plan before taking him on.

The six of us ran toward the back of the house, but instead of going through the wall like we were supposed to, we ran *into* it. We bounced off the wall and into each other like balls in a pinball machine.

"What the hell?" Ivan yelled.

"We can't get through," Seth replied.

"No shit, Sherlock."

"All right, that's enough," I said. They quieted and let me think. We had no other choice. We couldn't evaporate, we couldn't walk through walls, we couldn't break a window unless we wanted to give away our location. Other than being able to stay invisible, we were essentially human. Richard had robbed us of the powers that made us spirit-like. There was only one way out of here now. We had to fight.

CHAPTER THIRTY

I crossed through the kitchen and headed in the direction Richard had gone. Entering the hallway leading to the study, I jumped when one of his followers joined me from the bedroom on the left. He stopped and looked around with his hands open at his sides. He could feel me closing in on him.

Knowing I needed to be quick, I sprinted around him and went corporeal when I was at his back, digging my blade into the side of his neck. Blood squirted onto the wall, and he fell to the ground with a shout. I went invisible before anyone else could see me. And just in time. Richard ran into the hall from his study.

His nostrils flared as he took in the sight of his now-dead follower on the floor. I paused to see what his next move would be, gripping my blades tight. On the balls of my feet, I kept my gaze on his hands, prepared to jump out of the way if he tried to strike. Instead, he reached into his pocket and pulled out his mobile.

He pressed a button. My body turned cold as Kayla's voice filled the hall.

"Please. I'm sorry. No more," she said.

"I will send the Nightmares away if you give me a name. Who let you out of that room?" Richard asked.

There was a long pause. Then Kayla screamed.

My vision clouded, picturing her writhing around in a dark room while Nightmares filled her mind with images from her tortuous past. I squeezed my eyes closed as my heart raced and my ears roared. He was playing my weakness—and it was working.

"I'll make you a deal, Daniel," Richard said. "Come with me, and I will never again give her to the Nightmares. And just to prove you can trust my word, I will let your friends go. Do we have a deal?"

My hands were so clammy; I thought I was going to drop the daggers. Here was a chance to save my team and protect Kayla. And for my capture?

That was it? Seemed too good to be true. But what choice did I have? If I tried to attack him, he'd call it off, and then not only would I leave my friends open to attack, but he would definitely ensure Kayla spent another night as Nightmare fodder.

"Better make a choice soon, Daniel, or my offer will be off the table. You have ten seconds. Show yourself."

"Daniel, no," Samantha said from behind me. I hadn't heard her arrive.

I looked at her. She knew I had to. "Find someone to hack that hard drive, Sam. You're in charge now."

"Daniel, no!"

I went corporeal.

Richard smirked. "Knew you couldn't resist, mate. Put your blades down."

As he asked, I set them on the ground in front of me, never taking my eyes off him.

Richard snapped his fingers. "The seal is broken. Your friends may leave."

I turned to Samantha and whispered, "Run."

She shook her head.

"Now." I spoke the word more forcefully. With tears in her eyes, she obeyed. I waited until her blonde hair was out of sight then turned back to Richard. "I've surrendered. Now what?"

The sinister look in his hazel eyes sent chills down my body. "Now I reunite you with my daughter."

Sharp pain stabbed my head, like lightning struck inside my brain. The room spun, and I gripped the sides of my skull with my hands, falling to my knees. A hard blow to the back of my head was the last thing I remembered.

Ice-cold water poured over me, jerking me awake. I shook my head to get the water out of my eyes and shivered. This room was freaking cold. A boy not much older than Tabbi stepped away with a bucket in his hands. The wicked grin on his face sent another chill down my spine. He stepped into the hall.

I leaned forward in my chair and tried to struggle out of the bonds around my wrists. Going invisible—or evaporating—would be pointless. The chair and binds would go with me. Not to mention, I was positive Richard put up spells to keep me here. He was way too intelligent to make a rookie move. He'd kept us from escaping his house in a matter of seconds, after all.

Again, I tried to struggle out of the rope, but the binds were too tight. Whoever bound me knew what they were doing. I clenched and unclenched my hands, keeping the circulation flowing in my fingers.

Glancing around the room, I tried to get a feel for where I was. To my surprise, I wasn't in a dungeon-like cell as I'd expected. Instead, I was in some sort of large hospital-room-slash-science-lab. A window on the far side told me I was above ground. Metal tables stood sporadically throughout the area, and in a far corner was some sort of machine that reminded me of an electric chair. Cabinets lined the other side of the room from where I sat, and on them were chemistry-like sets, gizmos that I decided looked like prodding devices from an alien spaceship, and some sort of machine that reminded me of a lie detector.

Why would a warlock need all of this?

As if on cue, Richard strode into the room. Again, I fought against the ropes around my wrists when I saw who followed him. Giovanni. Baring my teeth, I swore at the both of them.

"Now, now, Daniel. Don't go injuring yourself," Richard said.

I avoided him and spoke directly to Giovanni. "Why'd you do it? Betraying us all—your own kind—the Protectors who swore allegiance to you. You're going to Hell for this."

Giovanni's stare was intense, fevered even. I'd never seen such hatred pouring out of him. "No. When I die, I will spend eternity in a black void, just like the rest of you. *This world* is Hell. Constantly slaving over pathetic humans who think they're so much better than the rest of the world's creatures. Never to be able to roam free, have a family, free will… never to be a member of society. I would've thought you'd understand, Daniel."

Oh, but I did understand. It's what I still wanted—to be able to live a normal life. But starting a war, killing people? "There has to be another way."

Richard jumped in. "There is no other way. What do you think humans would do if they found out a warlock or a vampire lived next door? They'd shun us, hunt us down and treat us like a plague. No, we need to take a stand against them and take this world for our own."

"And what? You'll destroy them all? How does that make you any better?"

"Because they destroyed my kind first!" He yelled at the top of his lungs then cleared his throat and smoothed his shirt. "Did you ever hear the real story of Tamesis?"

I rolled my eyes. *What did that bloke have to do with this?* "He was a warlock who used Nightmares to attack innocent people."

"Wrong. Those *humans*," he spat the word like it was coated with venom, "were far from innocent. He destroyed the people responsible for raping his mother, repeatedly, and burning her at the stake for what she was—a witch who had only used her powers to save her infant son from death. Now tell me, what would you have done if the woman was *your* mother?"

I pursed my lips and clenched my fists. Telling myself I would not have sought revenge would've been a lie. Still, there was no way I would ever compare myself to Tamesis. I wouldn't murder women and children in their sleep.

"So what—you're carrying out his revenge?" I asked. "You do know he died hundreds of years ago. The same people responsible for his mother's death are long gone, mate."

Richard's smirk sent a shiver down my spine. "Oh, but you're wrong. Those people responsible for her death had children, and those children had children. The families of those bastards lived on. The Lancasters, the Fletchers… the Grahams."

Richard's gaze cut through me like a knife. The hairs rose on my arm.

"So, you're going to make me pay for something my ancestors did, and for some warlock who's been dead for god knows how long? You're insane."

"No, my boy. I am far from insane. *I'm Tamesis.* And I'm going to make you pay for what your kind did to my mother."

After Giovanni had dealt a hard blow to the back of my head, I'd awoken to find myself strapped to a metal table, shirtless, and unable to break free of my bonds. Twice, Richard had cut into my chest, stomach, arms, legs… and twice he had healed me so he could start all over again.

Now, his knife cut into my stomach for the third time. I fought against the metal cuffs around my wrists and ankles, unable to stop the screams from escaping my mouth. A trickle of blood ran down my side. My chest heaved up and down from the rapid breaths entering my lungs.

"Ah, Daniel. This is so what I've been waiting for," Richard said. "As soon as I knew it was you my daughter loved, I waited for my chance to carve you into pieces. Not only am I getting some revenge, but I'm learning just how you Protectors work. Wouldn't it be amazing if I figured out a more permanent way to live forever?"

I lifted my hand as high as I could and flipped him off. Giovanni, standing by my head, stabbed his knife into my hand, and I screamed.

Richard leered at me then smiled at Giovanni. "I love when you fight for me."

"Anything for you, *amore.*"

Even in the midst of my pain, I picked up on the emotion behind their words. *No way.* I laughed. "You've got to be kidding me. You two? Wow."

Richard stabbed me right above my belly button. My body jerked, and I shouted as blood poured from my body. Then he removed the knife and held his hand over my wounds, healing me before I could die. I groaned and spat in his face. He punched me, splitting my cheek open.

"Isn't it time you let him die, Tamesis? You conducted all your research. He's of no further use to you," Giovanni said.

"Oh, no. I'm not done with him yet. I'm just taking my time before I use him to his full potential."

Again, I struggled against the binds that held me to the table.

"Oh? And what will you do with him?"

Richard turned and faced the door. "Gents!" he yelled. The door opened and footsteps entered the room. Then he spoke again, "Take Daniel to Kayla's room. And make sure you leave him bloodied and bruised. Maybe seeing him die before her eyes will be enough to get her to follow me."

Four warlocks appeared next to me. When Giovanni and Richard opened the metal cuffs from around my wrists and ankles, I took my shot. Jumping off the table, I grabbed a knife off the counter. But as my fingers wrapped around the handle, a body hit me from behind. My ribs smashed against the edge of the countertop. I cried out as something popped in my side.

A second warlock grabbed my arm as I swung around to slice his neck, and he slammed my hand against the wall. The knife fell. And within seconds, fists were flying at me so fast, I didn't know where to block.

CHAPTER THIRTY-ONE

I hit the crimson red carpet of Kayla's room with a thud and groaned, rolling from my stomach onto my back.

"Daniel!" Kayla shouted from across the room. She dropped to her knees next to me and brushed the hair out of my face. "Oh my god."

I tried to speak, but my throat was too raw from all the screaming. Tipping my head to the side, away from her, I coughed. The blood that came out of my mouth matched the carpet. I wiped my lips with my hand and closed my eyes.

"Oh, Daniel, what did they do to you?" Kayla took my hand in both of hers. She kissed it. A tear fell onto my skin. "I'm so sorry."

"Don't be." My voice was raspy.

"This is all my fault." Her voice broke.

I opened my eyes as she sobbed into my hand. Wincing, I lifted my other hand and wiped the tears from her cheek. "Stop talking like that." Then I spotted the bruise on her left cheekbone and gently ran my thumb across it. "I'm going to kill him for doing this to you."

Kayla opened her eyes and looked at me, her eyes wide. "How did you know?"

"Tabbi. Her connection with you lets her get into your head whenever she focuses hard enough. If I take her hand, I can see through your eyes."

Kayla let go of my hand, stood and wiped her cheeks. Then she walked away. Sighing, I rolled onto my hands and knees then groaned as I got up from the floor. Kayla stood near a white sofa by the fireplace, her back to me.

I walked over to her and wrapped my arms around her. She stood there like a statue. Had my revelation scared her? Before I could ask, her arms wrapped around me, and she buried her face in my shoulder. She shook with sobs. I held her tighter and kissed the top of her head. Her hands gripped the back of my shirt, and I rubbed her back as the tears flowed.

"I will get you out of here, Kayla, even if it's the last thing I do."

At that moment, the door to the room opened. Richard walked in from the other side, followed by four of his followers—the same four who beat me senseless minutes ago. All of them wore smug smiles.

"Oh, good. I see you two have reconnected," Richard said. "Let's get this over with, shall we?"

He snapped his fingers, and the four warlocks rushed us. I stepped in front of Kayla, poised to fight them, but my body filled with pain, like a hundred daggers penetrating my skin. I doubled over with a gasp.

"Daniel!" Kayla shouted. She reached for me, but two of Richard's men grabbed her and yanked her away. She screamed and fought against them, but they held her tight.

The other two grabbed my arms and hauled me up from the ground. I tried to fight them and clocked one in the jaw, but a crack of electricity hit me square in the chest. I flew across the room and landed on my back, gasping for air.

"Stop! You're going to kill him!" Kayla yelled.

"Then join me, and I promise I will spare his life," Richard replied.

Standing, I shook my head. "Don't do it, Kayla." A blast of air flung me across the room and pinned me to the wall. Richard's left hand rose in my direction.

"Your answer. Now!" Richard's voice echoed.

Kayla stared at me, teary-eyed, then returned her gaze to her father. "Please, let him go."

Another shock of electricity hit me, like Richard smashed me between a gigantic defibrillator. I yelped in pain, unable to control myself. Kayla struggled against her captors, refusing her father a response.

"Fine," Richard said, raising his other hand, palm up. A wraith dropped in from the ceiling. My heartbeat screamed in my ears, and I fought the urge to squirm like a frightened child. I needed to be strong, for Kayla.

"No, please. Stop!" she yelled.

Richard smirked. "You can see them? You're more my daughter than I thought."

"Daddy, please. Don't do this. I know this isn't you."

Maybe it was because she called him "Daddy," but his eyes softened slightly as he looked at his daughter. Chills rain down my spine.

"You know," Richard said, "the other three, their genes I manipulated. But you are my own. I do not enjoy doing this to you, seeing you cry. Maybe

I've gone about this the wrong way. Maybe you, like me, respond stronger to love than to fear."

He took a step closer to her, and I fought against the hold he still had on me. Richard waved his fingers at the two Magus holding Kayla. They let her go. Her eyes flickered to me, then fell on her father's face.

Richard placed a hand on each shoulder. "I told you—I am doing all of this for you. You are my first true child in almost two hundred years, and I want to make this world a better place for you. I do not want the world to dispose of you like they did to my mother, Gwyndolyn—your grandmother—like they did to my other children. Please, stand with me. Together we can change the world not just for ourselves, but for all of those like us."

Kayla stared at him, seeming to contemplate his words. Then her eyes turned cold. "Never."

"Fine. Goodbye, Daniel. *Occidere eum!*" Richard spoke with ferocity. In a second, the wraith was barreling down on me.

Two of the Magus grabbed Kayla from behind as she pushed away from her father with a scream.

Locking eyes with her, I spoke the words I should've said a long time ago. "I love you."

I closed my eyes and waited for the wraith to take my existence. *The pain will be over in a second.*

"No!" Kayla's voice was so loud the room shook. I snapped my eyes open. A crack slithered up the wall behind her, all the way across the ceiling. And to my disbelief, the wraith shrunk back from me in fear.

The gold in Kayla's eyes glowed like the sun. Flames from the fireplace exploded into the room, catching the floor and ceiling on fire. Kayla flung the two warlocks off her arms so hard they soared in opposite directions. They fell to the floor, unconscious. The other two rushed her as Richard stepped back, but with a swift turn of her hands, their necks snapped.

My mouth gaped. I'd seen Kayla's power in Bartholomew's office. Even Trishna had known what was stirring inside her.

Richard just forced it to explode.

Kayla stepped toward the wraith, her eyes still glowing. The air around me grew heavier, and while the flames from the fireplace rose higher into the room, everything around us darkened.

Kayla's hair flew behind her, as if someone held a fan to her face. Both of her hands were open at her sides, palms facing outward.

"Go back to Hell," she said to the wraith, her voice amplified like she spoke through a microphone.

With an earsplitting scream, the wraith folded in on itself, disappearing with a loud boom. Then Kayla turned to her father, her hands held out to him. "Let. Him. Go."

The room shook again, filling with smoke. Dust from the ceiling fell to the floor. If we didn't get out of here soon, we'd all either roast to death or die of suffocation. Richard took one wide-eyed look at his daughter, then smirked.

I fell to the ground as Richard reached up and magically dropped part of the ceiling down in front of him, trapping us on the other side with the flames.

CHAPTER THIRTY-TWO

I coughed and forced debris off my body. When Richard pinned me to the wall, he saved me from being trapped beneath the wreckage, unlike—

"Kayla!" I shouted, unable to see through the cloud of dust and smoke. Flames lined the back wall and spread across the floor and ceiling. It wouldn't be long before they reached us.

"Daniel!" Her voice was a shot of adrenaline.

I jumped up. "Kayla, thank god. I'm coming to get you. Are you hurt?" Waving my hands in front of my face, I moved across the room to where I knew she'd been standing when the ceiling collapsed.

She whimpered somewhere to the left of me. "My leg. I think it's broken."

At least it's just the leg. "All right. Keep talking." My eyes burned, but I kept them open, searching for her.

"I'm sorry, Daniel. I didn't mean—"

"I know. You don't need to apologize." I followed the sound of her struggling, and then I saw her through the haze, buried underneath a large piece of drywall. Blood trickled down her forehead. I sprinted the rest of the way to her, ignoring the pain in every part of my body, and dropped to my knees.

Kayla sobbed almost immediately.

"Hey, we're going to be fine," I said. "But I need your help, so you have to calm down."

She nodded and breathed deeply through her nose, setting her lips in a tight line.

The flames were just a couple feet away. Soon they would lick at her hair if I didn't get her out. Holding her hand, I closed my eyes, praying that Richard lifted the spell to keep me from evaporating.

But he hadn't. I swore under my breath and touched her cheek. "Take in as little oxygen as you can. Keep breathing slowly through your nose, all right?"

She nodded.

"Good. I'm going to get this drywall off you. When I lift, roll to your right. Don't slide back, or you'll hit the flames."

When she nodded again, I stood up and wiped sweat from my forehead. With a groan, I lifted the drywall, every muscle in my body aching. The depleting oxygen didn't help, either.

My arms shook. "Kayla, move!"

"I can't. My leg's caught."

The world around me tilted, and I lost my grip. Kayla cried out when the drywall landed on her again. I fell to one knee, apologizing, and shook my head, trying to put everything back into focus. The flames were inches from her now. My throat tightened.

Standing up, my vision blackened around the edges. I coughed and gripped the edge of the drywall again. *Come on, Daniel.*

A loud *boom* sounded to my right. I crouched low to gain my balance as the room shook. Someone had blown a hole in the debris. The smoke in the room lessened now that there was an opening for it to go through, and a blurred figure came toward us. I prayed he was a Dreamcatcher, but as he ran further into the room, I could tell he wasn't wearing a weapon belt. Balling my fists, I prepared to fight with every ounce of strength I had left.

Then he called out, his voice familiar. "Kayla!"

"Nolan!" she screeched from underneath the drywall.

Nolan? My jaw tightened. Not only had he carried her over his shoulder, but he'd been responsible for her botched escape attempt. I swung when he got close enough and clocked him in the jaw.

"Jesus!" Nolan rubbed his face. "I'm rescuing you, and this is what I get? What the hell was that for?"

"That's for carrying Kayla over your shoulder like a bloody rag doll," I said.

He smirked. "Oh, she's definitely not a rag doll."

I raised my fist again, but Nolan stepped back and held his hand out in front of him. Water shot from his palm, putting out the flames that were now centimeters from catching Kayla's hair on fire. Then the drywall covering Kayla went flying across the room.

"Can I get a 'thank you' now, please?" he said.

With a roll of my eyes, I bent over, scooping Kayla into my arms. She cried out in pain and struggled to get her arms around my neck.

A light film, like a bubble, enveloped Kayla and me.

"What are you doing?" I asked Nolan.

"What do you think? I'm shielding you. It's either this or put out the rest of the fire, but I can't tell the firemen I had a squirt gun in my back pocket and used my saliva to fill the tank, can I? Now, hurry up. You can evaporate us from the parking lot."

I glared at him, unsure if I wanted to trust him, but then Kayla winced in my arms, and I knew it didn't matter. She needed to be somewhere safe, now. As quickly as I could without hurting her, I ran out of the room then swore when the door opened at the end of the hall. Ten of Giovanni's Catchers ran in, weapons pointed at us. One pulled the trigger, but Nolan's bubble worked. The bullet disintegrated in front of my eyes.

"Get out, now!" Nolan yelled. He moved so the light film stood in front of the three of us like a shield. "I'll hold them off."

"What about you?" I asked him as the Catchers encroached upon us, firing their weapons.

"What do I look like? A Disney princess? I can take care of myself. On three. Ready? One, two—"

I took off, my body aching everywhere. Despite her small size, Kayla was becoming heavier, and she screamed with every step I took. But I could not stop, no matter how much my body protested—or my heart. True to his word, Nolan parted the group of Catchers like Moses and the Red Sea. Every one of them, as we passed, went up in flames, froze, or was blown into the wall.

When I finally reached the stairwell, I kicked the door open with a grunt and worked my way down the stairs. Footsteps followed and, for a moment, a hot wave of panic seized me. Then, I glanced over my shoulder to see Nolan following close behind.

"Hurry up, slow poke," he said.

I would've sworn at him had my lungs not already felt like they were going to explode. Then I noticed Kayla was silent and looked down at her. Her lips were pale.

No, no, no. How was this possible? She'd barely been injured. I forced my body to speed up, using every ounce of energy I had left. Finally, we reached the first floor and turned left out the emergency exit. Fire trucks lined the parking lot, and firefighters ran toward us in their gear.

"Somebody call the paramedics!" one of them yelled.

"Grab my arm!" I shouted over my shoulder at Nolan, not caring who saw us evaporate.

He wiggled an eyebrow, but did as he was told. As soon as his fingertips touched my shirt, I evaporated to Alaska, where I prayed the others would still be.

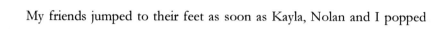

My friends jumped to their feet as soon as Kayla, Nolan and I popped into the room.

"Oh my god. Daniel," Samantha said as she sprinted forward to help me get Kayla on the bed.

I set Kayla down gently and stepped back when I noticed Bartholomew running across the room. I'd have been more shocked to see him if my heart didn't feel like it would jump out of my chest, or if the room ceased spinning for one blooming minute.

The sensation of falling hit me, and it wasn't until someone caught me from behind that I realized my knees had buckled.

"Seth, help me," Ivan said. Seth ran to my other side, and the two of them led me to the other bed.

I passed out before my head hit the pillow.

CHAPTER THIRTY-THREE

I awoke to whispers and regretted opening my eyes. The light burned, like someone held a flashlight in my face after months of blackness, and I covered my eyes with a groan.

"Sam, get Trishna," Seth said. "Daniel's up."

Someone ran from the room, then there was a hand on my arm.

"Drink this," Tabbi said.

Without opening my eyes, I held my hand out. Tabbi placed a cold glass into my hand. Sitting up a little, I held the cup to my lips and drank the liquid deep. It tasted like mint chocolate. Was this one of Bartholomew's concoctions?

"You took in a lot of smoke and lost a lot of blood," Seth said. "You've been out for almost two days."

Two days? So much could've happened by now. I passed the cup back to Tabbi. "Kayla—how is she?"

The door to the room opened. "She is stable," Trishna said. "Right now, let's worry about you. Can you open your eyes and sit up, please?"

I didn't like the way she dodged my question, but I obeyed. The light still burned my eyes, but not as much as the first time. My body was stiff, but there was no pain. I leaned against the headboard.

"I saw Bartholomew alive," I said.

Samantha nodded. "He found us only hours after Richard took you. We were in the midst of making plans to come get you when you evaporated to us."

I winced when Trishna shone a bright light in my eyes. "And if I can, that means Giovanni can, too. We need to move."

"No need. I've already put up spells around here to ward off any unwanted visitors," Trishna said. "Only those who don't intend to harm us can evaporate here. You are all safe. Now, hold still while I make sure you don't need any more care."

Bartholomew had said she was powerful, but I wondered if her spells would hold up against Richard. I let her finish her thorough inspection, and when she said I would be fine with a little more rest, I stood up.

"Where's Kayla? I want to see her."

Seth's frown sent my heart hammering.

"Daniel, she's fine. I am monitoring her closely," Trishna said.

"'Monitoring her?'" I knew what those words meant. Kayla was still in critical condition. I stared at Seth. He'd give me the answers I wanted—needed. "Where is she?"

He held his breath, but it didn't take long for him to break. He spoke so fast, everything blurred together like they were one word. "Next door. Room five-oh-seven." He covered his face with his hands.

Trishna glared at Seth as I bulldozed passed her and into the hall. The door to room 507 was cracked open, like people didn't want to bother with having to get in with a key, just in case. My chest tightened. I took a deep breath and opened the door.

Lian sat on the bed next to her, her black hair tied in a bun, holding a towel to Kayla's forehead. Bartholomew stood with Ivan and Nolan in the far corner of the room, the three of them speaking in hushed voices. Seeing me enter the room, they broke apart.

"Daniel, how do you feel?" Bartholomew asked. Stubble lined his tanned face, and deep circles framed his brown eyes.

"I'm fine." My voice was stern, and I moved past him, not wanting anyone else to get in my way of seeing Kayla. Lian stood from the bed, eyeing me with sympathy, and I sat in her place. I touched Kayla's cheek. It was on fire. This time my voice was weak. "What happened?"

"She was hit, Daniel," Nolan said.

"Yeah, with a piece of drywall. She shouldn't be like this."

"He doesn't mean like that," Bartholomew said. "Richard tagged her, probably as the ceiling was collapsing on her."

"English!"

"There was a wound on her left side," Lian said, her almond eyes sad. "A burn mark, like a brand. From what Trishna said, it was left there by a spell. A dark spell. *Cuīmián*. Hypnosis. She thinks the reason she isn't waking is because Richard connected himself to her. Right now, he's in her head. He'll let her go when he either gets what he wants from her, or when…"

I closed my eyes, tears looming behind my lids for the first time in years. I finished her sentence. "Or when she dies."

For hours, I sat with Kayla, holding her hand, until my heart couldn't take it anymore. I'd felt all sorts of pain over my two hundred years as a Protector—broken bones, pierced organs, my skin melting off. But all of that combined couldn't compare to the pain in my chest as I watched Kayla's pale eyelids flutter, wondering if her next breath would be her last.

No one had been able to crack the hard drive we took from Richard's house. Not even Nolan, who'd spent most of his life in Richard's coven. By now, he told us, Richard would know that Nolan had betrayed him. Any communication he used to have with the warlock would be cut off, and any attempt at rekindling it would be dangerous for us. He promised he'd try his best to locate Richard's preferred hideout, but he'd only ever been there as a child, and since then, he'd been out in the field.

Desperation floored me as I watched Kayla. Sitting here was doing her no good. I needed to be out there. I needed to kill Richard. She was not going to die while I could be doing something.

After setting her hand down gently on the bed, I stormed out of Kayla's room. The others had left me alone with her; they would all be next door. I barreled into the other room, and they jumped to their feet. All except Nolan, who lay on the bed with his eyes closed.

Seth's eyes widened. "Oh, no—"

"Please tell me you guys have something. I cannot sit here any longer."

"My coven is ready to fight as soon as we find him," Trishna said. "What he's doing to Kayla, playing with her memories, intruding her thoughts, is the last straw. I know I said a war between Magus would be catastrophic, but we're past that now."

"Then where is he?"

Bartholomew held up a hand. "Nolan is working on finding him."

"Well, tell him to hurry up. I've about had it with his—"

Nolan sat up and stared at me. "Dude, you're ruining my mojo." He flopped back down onto the bed and covered his eyes with his arm.

"Nolan is attempting to go back into his memories and pull out clues as to where Richard used to take him when he was young," Trishna explained. "It takes a lot of concentration to revisit the parts of the brain you've locked away."

"And how do we know he's not just stalling so Richard can kill Kayla? He spent how many years with the guy?"

"Thirteen," Nolan replied with his eyes still closed.

I glared at him. "My point exactly. So he got Kayla and me out of that place? What if that was Richard's plan all along, and he's lying on this bed right now," I gestured toward him, "laughing on the inside because you're all bloody morons listening to his bullshit."

Trishna scrunched her nose. "No, his aura's off. If he was really evil—"

"He doesn't have to be evil to be manipulating us!"

Nolan sat up. "True. One doesn't have to be evil to be a good con man. I mean, I could probably give that Frank Abignale guy a run for his money, but does that make me evil? No."

My fingers twitched, itching to throttle him. I'd had just about enough of his snark.

"Oh, calm down, Daniel, and pick your wedgie. It's not *you* I'm conning. I've been after Richard for years. Now, if you don't mind, I'd like to get back to figuring out how I can—"

He stopped dead cold, the color draining from his face. The hair on the back of my neck rose on end.

"Nolan?" Trishna said.

Nolan's eyes squeezed shut. "It's Richard. He told me where they are, and he has a message for you. He says, 'I'm waiting.'" He flipped over his left wrist. A black tattoo in the shape of a "G" was branded into his skin.

CHAPTER THIRTY-FOUR

Y ou're *linked* to him?" Samantha yelled. We all knew the rumors of the Unity spell. Only the most powerful Magus could cast it, but the enchantment gave a coven the ability to communicate solely through their thoughts.

Nolan raised his hands. "I have not been talking to him, I swear. And until now, there's been radio silence on his end, too."

Samantha gripped the blade in her belt, but then Trishna grabbed Nolan's wrist.

Nolan yelped. "God! What the hell was that?"

"You are not of his coven anymore."

She let go, and Nolan looked at his wrist. The "G" was gone. "*You* can do the spell?"

Trishna lifted her shirt sleeve to reveal a fancy "T" branded inside her own left wrist. "I am the leader of my coven. Tamesis isn't the only powerful Magus."

I fought the smirk that wanted to rise on my face. I liked Trishna more and more with each passing day.

Bartholomew stepped forward. "Nolan, where did Richard say to find him?"

Nolan was still rubbing his now-sore wrist. "Columbus, Ohio. There's an abandoned factory in the bad part of town. It's one of his better-known hideouts. Has been for a long time. I didn't think he'd go there."

My fists clenched. Richard had been watching Kayla for years. "Well then, let's go."

Trishna turned to me. "Now, wait. The five of you Catchers against his coven is suicide."

"So, what do you suggest?" Ivan asked.

"You're going to need help. My help." She looked around the room at us, her face tight in contemplation. Then, finally, she spoke. "I've never done this before, but the same rules cannot be followed any longer. Seth, hold out your left arm, please."

He did as she asked. Trishna turned his arm over so his palm was facing up. Realizing what she was about to do, Bartholomew startled. "Trishna, no. They were made Protectors by the Angels. You can't unite them to you using dark magic."

"My coven cannot see Nightmares. Richard is going to have them on leashes like pets. Without the help of the Protectors, my coven won't make it out of there alive. And your kind cannot battle magic the same way we can. We need each other, and we need to be able to communicate. This is the only way."

Bartholomew's mouth opened to protest, but I didn't care anymore if I wound up in Hell. Richard would not win. I stuck my arm out, palm up. "Unite me."

The room was so quiet, I could hear someone riding their bike twelve stories below. I'd gone over the Keeper's head, offering up my eternity. I knew enough about Protector history to know I'd be the first one ever to wind up in Hell. Binding yourself to anyone with demonic blood was strictly forbidden. But my stomach didn't churn. My heart beat steady. My head was clear. If this was the only way to save Kayla, I would gladly pay the price.

To my surprise, Seth spoke before Trishna could cross the room. "Me too. I'm in." Then Samantha, Ivan, and Lian followed suit. Only Tabbi and Bartholomew stood silent.

Trishna turned back to Seth. "Are you sure?" He nodded once, then Trishna clasped his wrist, speaking in Latin. "*Lunctus nos unum sumos.*" She let go when Seth shouted.

"Man, I was not expectin' that."

"Yeah, it's like a cattle prod," Nolan said.

Nolan went next—most Magus were bound to a coven leader—and, knowing what to expect, didn't even flinch.

The rest of my team replied with some sort of "ouch," and then it was my turn. Trishna looked me straight in the eye, grasping my arm tight, her palm against the inside of my wrist. Again, she spoke the Latin words. Red hot pain exploded into my arm, up my shoulder and into my chest. I clenched my jaw to avoid wincing, and when she let go, I looked down. On my wrist was a brand in the shape of a fancy "T."

"Until you get used to the feel of sending one person a message, do not attempt to try to communicate to the entire group at once. Doing so will result in a terrible headache and will weaken you. But, you should be able to speak directly to each other." She turned to Seth. "The magic should have worked through you by now. Try. Send a message to someone. Use only your thoughts, and you must focus on directing it *to* them. Understand?"

Seth nodded before looking directly at me and scrunching his face like he had to take a massive bowel movement. A few seconds later, I heard his voice in my head.

My butt itches.

I couldn't help myself. I burst out laughing.

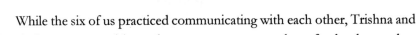

While the six of us practiced communicating with each other, Trishna and Bartholomew popped in on her coven to prepare them for battle—and to bring some weapons back for me. The last place I'd seen mine was in Richard's house before he dragged me to his torture facility. By the time they returned, we were all pretty confident we'd be able to communicate during battle.

Trishna passed out long-sleeved black shirts and black pants, spelled to be body armor against magic. Nightmares and weapons could penetrate the fabric—Magus rarely had to worry about such things—but the outfits could take a few hits from the Magus before we'd be injured.

Bartholomew handed me a weapon belt and blades. "The coven is on their way to Columbus. They should be ready to go within the hour. If I were you, I would take a moment to relax and strategize because once you're in there, your abilities are going to be limited."

I nodded, but there was no way anyone would be relaxing. Every muscle in my body was tight, and I had an unbearable urge to run or do jumping jacks. *"Within the hour"* better mean in the next ten minutes.

Bartholomew grabbed my arm before I could turn away. "And Daniel, be smart. I know you fear for Kayla, but don't do anything rash. You're no good to her dead."

Again, I nodded, not wanting to respond in case my voice gave me away. I wanted to live, to have another day with Kayla, but either Richard was going to die tonight or I was. There'd be no coming back unless I knew Kayla was safe.

I left the room to sit with her until it was time to go. Her face was still ghostly white, and the way they had laid her hands on her stomach already made her look like a corpse. My chest tightened as I sat down. I reached forward and grabbed her cold hand, bringing her fingertips to my lips.

"Hold on just a little longer for me, love. Don't let go yet," I whispered.

"You really do love her, don't you?" Samantha said from the doorway.

I couldn't reply. My throat was too tight. Instead, I let my newfound gift of telepathy do the talking for me. *You should've known that by now.*

Samantha sat next to me. "I'm sorry, Daniel, for what I said back at the mansion. I hope you know—"

It's all right, Sam.

She continued anyway. "I hope you know that I'm happy for you. You deserve this, and I've been a terrible friend for not saying it sooner."

I looked up at her. Samantha's lips were tight, and her eyes glistened. Knowing her as well as I did, this act of selflessness was an effort for her. She never gave up on the things she wanted. Touching her hand, I spoke, my voice tired. "And you deserve someone who cares for you as much as I love Kayla. It's only a matter of time before you find him."

Samantha gave me a weak smile, then Trishna's voice filled our heads. *We're ready.*

CHAPTER THIRTY-FIVE

Bartholomew and Tabbi stayed behind. Neither were equipped to fight, and Bartholomew needed to keep an eye on Kayla. The rest of us evaporated together to an empty hotel down the road from Richard's hideout. Trishna's coven stood in the lobby, dressed in black gear. My pulse quickened when I saw how many there were, especially when about a fourth of them wore daggers at their sides.

Bartholomew had found more Protectors.

Trishna's coven—Protectors and Magus alike—silenced and listened for her direction.

"You've all heard the stories about Tamesis. Tonight we take him down. Nolan, you said you knew how to get in?"

Nolan nodded. "Down the road is an abandoned factory that used to manufacture... well, I don't know what. But a barbed wire fence surrounds it to keep people out. Once you get inside the factory, though, it'll be easy to find Richard. The first room is some kind of office or security area or whatever, then there's a second set of double doors you have to go through. Knowing him, he'll be waiting right inside those doors."

"And you said the place is heavily guarded by Nightmares?"

Again, Nolan nodded. "They're Tamesis'—or, Richard's—favorite pets. They'll be infesting the parking lot and surrounding yard. But, he doesn't let them come inside. He doesn't want his coven to be feasted on in their sleep."

"Then, it's simple," I said. "We'll go in first and clear a path for the rest of you. Then, while they're distracted, you can run into the security area. We can regroup there."

"No, we're better if we stick together," Trishna said.

I shook my head. "You can't see them. We can. Richard uses these creatures to physically attack people now, not just torture them with evil thoughts. If you get too close to one, they will kill you. We can at least give you a shot at reaching that door in one piece. We're no good against Richard and his Magus. But we can take down these Nightmares, and then we'll be ready for any of Giovanni's followers on the other side."

Trishna's eyes fell, but she nodded. It was our only shot at getting most everyone inside. "Protectors, follow Daniel. The rest of us will wait in the shadows for his signal."

When everyone shouted their affirmation, Trishna held out her hand, signaling it was time for me to lead my team. I shoved down the queasiness in my stomach and stepped outside.

The stench of rotting flesh and sewage floored me. I covered my nose with my arm and gagged. Dead humans lined the street, and fires blazed from every collapsed building, illuminating the night sky with an ominous, orange glow. Richard's return to Columbus had meant death for this city. It was a good thing Kayla wouldn't be here to see this.

Soundless, we walked down the decimated street, invisible to the police that ran from building to building, looking for survivors. When we reached the gate to the factory, I held up a hand and paused. At least one hundred Nightmares paced like soldiers in front of the building. Sensing us, they turned, hissing, like someone held up a rattlesnake to a microphone.

"Oh my god," one of the Protectors said.

"We'll never make it," echoed another.

I glanced at the white faces of my comrades. "Yes, we will. Sprint to the right, drawing them away from the entrance. Then circle up, facing out, and take them down. Stay together."

My team nodded and stepped so close to each other their arms were touching. I took a deep breath, returning my attention to the Nightmares on the other side of the fence. "On three. Ready? One, two, three!"

We raced through the fence, our invisible bodies passing through the barrier. The Nightmares roared at our arrival. Every now and then, one would reach out for us, but together we hustled forward. To my right, one of my Catchers screamed, and I gripped my daggers tighter. Then finally, we reached our target and formed a circle.

I stepped out enough to give myself room to battle, and when the first Nightmare reached for me, clawing at my face, I sliced its hands off and kicked the creature away. With a cry, the monster ran at me again, black blood oozing from its arms. I waited until the beast leaned in to bite me with its fanged teeth then jammed my blade into its neck. The Nightmare fell to the side with a gurgle.

Before I could breathe, two more lunged at me, one of them missing an eye. I ducked in time to avoid my throat being slashed, but then hot pain whipped my back as a Nightmare clawed my skin. I mule-kicked the one-eyed bastard away from me, then dug my blade under the other's ribs. With a grunt I jerked up, piercing the creature's heart. It fell as I turned around, crouching low to the ground. The one-eyed Nightmare swiped at my face and ran into my knives. I shoved the beast away, gutting it.

Before the next Nightmare swung at me, I took a second to glance around the lot. We were down five Protectors, and though we'd taken down many Nightmares, we wouldn't be able to hold the rest much longer. I disposed of the next Nightmare then shouted at Trishna.

Go now!

Within seconds, Trishna and her coven burst through the chain-link fence, their hands stretched out in front of them.

Protectors, go corporeal now! Trishna yelled.

When we did, all around us, fire lit up the scenery, sometimes hitting a Nightmare, sometimes missing them. The Magus were fighting blind, but damn it, they were still fighting. The Magus ran for the entrance to the factory, one after one slipping through the door Seth held open. We Catchers sprinted after them, surrounding and protecting them from the Nightmares they couldn't see.

One neared Nolan's face, and I threw my dagger into the Nightmare's skull. I stopped to pull the blade out of the creature's head and in the same motion sliced through the neck of another that reached for me. The monster's claws caught my arm as it fell. Swearing at the hot pain, I pressed forward, desperate to get into where Richard waited.

Nolan stood on one side of the door, shooting fire from his hands and ensuring everyone got inside. I stopped next to him, protecting him and ushering the coven inside.

This is fun, isn't it? Nolan said.

Your definition of fun is warped, mate. I pointed to his right where a Nightmare was closing in. Nolan lit the beast on fire.

Aw, you called me 'mate.' That's like 'friend' in your language, right? I'm so touched.

Don't get used to it.

When the last person finally crossed through the opening, I elbowed Nolan toward the door, but he fought me.

What are you— I was about to say when fire spit out of his hands. Flames lined the ground in front of the door. The Nightmares halted, hissing at us for blocking their path.

Nolan handed me a small, glass box. *Throw this. Tell me when it's over their heads.*

What is this?

Just throw it, already.

I lobbed the box as hard as I could. When it was dead center over the group of Nightmares, he hurled a ball of fire at the glass box. Sunlight exploded out, so much that satellites in space would wonder what the hell was going on, and I covered my eyes. The shrieks from the Nightmares were deafening. We turned and ran into the factory, Nolan laughing as he closed the door.

CHAPTER THIRTY-SIX

I s anyone seriously injured?" Trishna asked as we all stopped to catch our breaths. When no one answered, she wiped her tanned brow with the back of her hand. "Thank the stars. We've already lost too many. All right, it's our turn to protect you, Catchers. On my lead."

Trishna slowly opened the doors to the main factory, then paused, her hands in front of her, prepared to fight off an attack. But none came. With a nod to two of her coven, Trishna entered the room. The two went right or left, and just like that we split into three teams.

After you, miss, Nolan said, holding out a hand for me. I glared at him then followed the rest of the coven into the room, flanking left. The factory was so dark, only a little starlight from the few windows provided light, and only the faint *thump* of footsteps filled the room. I clutched my daggers in my sweaty hands as my pulse raced in my ears. If Richard was waiting for us, he was hiding very well.

Lights flipped on, illuminating the vast, empty space, and from every corner of the room came hostile Magus and Catchers alike. I sprang into action, going invisible. As long as only Giovanni's Catchers could see me, I'd have a chance of finding Richard and putting my dagger through his heart.

Turning in a circle, I scouted the vast room for a sign of him. But there was none. *Come on, you bastard.*

Three conveyer belts away, Giovanni's head popped into view. His black hair had come loose from his ponytail, and the strands flung around his face as he spun, digging his blades into the bodies of those who'd once looked up to him. I sprinted across the room, weaving through the battles taking place around me. One of Giovanni's Catchers jumped in my way, and I kicked his feet out from under him before bringing my blade down into his chest. He gripped my wrist as the life left his brown eyes. Hot bile rose in my throat. I'd never killed one of my own before.

Drawing my dagger from the Catcher's chest, Giovanni stared right at me, a twisted grin on his face. With a snarl, I closed the gap between us until we circled each other, waiting for the other to make a move.

"How's Kayla?" Giovanni leered.

My grip tightened on my blades. "Where's Richard? I'm surprised he'd miss all the fun."

"Oh, he's here. You just can't hear him." Then I spotted a familiar "G" branded on the inside of Giovanni's left wrist, and it clicked—Nolan had worn the same unity mark. Richard wasn't here at all. He was hearing the play-by-play through Giovanni. My hands shook as a heat wave flooded my body. I was going to lose Kayla.

My moment of weakness gave Giovanni his opening. He kicked my left hand, sending my dagger flying, and threw one of his own blades at my chest. I spun out of the way in time to avoid a major hit, but groaned when the blade sliced my shoulder.

"Not bad. But I have four hundred years on you, Daniel. You have a long way to go."

And just like that, he charged me. His dagger sliced at my neck, but I smacked his arm away and punched him in the nose. Instead of staggering back like anyone else would have, Giovanni grinned at me, blood gushing down his face. Chills rushed down my spine.

Again, he lunged at me, his arms moving so fast I barely had time to breathe. For someone who'd spent so many years behind a desk, Giovanni could *move*. He swung at my face with his knife, but I raised an arm just in time, blocking his attack. His other fist collided with my jaw. I swore as I ducked to avoid Giovanni's dagger and jabbed him in the stomach. A soft grunt escaped his lips, but his arms never stopped moving. His blade caught my cheek.

Two more times I managed to block his hits, unable to get in a jab of my own. Then, as I spun out of the way a third time, I found my opening. While he was focused so hard on his handiwork, he completely forgot about his feet.

I ducked one of Giovanni's punches, spinning and crouching low to the ground. Swinging my leg out to the side, I caught the back of his ankles. With a shout, he came tumbling down. I dug my dagger into his leg and stood, kicking Giovanni's blade out of his hand.

"Where is he?" I shouted as Giovanni tried to rise to his feet. I kicked him in the side of the head, and he fell onto his back with a groan.

"Tell me where Richard is, and I'll spare your life."

Giovanni laughed. I stepped on his leg, digging the heel of my boot into his knife wound. He screamed and reached for my foot, but I kicked him in the face. Blood spurted from his mouth.

"I will ask you one more time. Where is Richard?" I raised my blade to his throat.

"Stop!" he shouted.

The room around me silenced as the fighting ceased. Richard's coven and Giovanni's followers dropped their hands and weapons. Giovanni's body convulsed, and his eyes rolled back into his head. I stepped back as a cold chill ran through me. When his eyes opened again, they were black—just like Seth's had been in the club.

"You win, Daniel. Let Giovanni live, and I will give you what you want most. This was never really about finding me anyway, yeah?" Richard spoke through Giovanni's body.

My jaw clenched. He knew that if I had to choose between his location and Kayla, I'd choose her.

"Now, step back and send one of your friends to see if Kayla's awake."

I did as he said. *Sam, check on Kayla now.* "Why are you letting us go?"

Giovanni's face smirked. "Because simply destroying the world wouldn't be much fun, now would it?"

Daniel, she's waking up, just like he said, Samantha said. *The mark is gone.*

I let out a deep breath, closing my eyes for a brief moment. Then I opened them and stared down Giovanni, a smug smile on my face. Richard had shown me his weakness. He cared as much for Giovanni as I did for Kayla. He was going to get what he deserved.

Twirling my blade in my fingers, I dropped to my knees. "Thank you, Richard, for holding up your end of the bargain. But see, I'm not interested in playing your game."

Giovanni's eyes opened wide as my blade entered his throat. All around the room, Richard's coven and Giovanni's followers retaliated. But we were a bit quicker. Because they had dropped their weapons, within minutes, Giovanni's Catchers were dead, leaving us to team up with the rest of Trishna's coven. Richard's Magus didn't stand a chance. The thirty of us who remained took them out, and by the time the battle ended, the floor was coated in red blood.

"You can see her now, Daniel," Trishna said.

I lifted my head out of my now-clean hands and jumped off the bed, forcing myself not to sprint into the other room. Instead, I entered slowly, holding my breath. Tabbi and Kayla stood, embraced in a hug. Seeing me, Tabbi grinned and whispered something into Kayla's ear. Then Kayla turned. With a soft cry, she ran into my arms.

Holding her tight, all the emotions I'd held bottled inside exploded. I kissed her, hard, as a single tear fell from my eye—the first one in a long time. She was safe. Resting my cheek on her head, I breathed in the scent of her strawberry shampoo. The tension that had plagued every part of my body for weeks disappeared. I closed my eyes and let the feeling of floating take over.

Kayla didn't move as she spoke. "My dad?"

My eyes opened. "Nolan's going over all of his known hiding spots with Trishna. It won't be easy, but we'll find him."

She was quiet for a few minutes, then she spoke again. "I won't turn out like him, right?"

I leaned back to look into her eyes. They were framed with red. "Where is this coming from? He might be your father, but you're nothing like him."

Kayla shook her head. "I killed those two guys and started that fire. What if I can't control myself?"

"You're part of Trishna's coven now. She will train you. And don't forget, your father didn't have something you do."

"What?"

"Me." I touched her cheek. "If you ever feel like you're going to fall, I will be here to catch you."

Kayla smiled softly. "I forgot you were invincible."

I grinned. She'd used the same line when we'd visited Paris. "Invincible, no. But you'd be surprised how much I'd do for the girl I love."

Her hazel eyes sparkled as her arms wrapped around my neck and her lips met mine. I squeezed her tight in my arms. The war was far from over, but right now, even if only for a few minutes, the world was perfect.

ACKNOWLEDGEMENTS

"Writing a book is [an]…exhausting struggle. One would never undertake such a thing if one were not driven on by some demon whom one can [not] resist."
—George Orwell

To my agent, Sarah Negovetich: Thank you for helping me navigate the publishing waters and find the perfect home for my novel. Your advice and expertise are invaluable! I'm so blessed to be going through this journey with you—and to have someone in my corner who doesn't mind answering a thousand questions. One of these days, I'll make your Superagent cape.

To my editor, Jessa: I owe you thanks for not just making my book a thousand times better but for giving this manuscript a chance to shine in PitchMas. You, in more ways than one, have helped make my dreams come true. So glad it was you who helped me whip my story into something beautiful.

To my team at CQ: Thank you to everyone who had a hand in helping this book get into readers' hands. You all have been so fantastic to work with and have really made my first publishing experience an exciting adventure. And Dean, what an awesome cover. Your ability to read my mind and put together such a stunning picture is truly a superpower.

To my amazing critique partners: Ava, Emily, Laura, and Jessica. I definitely could not have written this without you four. You saw my manuscript when it was at its conception and helped me make it into something beautiful.

To the thirteen others who had a hand in helping me shape my novel: M. Andrew, Angi, Bess, Catherine, Jen, Marika, Nikki, Sarah, Stephanie, Summer, Tabitha, and Vikki. Thank you all for your encouragement and wisdom.

To my street team: I cannot wait to share this journey with you, Dreamweavers. You guys rock, and I'm so lucky to have so many awesome people in my corner.

To my friends and family: It's such a blessing to have people in my life who get as excited by book news as I do, even when you have no idea what I'm talking about. Your love and enthusiasm keep me going on the toughest days.

And to my parents, who supported me before I even knew this was possible: Thank you for sending me to all those writing conferences and for investing not just your dimes but your hearts in me and my book. I love you both.

ABOUT THE AUTHOR

Adopted at three-days-old by a construction worker and a stay-at-home mom, **Vicki Leigh** grew up in a small suburb of Akron, Ohio where she learned to read by the age of four and considered being sent to her room for punishment as an opportunity to dive into another book.

By the sixth grade, Vicki penned her first, full-length screenplay. If she couldn't be a writer, Vicki would be a Hunter (think Dean and Sam Winchester) or a Jedi. Her favorite place on earth is Hogwarts (she refuses to believe it doesn't exist), and her favorite dreams include solving cases alongside Sherlock Holmes.

Vicki is an editor for Curiosity Quills Press, a co-founder of The Writer Diaries, and is represented by Sarah Negovetich of Corvisiero Literary Agency.

THANK YOU FOR READING

Please visit http://curiosityquills.com/reader-survey to share your reading experience with the author of this book!

Exacting Essence, by James Wymore

Megan's nightmares aren't normal; normal nightmares don't leave cuts and bruises on waking. Desperate, Megan's mother accepts a referral to a new therapist; a doctor dealing with the business of dreams—real dreams. The carnival of terrors that torments Megan nightly is all just a part of the Dreamworld, a separate reality experienced only by those aware enough to realize it.

On her quest to destroy the Nightmares feeding from her fear, Megan encounters Intershroud, the governing entity of the Dreamworld, and must work with her new friends to stop the agency from continuing its evil agenda, and to destroy her own Nightmares for good.

Sweet Dreams are Made of Teeth, by Richard Roberts

How does a nightmare hunt? He tracks your dreams into the Light, and chases them into the Dark. How does a nightmare love? With passion and obsession and lust and amazement. How does a nightmare grow up? With pain and grief and doubt and kindness and learning and dedication and courage. First Fang hunted, now he loves, and soon he'll have to grow up.

Five: Out of the Pit, by Holli Anderson

The FIVE find their way to Moab, Utah where, before they're even settled in, evil finds them.

As Paige fights the pull of an Incubus that has her marked as his next conquest, Johnathan seeks to find a way to rid her of a curse she willingly accepted in order to save him.

A surprising revelation initiates a long-awaited, yet unexpected, reunion for Alec who discovers a new magical talent he possesses.

The FIVE, along with their mentor, Joe, must decipher the final words of a Demon banished to the Netherworld, and prevent the promised gathering darkness before it is unleashed on Moab - and the world.

Fade, by A.K. Morgen

When Arionna Jacobs and Dace Matthews meet, everything they thought they knew about life begins to unravel. Neither understands the frightening things occurring around them, and they're running out of time to figure out what it all means. An ancient Norse prophesy of destruction has been set in motion, and what destiny has in store for them is bigger than either could have ever imagined.

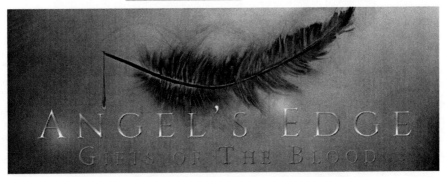

Gifts of the Blood (Angel's Edge, Book 1), by Vicki Keire

Before her world tilts towards impossible, Caspia Chastain thinks the only strange thing about her is that she sometimes draws the future. When she draws a man surrounded by brilliant light, dark wings, and frightening symbols, she can only hope the vision won't come true.

But when a stranger named Ethan appears, determined to protect Caspia from dangers he won't explain, she's unsure what to think. Strangers never come to Whitfield. They certainly don't follow her around, frightening her one moment and treating her like glass the next. And they definitely don't look exactly like her most violent drawing.

Darkness Watching, by Emma Adams

Eighteen-year-old Ashlyn is one interview away from her future when she first sees the demons. She thinks she's losing her mind, but the truth is far more frightening: she can see into the Darkworld, the home of spirits– and the darkness is staring back. At her new university in the small English village of Blackstone, she meets a hidden group of sorcerers and, for the first time, finds a place where she belongs. But her new life turns dark when she's targeted by a killer. The demons want something from her, and not everyone is what they appear to be...